THE LEGACY

This Large Print Book carries the
Seal of Approval of N.A.V.H.

THE LEGACY

DAN WALSH
AND GARY SMALLEY

THORNDIKE PRESS

A part of Gale, Cengage Learning

GALE
CENGAGE Learning·

Farmington Hills, Mich • San Francisco • New York • Waterville, Maine
Meriden, Conn • Mason, Ohio • Chicago

GALE
CENGAGE Learning®

LIBRARY OF CONGRESS CATALOGING-IN-PUBLICATION DATA

Walsh, Dan, 1957–
 The legacy / by Dan Walsh and Gary Smalley. — Large print edition.
  pages cm. — (Restoration series ; #4) (Thorndike Press large print Christian fiction)
  ISBN 978-1-4104-8138-2 (hardcover) — ISBN 1-4104-8138-7 (hardcover)
  1. Large type books. I. Smalley, Gary. II. Title.
 PS3623.A446L44 2015b
 813'.6—dc23   2015012483

Published in 2015 by arrangement with Revell Books, a division of Baker Publishing Group

Printed in Mexico
1 2 3 4 5 6 7 19 18 17 16 15

But while he was still a long way off, his father saw him and was filled with compassion for him; he ran to his son.

— Luke 15:20

1

Jim Anderson watched his son back his red Mazda out of their driveway, drive it down the one lane road behind their home, turn left at the road's end, wave once, then disappear behind a row of ligustrum hedges. Jim knew Doug hadn't really disappeared. He was simply leaving River Oaks and driving back to college and his graphic arts degree. But on the level that mattered most, Doug had disappeared.

Not just now. Years ago.

Jim couldn't shake the sick feeling in his stomach that something new was going on with Doug. Not good new, either. Just what, he couldn't figure out. Soft hands reached around his waist, followed by a kind embrace. It was his wife, Marilyn.

"Are you doing okay?" she said. "I could tell what you were trying to do back there, but he wouldn't open the door."

"Was I being too obvious?"

"Not in a way Doug could tell," she said. "I just know you and how much pain you feel about this . . . this gap."

"It's more than a gap. Feels like the Grand Canyon." He reached down and intertwined his hands with hers. They were still standing in the driveway, facing the direction Doug had gone. "It doesn't bother you?"

"It does. I just handle it differently."

Jim knew what she meant. It wasn't said as an insult. She was referring to her level of faith for the situation, which clearly exceeded his. Her faith always seemed to exceed his, especially when it came to relationships. They had talked about this many times. Jim had a hard time recognizing the moments when words did more harm than good. When faith and silence were better tools to reach for.

He'd always had that problem, especially with the kids. More so when they were younger, but it was still a weakness. With Marilyn's help, he'd made some progress with the *silence* part. Shutting up was something he could do. Stopping the pain in his heart or trusting God to fix things with Doug was another matter.

"He's in God's hands now," she said. "He's working even when we can't see."

"I know." But it was just something to say.

It didn't feel true. At least not to him.

Marilyn released her hug but kept her arm around him as they turned and walked back into the garage.

"Did he find the box he was looking for?" Marilyn asked.

"It took awhile, but he did." Jim looked down at the empty space in the garage where the box used to be. Doug had come home for one of his rare weekend visits. Apparently, he and a friend, Jason, had started working on a graphic novel. He'd come home to get a certain box of comic books from his old collection.

"What was so important about that one box?" she asked.

"Doug said he needs to make sure some of the ideas for their new graphic novel aren't rip-offs from his old comic books. Jason's writing the story and Doug's doing the artwork. Jason thinks they're fine, but Doug's pretty sure some of Jason's ideas might be too close for comfort."

"Well, I'm all for whatever gets him home."

Jim was too. He was tempted to just insist Doug came home on a regular schedule. That didn't seem too much to ask, considering they were paying for his college education. Jim's real estate business was doing better now than it had been a couple of years ago, but money was still tight. It was a serious sacrifice keeping up with Doug's expenses. They shouldn't have to beg him to come home for a visit a couple times a month. And would it kill him to call his mother once a week to let her know he was still alive? But Jim knew that if he said anything, it would just push Doug further away.

"What are you doing?"

Jim looked at her. "What do you mean?"

"Your face. You're doing that thing, aren't you?"

"What?"

"Giving it to Doug in your head."

Jim laughed.

"I knew it," she said. "Well, I guess it's better if it only happens in your head. Two years ago, you would have let him have it out loud."

She was right. He would have. And it would have made things worse. Now if he could only add faith to the silence. Find a way to trust God so that he wouldn't worry about Doug so much. Another thing that talking with Marilyn had helped him see was that anger was a secondary reaction for him, the place his heart went after worry. Neither one was better than the other; both

10

left God totally out of the equation.

For that matter, was God even in this equation? It didn't feel like he was. Jim restacked the boxes of comic books to make a little more floor space in the garage. "I suggested he just bring the rest of these back to school with him. Try to sell them or something, but he didn't want to."

"I'm kind of glad he said no." Marilyn opened the top box and pulled out one of the comic books. "If he did, it would be the last of his things left in the house."

"None of the things in the apartment upstairs are his?"

She shook her head no. "They either belong to us or Christina." Christina was a young woman who'd come to live with them last year. Marilyn had been her counselor at the Women's Resource Center, helping her through a crisis pregnancy that had ended with Christina placing her child for adoption with a young Christian couple. Now, Christina was like family. "Little by little over the past year, Doug's been taking more of his stuff back to school with him. These boxes are all that's left."

Then Jim didn't want them gone, either. "I wish there was some way to get him to open up to me, let me know how he's really doing."

"He's been this way since the last few years of high school."

"I know," he said, "but it's worse now than it was then. Right after you and I went through our difficult time, I thought Doug and I were starting to connect a little better. Last fall when Christina came to live with us, he started coming home more often, remember?"

Marilyn nodded then glanced at Christina's car on the far side of the garage, signaling she was upstairs. Jim got the message. But he hadn't said anything inappropriate, had he? Still, he lowered his voice. "Now he's back to hardly coming home at all. And when he's here, he doesn't seem like himself."

"I know," she said. "It feels like that to me too."

Jim sighed. "I get the impression he's not doing well at all. Spiritually, I mean. I'd be surprised if he's even going to church anymore."

"I don't think he is," she said. "I almost asked him this morning, but I stopped. I didn't want to hear his answer."

They both heard the sound of footsteps coming down the last few stairs from the apartment. They turned to find Christina carrying a laundry basket.

"Sorry if I startled you," she said. "I started down the stairs then heard you guys talking. I didn't mean to eavesdrop, but I couldn't help overhearing. You're talking about Doug, right?"

They nodded.

She set her basket on the dryer. "Are you guys on Facebook?"

2

Christina wasn't sure this was a good idea, talking about Doug like this with his parents. It didn't feel right keeping things from them, considering how close they had become this past year. On the other hand, it didn't feel right talking about Doug behind his back. She hated being caught in the middle.

"I go there sometimes," Marilyn said.

"I signed up a while ago," Jim said, "but I hardly ever use it."

"To be honest," Marilyn said, "some of the things I've been seeing lately concern me."

Christina leaned back against the dryer. She had to agree. It seemed like Doug was starting to head in a different direction.

"Like what?" Jim said.

Marilyn sighed. "He seems to be developing some new friends this year. Hanging out with a lot of people I've never seen before."

"What about them bothers you?" Jim said.

"It's nothing serious, not yet anyway. I'm just seeing a lot more party pictures lately. Lots of people his age laughing, holding glasses of beer. Definitely not a youth group crowd."

"Is Doug drinking beer in these pictures?" Jim asked.

"No, not in any I've seen. It seems like most of his friends are."

To Christina, in a few of the pictures, Doug's eyes looked a little too red, but she couldn't tell for sure if he'd been drinking. He could have just been overly tired. Then again, Doug would have enough sense not to be caught holding a beer when someone was taking pictures that could show up on the internet.

"Are any of them in bars or nightclubs?" Jim said.

"Doug's not old enough to go to bars," Marilyn said. "Of course, he could have gotten a fake ID somehow."

Jim sat down on one of the steps. "They're a lot harder to get now than when we were his age."

"Not really," Marilyn said. "You can get anything online these days. But I didn't see any pictures in bars. They were mostly in dorm rooms and people's houses. It's just

15

there were lots of these pics, off and on over the last several months. Before that, most of his pics were with a different group of friends around the campus."

"What about Jason?" Jim said. "I know they're still hanging out. That's part of the reason Doug came home this weekend, for some project they're working on together."

"Oh, he's still with Jason," Marilyn said. "I see them together on Facebook sometimes."

Christina almost added that Jason always looked totally smashed in these pics, but she didn't say it. She rarely saw Jason without a beer in his hand. Occasionally, he was even holding a "handmade cigarette." That was what it said in the caption. She was sure it was pot.

Marilyn set a comic book down on top of a box and looked at Christina. "What do you think of Jason?"

She didn't mind talking about him. "Let's just say, I'm not a fan. I don't really know him that well. But I've known lots of guys like him. Doug's totally different than Jason. I talked to Doug about it a few months ago when we were closer."

"You two aren't that close anymore?" Marilyn asked.

"Not really. Not like before." She thought

16

they had been getting really close around the time her baby was born. They were texting, messaging back and forth on Facebook, occasionally exchanging emails, even talking on the phone sometimes. But something brought all that to a halt a few months ago. She was pretty sure she knew what it was. Or rather, *who* it was.

And it wasn't Jason.

"What were you saying about Jason?" Jim said.

"I know they're like best friends," Christina said, "and they've been going to school together forever."

"Jason's family lives just a few blocks away from here," Marilyn added.

"The thing is, Jason's kind of wild. A real party guy."

"The guy with the lamp shade on his head," Jim said.

Christina had no idea what that meant.

"It's just an expression," Jim said. "That's what we used to call guys like Jason."

"Oh."

"But isn't Doug really the leader in their relationship?" Marilyn asked. "Doug wouldn't just do something because Jason was, would he?"

"I used to think Doug was the leader," Jim said. "But I'm not so sure anymore."

With Doug, Christina couldn't tell who was leading whom. She'd read something in her Bible a few mornings ago, something Jesus said about the blind leading the blind and both of them falling in a ditch.

"Reminds me of that Scripture in Corinthians," Marilyn said, "about bad company corrupting good morals. The thing is, Doug wasn't all that strong before he left for college. I've been worried it was all going to be too much for him." She looked at Jim. "What can we do?"

Jim stood up, shook his head. "I don't know. It's not like he's a little kid anymore. We can't tell him who he can and can't hang out with."

"I just keep praying about it," Christina said. "I wish I could do more."

Marilyn put her hand gently on Christina's shoulder.

"It's not the best of news," Jim said, "but it's not really much of a shock. We'll all just have to keep praying and ask God for wisdom to see if there's anything more we can do besides pray."

Marilyn looked at Christina. "Do you want to join us for dinner tonight? I'm just reheating some meatloaf."

"Are you kidding?" Christina said. "I love your meatloaf. What time?"

"Maybe an hour. Is that enough time for you?"

"Plenty. I'll just finish up my laundry then get cleaned up and come right over."

Jim opened the back door for Marilyn and they headed over to the main house. Christina put a load of clothes into the washer, set the dials, and hit the start button. She made her way up the stairs toward her apartment, thinking about what they had talked about. Doug's friend Jason was certainly part of the problem, but she didn't think he was the biggest concern. Jason was just being Jason, like he had been ever since she had known Doug.

She was sure the changes in Doug had more to do with this cute blonde girl who had started showing up in his Facebook pictures. In the very first one, Christina had recognized the look the blonde was giving Doug. It was the same look in every pic after that. As Christina had clicked through more pictures, she could see that this girl was hanging all over Doug.

That bothered her some, but it wasn't the most disturbing thing. In the last few weeks, it had become clear Doug was now returning her advances.

The girl's name was Courtney.

3

Doug arrived back at his apartment in St. Augustine, a few blocks from the campus of Flagler College. He dropped off his things and rushed out to a party Jason had texted him about. Some house in an upscale subdivision off 207. Jason was already there. So were all their friends. Courtney too, and about thirty other kids Jason said he didn't know. The parents of one of them owned the place, but they were out of town.

Doug's GPS got him to the neighborhood. Jason's text included the street but not the house number. It was easy enough to find. Doug drove until he found a crowd. The houses were on large lots with lots of space in between. Hopefully, they were far enough from the neighbors to keep them from calling the cops.

The sun had pretty much set for the day, but Doug could still see well enough. Jason had been right; the house was almost as big as their homes back in River Oaks. Doug's parents would have died if they'd driven home to this scene. Cars all over the place. Music blaring. College kids stumbling around carrying red Solo cups filled with beer. Most were probably underage.

Drinking wasn't a big problem for him. Doug didn't really like beer or the various drinks his friends made with beer, like Black and Tans and Boilermakers, Jason's favorite. That sometimes subjected him to ridicule. *"How can you not like beer? What are you, a complete moron? What's not to like?"* His closer friends were okay with it. Jason would defend him if someone made too big a deal out of it. *"Doug's an artist, man. He's got a refined palate."* Jason always drank enough for both of them. If Jason wasn't around, Doug would tell scoffers he only drank fine wines. A safe bet, since no one ever had any at these parties.

When he and Courtney first met, he thought this issue might be a problem. She could really put it away, and he didn't like the way she changed after two or three drinks. So she started cutting back. Now she drank just enough to get a buzz. At least, that was what she did when she was with him.

Doug got out of the car and walked down

21

the driveway past a dozen people he didn't know arguing about some movie that had just come out last weekend. He glanced at the front door, saw Drew waving at him from the porch. Jason must've sent Drew out to get him. One look at the dumb smile on Drew's face and Doug knew the beer in his hand was not his first.

As he walked toward Doug, he tripped on the second step. "Whoa, man. Somebody needs to put a sign out here." The beer spilled, but he didn't fall. "Doug, great to see you, man. Everybody's out back. Courtney's been asking for you, wondering when you were gonna get here."

"I just got back into town," Doug said. "Spent the last few days back home with my folks. Where's Jason?"

"He's somewhere in there, making the moves on some girl. He asked me to get you." They walked back toward the front door, up the porch steps, then stepped through the doorway. "I'll show you around. The kegs are on the screen porch out back. The kid who owns the place asked everyone to be careful not to spill any beer on the rug."

"Thanks, Drew, think I should connect with Courtney first. Know where she is?"

"Sure, man. She's out back with the others, sitting in deck chairs around the pool."

They threaded their way through the crowd. Doug hadn't seen anyone he recognized other than Drew. They walked through a set of open French doors into a large screened porch. On the left, a small line had formed in front of a table holding two beer kegs. Through the screen, Doug saw another group standing around the pool. He scanned the folks sitting in chairs until he found Courtney and a few other friends.

She noticed him as soon as he stepped out of the porch. Setting her beer down, she got up and hurried toward him, almost knocking a guy into the pool. Doug still wasn't used to the way she greeted him. Hugs and kisses every time, like he was a soldier coming back from the front.

"I'm so glad you're here," she said, throwing her arms around him. She kissed him, he kissed back.

He did like her, and they were officially a couple now, but it was obvious she liked him a lot more than he liked her.

"Come on, we're sitting over here. I saved you a seat. It's so nice out tonight, isn't it?"

She led him by the hand through the partiers, making a wide arc around the guy she almost knocked in the pool. He glared at Doug as they walked by. The rest of the group, minus Jason, sat in plastic Adirondack chairs near the deep end. Drew was heading their way from the other side of the pool, holding a fresh cup of beer.

Doug was actually a little thirsty. As they reached their friends, he stopped.

"What's the matter?" Courtney asked.

"Nothing. I just want to get something to drink before I sit down."

"All right," said Brian, another guy in their group. "Doug's finally seen the light."

Courtney knew better. "There's ice water in the refrigerator door."

"You can do better than that," Drew said. "Some guy showed up with Bacardi and Coke. I just saw him. He set them up on the far end of the kitchen counter."

"Now you're talking," Brian said. "Rum and Coke."

"I'll be right back," Doug said.

As he walked through the crowd, he kept an eye out for Jason. Jason was his best friend, but sometimes he got pretty stupid in crowd situations. Especially when he drank too much, and he always drank too much. Doug didn't see him in the pool area or the screened porch. He stopped at the keg to grab a Solo cup and almost got into a fight with a guy who thought he was jump-

24

ing the line. Doug held up the plastic cup. "Just getting this for a rum and Coke," he said. The guy calmed down.

He weaved his way into the kitchen, spotted the two-liter bottles of Coke right where Drew said they'd be. Beside the Bacardi bottle sat a big bowl of ice. He poured himself a Coke and started making his way back toward the pool area. As he turned a corner by the shallow end, he heard male voices yelling in the side yard. Courtney and her friends sat up, staring in that direction.

"Sounds like some guys need to chill out," Brian said.

"Sounds like a fight starting," Drew said.

Doug walked past his friends, trying to get a better look.

"Don't get involved, Doug," Courtney said.

He didn't want to. He hated fights, had done his best to avoid them growing up. The problem was, through all the yelling, he recognized one of the voices, slurred speech and all.

Jason.

4

The yelling got louder and angrier as Doug hurried toward the scene. The side yard was darker than the pool area, sandwiched in the shadows between the house and some large trees. A circle had formed around two guys shoving each other.

"Cut it out, you guys," someone yelled.

"Let it go, Rob," a girl said.

"I will not let it go," said one of the two guys starting to fight. Doug knew now that Jason was the other guy.

"Hey, man, I didn't know she was taken. She didn't say anything."

"I am not taken," the girl said. "We broke up last weekend."

The other guy, Rob, turned and faced the girl. "We did not break up. I'll talk with you later." He was holding Jason's shirt like they did in the movies.

"Get your hands off me," Jason yelled, grabbing Rob's forearms and pushing them down. Rob took a swing at Jason's head. Jason ducked but got it in the shoulder. He threw an uppercut that landed square on Rob's jaw.

Rob fell back, landed on his butt. He rubbed his chin. "You're a dead man." He leapt to his feet.

"Do it, Rob," some guy yelled. Other guys shouted similar things.

Jason instantly switched to a boxing stance. But Doug knew that Jason was no fighter. And this guy had two inches on him and at least thirty pounds.

"Stop it, you guys!" the girl yelled, more at Rob.

Rob didn't listen. He came running at Jason like a lineman out to sack a quarterback. When they collided, the men flew back the other direction. Jason got off one punch, square on the guy's back, then went down with a thump. Rob quickly straddled Jason and began hammering him with blows. Some kids yelled, "Fight, fight!" Others screamed for him to stop. Jason blocked some of the hits with his forearms, but some were getting through.

Doug couldn't let this go on. He ran at Rob full speed, aiming his shoulder at Rob's head. Behind him, Courtney screamed for him to stop. The hit knocked Rob completely off Jason. He got up and looked down at Rob, who seemed momentarily disoriented. Doug ran over and pulled Jason to his feet. "C'mon. We're getting out of here. Now."

"What?" Jason said, holding the left side of his face. It was already swelling.

"C'mon." Doug dragged him into the shadows toward the front of the house.

"Doug," Courtney said, "wait! Where are you going?"

But Doug couldn't wait. He had to get Jason into the car now. They had just cleared the house. Doug looked up ahead through all the cars for his.

"I'm coming," Jason said. "Would you stop pulling my arm?"

Doug let go. "We've got to get out of here. You got a lucky punch in, but that guy was creaming you."

"I was doing all right."

"You were not. And didn't you hear his friends? Three or four of them were standing around, ready to pounce."

"I've got just as many friends."

"Maybe. But your friends are smaller than his and none of us are fighters." Jason said nothing back. Doug walked a few more steps and was just about to say something else when he didn't hear Jason's footsteps anymore. He turned. Where was he? The property was bordered by a row of trees that darkened the whole area they had just walked through. A double row of cars lined the driveway. Back by the house, guys were yelling things like, "Where is he? Where'd he go?"

Was Jason going back for more?

A dark figure came out of the trees. It was Jason cradling something in his arms. "C'mon, Jason. We've got to go. They'll be out here any second."

Jason ignored him. He wandered into the row of cars. "I know which one is his."

"What are you talking about? C'mon."

"You get the car started, I'll be right there."

"What are you doing?"

"Go on. I'll be right there."

What was he carrying? Doug couldn't see. Moments later, he didn't need to see. He heard the crash. The sound of a large rock impacting a windshield.

"There!" Jason said as he turned toward Doug.

"You idiot." Doug ran up and began dragging him toward his car. He looked back to see a mob heading their way from the side yard.

As he reached his car, Doug heard a guy

yell, "Rob, that guy bashed in your windshield," followed by a string of obscenities.

"Get in," he said to Jason. Fortunately, there were no cars blocking him in. He pulled out with the lights off. Backing into the street, he tore off down the road, looking in the rearview mirror every few seconds until they made it out of the subdivision. Jason slouched in the seat beside him, holding his face. Doug didn't know how many times he'd been hit. "Does it hurt much?"

"It doesn't feel good."

Doug was sure it would hurt ten times more in the morning, once the booze had worn off. "That was a stupid thing to do."

"I didn't know she was the guy's girlfriend. She never said anything."

"I'm talking about throwing the rock at the guy's windshield." Doug looked at his speedometer then hit the gas pedal. He turned onto the main road, which would take them back toward town. "Did you know him, the boyfriend?"

Still slouched against the side door, Jason said, "I heard them call him Rob."

"I heard that. But do you know him? Does he know you?"

"No. First time I saw him was when he shoved me."

"How'd you know that was his car?"

"As we were walking by, that car had a front license plate that said 'Rob.' "

"Did you know any of his friends? Or that girl, before tonight?"

"No. I just met her tonight. It was going pretty good too, until —"

Doug looked in his rearview mirror, saw a pair of headlights way back at the subdivision entrance. He swerved and made a quick left. "I'm taking another way home. The long way. They're coming after us. They'll probably stay on 207." He floored it. If he got a ticket, so be it. He wasn't drunk, so it wouldn't be that serious. Whatever it cost, it was better than getting beaten to a pulp. "You shouldn't have done that, Jason."

"I had to get even. I only hit him once, and that was in self-defense. He must've hit me a dozen times." He paused, did something with his mouth. "Crap, I've got a loose tooth."

"Well, it's a good thing they don't know who you are. It'll make it harder for them to come after you at school."

"I'm not even sure they go to Flagler."

"Maybe not, but half the kids at that party do. A guy like that won't let this go. He'll be asking around the school. You know what that means?"

"What?"

"It means you need to stay off the campus for a week or so."

"Why? I already told you they don't know who I am."

Doug glanced at Jason. "Your face. It's already swelling. And your right eye's starting to close up. Can't you feel it?" Jason shrugged. "You're going to have at least one black eye, maybe two. And a fat lip. And the left side of your face . . . you're going to look like a guy who lost a fight."

"I didn't lose."

Doug let it drop. It didn't matter. "The point is, if they start asking if anyone knows a guy who looks all beat up, they'll find out who you are. You need to lay low until your face heals up some. You have any tests this week?"

"I don't think so."

They drove a few minutes in silence. Doug kept checking the rearview mirror. They were still alone on the road. His phone rang. It was Courtney. "Hey."

"Where are you?"

"Driving Jason home."

"Is he all right?"

"His face is all banged up. Didn't you see that guy pounding him?"

"I did, and I saw what you did."

"I had no choice."

"I know."

"What's going on there now?"

"We're all getting ready to leave," Courtney said. "The guy he was fighting is furious about his car. So are his friends. They took off after you in another car. That's part of the reason I'm calling."

"Well, they won't find us. I'm taking a different way home. Jason says they don't know who he is."

"They don't. I heard them asking if anyone knew who he was, or who you were. No one seemed to know. Drew and I slipped away and headed back to the pool area." A few moments later, "Are you okay?"

"My shoulder stings a little from crashing into his head, but I'm fine. I'm just going to take Jason back to his dorm then head back to my apartment."

"This really stinks. You've been gone all weekend, and I haven't even seen you."

"I know. But I couldn't leave him there."

"I know. I think it was great that you saved him."

"I didn't really *save* him."

"Save me?" Jason said. "Is that what she said? You tell her you did not save me."

"Shut up. I already said that." Doug could

hear Courtney laughing.

"How about I head over to your apartment?" she said. "I know where you hide the spare key. I could be there waiting for you when you get home."

Doug knew what she had in mind. "That might be a better way to end this evening."

"If you're really nice," she said, "I can stay long enough to make you breakfast in the morning."

5

Christina pulled into the employee parking lot of Odds-n-Ends, the gift and craft store in River Oaks's quaint downtown area. Marilyn had helped her get the job last year. It didn't pay a lot, but she loved working there, especially getting to work with Marilyn. Besides, since she lived in Jim and Marilyn's garage apartment, her expenses were quite low.

Just then, her car provided a reminder that she might need to reach for some higher financial goals. It kept running after she turned it off, sputtering and coughing for several seconds. She needed a new car. At least a new one for her, one that wasn't about to die any minute. For that, she'd need more money than what she got paid here at the store.

When the car finally settled down, she got out. Was it her imagination or was it smelling bad too? Like burnt coffee. Halfway across the parking lot, she remembered her cell phone on the front seat. She went back to retrieve it, and before putting it in her purse, she took a look at Twitter. There was a tweet from Doug sent last night, not to her but to anyone following him: *Back in St Aug, heading to a party. Jason, Courtney, and the gang already there. Should be fun.*

That was it. No other tweets, no pics on Facebook or Instagram.

She hated where their relationship was now and wished she didn't care about him so much. Was he all right? Did he get back to his apartment safely last night? An image of Courtney flashed in her mind. *Did he go home alone?*

Walking back across the parking lot, she tried blocking thoughts of their relationship from her mind. She and Doug were just friends, and that was all they had ever been. Really, not even close friends anymore. She was sure he and Courtney were a couple now and just as sure that Courtney was the reason Doug had stopped interacting with her online.

She was torturing herself, keeping track of him this way.

Her phone also told her the time, a few minutes before nine. The store opened in an hour. As she walked into the back

36

hallway, the fragrant aroma of freshly ground coffee filled her nostrils. The pleasant sound of Marilyn's humming added to the ambience. Marilyn must be making coffee for the customers. Harriet, the store's owner, had purchased a big commercial brewer a few months ago. She'd thought customers might stay and browse a little longer when that coffee urge hit them at midmorning and midafternoon. It seemed to be working, and the best part was, employees got to drink it too. As much as they wanted.

"Oh hi, Christina," Marilyn said. "Would you mind cleaning out the decaf pot while I grind some more?"

"I don't mind doing anything as long as you keep putting that wonderful smell in the air."

Marilyn laughed. "I know. Coffee smells even better than it tastes."

After Christina finished cleaning the pot, she returned to the back aisle where she'd been working on Saturday. Just a little inventory project, trading out some winter items that hadn't been selling very well for some new stock that spoke more of spring. She wanted to finish before the store opened.

Almost an hour later, Marilyn came down

her aisle. "I wanted to thank you again for talking with Jim and me yesterday about Doug's situation."

Christina had just bent down to begin working on the lower shelves. She looked up. "You're welcome. I'm not sure what I did deserves any thanks."

"I guess we're just thankful that you're still connecting with him. After you left last night, Jim and I talked about how disconnected we both feel. In some ways, we know it's natural. Kids have to grow up and move out. And when they do, parents always feel less involved. It happened with both Tom and Michele. But somehow, it seems worse with Doug."

Christina wasn't sure she *was* still connecting with Doug. "Do you think it just feels that way because Doug is your youngest, the last one to leave home?"

"We talked about that," Marilyn said. "I think it's more than that. If anything, you'd think we'd be more used to this after going through it twice already. It's always hard on a parent when a child leaves home, even for the right reasons. Listen to me, calling Doug a child. But that's the problem. When I look at all my kids, no matter their age, I can see them as the adults they are now, but right near the surface are flashbacks of them at every age between now and when they were babies."

"That must be hard," Christina said.

"Sometimes it is. Because you remember when they were totally dependent on you and came to you with all their questions and shared all their fears."

Christina could only imagine. Sadly, that didn't describe her childhood. Her mom had always seemed more focused on her latest boyfriend and having a good time. The ironic thing was, Christina was experiencing the benefits of Marilyn's motherly skills now, while her own son took her totally for granted. Marilyn was the person Christina turned to with all her questions and shared all her fears. "It doesn't make any sense to me," she said.

"What doesn't?"

Christina stood up. "This thing between parents and kids. I mean when the kids get older. I see it happening with Doug. But I see it all the time at church too, with the youth group kids. They reach a certain age, and all of a sudden, they don't trust their parents anymore. They forget how their parents treated them when they were younger, and now they're totally suspicious of anything their parents say. They might even listen to another adult say the same thing, but if their parents say it . . ."

Marilyn laughed. "I'm not laughing because it's funny. It's just true. I have no idea why it happens. It's sad when it does. As a parent, you feel so helpless." She looked up at the front door. "I guess we need to open the store in a few minutes."

Christina remembered something she had read in the Bible a few mornings ago. She hadn't thought about it then, but it kind of connected to what they were saying. "Remember that story in the New Testament when Jesus went back to his hometown. What was it called?"

"Nazareth?" Marilyn said.

"Yeah, that was it. By that time, he'd already gotten famous everywhere else from his preaching and especially the miracles. But back home, they couldn't see it. It said he could hardly do any miracles at all there because of their unbelief. All they could see when they looked at him was the kid who grew up there. Jesus said something that explained it, but I can't remember what it was."

"A prophet is not without honor," Marilyn said, "except in his hometown and among his own people."

"That's it. Because they had all that history with Jesus, they couldn't see past it.

They couldn't see who he was now and how much he could help them. But other people, the ones who had just met Jesus, didn't have to work through all that."

"I think that does relate to what we're dealing with here," Marilyn said. "Doug doesn't really see us. Not as people who could help him. To tell you the truth, I don't know how he sees us or what he thinks about us anymore."

"I'm sure he loves you," Christina said.

"I think he does too. In his own way."

Harriet, the owner, suddenly appeared. "Uh, ladies." Her eyes pointed toward the front door. "It's ten o'clock. I see customers standing outside."

"Sorry, Harriet," Marilyn said. "I'll take care of it right now." She hurried toward the door.

Christina also apologized and looked at the customers through the glass.

"Look, Christina," Marilyn whispered loudly. "One of them is that nice boy from church. What's his name again?"

"Ted," she said. "His name is Ted."

Ugh. What was he doing here . . . again?

6

Christina quickly dropped out of sight. She was pretty sure Ted had seen her through the glass. She heard the bolt unlatch as Marilyn opened the front door. Joyful voices entered the store; Marilyn greeted each one. One of them was Ted's, the only guy in the mix.

This was Ted's third visit to the store in the past week. At least the third Christina knew about. Each time he'd pretended to shop. The second time he'd actually bought something. Something small, judging by the bag. Harriet had waited on him. Christina didn't ask what he'd purchased, because she didn't want to appear interested.

That was because she wasn't interested in Ted.

Not at all.

It was pretty clear Ted was interested in her. Guys hardly ever shopped at Odds-n-Ends, at least by themselves, unless they were looking for gifts for their wives or girlfriends. Harriet didn't even try to carry items men cared about.

But here was Ted, again, by himself.

It wasn't just his visits to the store. Several times at church, especially over the last few Sundays, she caught him looking at her from across the auditorium. He'd quickly turn away, and so would she. But it happened way too often to be a coincidence. She stuck a price sticker to a cute little ceramic frog, set it on the shelf, and listened for his voice. He was talking to someone, probably Marilyn.

"Yes, she's working today," Marilyn said. "She's probably down one of the aisles. Don't you have school today?"

Ted said something. She heard the word *canceled.* She remembered him saying during his last visit that he attended UCF, a college near Orlando. They had a smaller regional campus even closer, in Sanford. He mentioned he wanted to be a banker someday. That seemed about right.

She lifted the next frog in the box, priced it, and set it on the shelf. She had better just accept it — in a few moments, Ted would find her.

He wasn't that bad, she told herself. He was interested, not stalking her. People at church liked Ted. Marilyn certainly did. And he wasn't bad looking. Fairly tall with short dark hair, likely cut by a barber not a stylist. He dressed in preppy-type clothes, which was different. For her. She was used to guys wearing jeans and T-shirts.

"Oh, there you are. Mrs. Anderson said you were working today."

Christina looked up into Ted's smiling face. Ted was always smiling. "Here I am."

"What are you working on?" he said.

"Frogs at the moment. Interested in buying a frog?" She held one up.

Ted laughed. "Maybe. I'm actually here to buy something for my older sister. It's her birthday Saturday. Maybe you can help me."

"How does she feel about frogs?"

"She's terrified of them."

Christina laughed. She didn't expect that. She stood. "Then we'll have to try a different direction. Is she interested in anything else?"

"I'm sure she is," Ted said. "Though what, I don't know."

"Well, think about it a minute. How much older is she?"

"Three years."

"Well, that's not *that* much older. When you guys were growing up, was she into anything? Like gymnastics? Did she like

44

sports? We don't have any guy-type collectibles, but we have some cute ones for women fans."

Ted laughed. "Hardly. I don't think I've ever seen her play any kind of sport."

"Guess that means she didn't have any favorite teams."

He shook his head no.

"We're making progress," Christina said. "That eliminates an entire aisle." She walked past him into the main aisle.

He turned and followed. "I'm sorry. Before she went off to school, we weren't really all that close. She ran with a different crowd than I did in her high school years. She wasn't home all that much even when she lived here."

"Have you talked to your mother about this? I'm sure she knows things your sister might like."

"You're probably right. I should have done that first. Coming here was kind of a spur-of-the-moment thing."

Christina walked down another aisle. She wasn't sure why. Maybe just to create some space between them. "Did your folks keep her room the way she left it, or did someone else take it over?"

"It's still the same."

"Okay, then think. You must've spent

some time in her room, right?"

"A little, maybe. I certainly didn't hang out in there."

"Don't get defensive. I wasn't insinuating anything. Now, close your eyes."

"Why?"

"Don't be difficult. Just do it." He did. "Think about the walls in your sister's room. Is there anything hanging on them? How about her dresser? Does she have any bookshelves? Do you see any knickknacks or any ceramic figurines? Anything she might have collected?"

"She had some posters on the walls, some rock bands, I think."

"What were their names?"

"I don't know. We didn't listen to the same kind of music."

"Anything else?"

"On her dresser, there was a little ceramic hummingbird and a big pink flower." He opened his eyes. "But it's not there anymore. She took it with her to college."

"See? You do know something she likes. Hummingbirds. If she brought it with her to college, then she definitely likes it. Follow me." Christina stepped around him, walked past the aisle she had been working in toward the back of the store. She stopped at some boxes piled in stacks of three.

Coming up behind her, Ted said, "What are these?"

She picked up a clipboard. "These are boxes of stuff for the spring. That's what I'm working on today. Changing out some of the winter stuff and replacing them with these. We don't have any hummingbirds out right now, but I remembered seeing something about them on this list."

"Really?" He stood closer.

A little too close. She took a step sideways as she flipped through the first few pages. "Here it is. Hummingbirds. Four different kinds. All in the same box." She circled the box number then began looking for a matching label. She had stacked them so that all the labels faced outward. She pointed to one. "Wouldn't you know it? It's on the bottom row."

"Here," Ted said. "I'll move the ones on top."

"Just stack them right next to it. I'm hoping to get through all of them before I finish today."

"What time do you get off?"

Rats. She played right into that one. "I'm supposed to get off at six. But it might be later if I don't finish." That wasn't exactly true. Harriet would never make her stay late.

"Oh." He set the boxes down.

She pulled out her box cutter, hoping to redirect the conversation, and quickly sliced through the shipping tape. "We should find what we're looking for in here." She gently set the non-hummingbird items aside. "Here we go. Hummingbirds. Oh, these are nice. I'm sure we can find some your sister will like here." She felt him hovering above her.

"Those are nice."

She grabbed hold of one of each. They came in nice gift boxes with a picture on the lid of what was inside. She looked up. He stood up straight.

"Can I see that shiny green one?"

She laid the other three boxes down. "Now, this one can also be used as a Christmas ornament. It's got this little loop and a hook." She lifted the lid. "You don't have to use it as an ornament. We also sell little stands that look nice on dressers and shelves. People can hang things like this on one and enjoy them all year long."

He reached for the box, so she gave it to him. "Yeah, this looks really nice. I'm pretty sure she'd love this. Do you know what it costs?"

"I'll have to look it up on the sheet. Excuse me." She stood and reached for the clipboard. "We sell it for $19.95. The stands start as low as $4.95. So for about twenty-five bucks you can give your sister a really high-end-looking gift."

"That's a few dollars more than I was thinking but, what the heck. Let's do it."

"Great. I'll just walk over to the other side of the store and grab that stand. Why don't you meet me at the counter?"

He gave her a strange expression, like he was going to ask if he could come with her to get the stand. "Okay, let's do that."

She turned and quickly walked away, passing Marilyn down the aisle with the stands.

"How is Ted?" Marilyn asked.

"Ted's fine. He's here getting a present for his sister's birthday. Found something in one of the spring boxes. Wasn't even opened yet."

"That's nice, a brother buying his sister a gift."

"A nice one too. A fancy hummingbird ornament. Just need to get one of these stands." She paused a moment, then decided on the brass-plated one. She carried it back to the counter and stepped behind the register.

Ted held up the stand. "Yeah, she'll like this. Thanks a bunch, Christina. I had no idea what to get her when I walked in."

"No problem." She rang up both items

49

then looked at the small line of customers that had formed behind him. "If you can come back a little later, I can gift wrap them for you."

"Really? I stink at gift wrapping. Let's do it."

"Oh no." Did she just say that out loud?

"What's the matter?"

"Oh, nothing."

But it wasn't nothing. She had just given Ted a reason to come back to the store.

7

Addis Ababa, Ethiopia

Michele slipped quietly out of Ayana's room and gently closed the door. She had just read a bedtime story to her and the two little girls sharing her room. It was a few minutes before nine; time to call Allan back home in the US. If she could get a decent connection. She had been here for three weeks already, visiting with Ayana and doing everything she could to help move their adoption date forward.

Seven months had passed since she and Allan had first come to Ethiopia, specifically to Korah, the little village near the city dump where Ayana had been born. That was where they had met her, where God had first spoken to their hearts about adopting her and bringing her back to the States. She couldn't have imagined then that Ayana would still be stuck here, seven months later, and still not legally their little girl.

Henok, the orphanage director, had said it could take six months or more, even though the government had given their preliminary approval. She had met with him earlier that day, which was one of the things she hoped to talk to Allan about tonight. As she walked through the living area, Michele nodded to Adina, one of the two women who lived and worked at the orphanage. Adina sat under a lamp on the corner of the couch, reading a book.

Michele held up her cell phone and pointed to the front door. Adina smiled and made a praying hands gesture. She knew how spotty cell phone service could be here and how much Michele missed Allan. Michele opened the front door and stepped into the cool night air. The newspaper said it might rain tonight. Michele hoped not, at least while she was on the phone.

Standing in the spot where she seemed to get the best connection, she dialed Allan's number. Nothing but silence for several moments, then the wonderful sound of his phone ringing. *Please pick up.* With the time difference, he should be on his lunch hour.

"Hello? Michele, can you hear me?"

"I can," she said. "You're coming through pretty strong. It's so good to hear your voice."

"Yours too. I miss you so much."

"I miss you too, Allan."

"Is Ayana asleep?"

"Just put her down a few minutes ago, after reading her and her friends a bedtime story."

"Which one?"

"The one you sent. It's her favorite now. She wants me to read it every night."

"Every night?"

"Every night."

"That's sweet. How is she doing? Besides at bedtime."

"She's being totally adorable. I wish you could be here with us. I know she's not a baby, but every day feels special, like something new happens and I want you to see it."

"What happened today?"

"We played patty-cake. Nothing fancy. Just the old-fashioned 'patty-cake, patty-cake, baker's man. Bake me a cake as fast as you can.' But she loved it."

"In English?"

"Yes, in English. I had to explain what it meant, but you should hear how well she's doing. Henok said she's learned more English these past three weeks than she has since she first moved into the orphanage."

"Are you learning any Amharic?"

"A little. My accent must be terrible."

"Why?"

"Every time I say something in their language, the people around me laugh." Michele heard a rumbling sound off in the distance. "Uh-oh."

"What's the matter?"

"I just heard thunder."

"Then we better get off the phone."

"No, not yet. It was way off in the distance. We've still got time."

"Just in case, maybe you better tell me anything you want to say before any more small talk."

"Hey, this wasn't small talk."

"You know what I mean."

She did. "Well, I did talk with Henok today. He thinks we're making good progress. Things seem to be happening at a faster pace now that I'm here."

"Anything firm? Anything like a date when the two of you can come home?"

"Not exactly. I asked him to make an educated guess. He thought it could be within two to three weeks. But then he was quick to add he couldn't be certain. Right now, they're working on securing Ayana's birth certificate and passport so we can get her US visa. He's sure they'll be able to get everything together soon."

54

"That's good. I hope he's right. I'd hate for you guys to still be stuck there once the rainy season starts."

"When's that?" she asked.

"Supposed to start in May. But you'll probably start seeing more rain than you've been seeing even before that. It gets really bad in July and August. I've never been there then, but Ray says it's awful."

"I hope we're not still here," she said. "That would be awful. Not so much because of the rain. I'd just hate not being with you that long. Or waiting that long to bring Ayana home."

"Are you having any second thoughts about going over there when you did?"

Michele sighed. When she'd left the US, she'd had no idea she'd be gone this long. She was only required to come here when Ayana's visa was ready to be approved, a trip that might take only three to five days. "At times, I wonder if I made the right choice. Like now, hearing your voice. I miss you so much. But getting to spend all this time with Ayana has been so precious. We're really connecting now. I can't imagine missing out on all the moments we've had. So no, I'm glad I came when I did. I just hope there aren't any more unexpected delays."

"We've got a lot of folks back here praying

for that very thing. God's already taken care of the biggest hurdle."

She knew he meant the money. "I know." A loud crack of thunder came out of nowhere, startling her. "Whoa, that was close."

"I heard that," Allan said. "You better get inside. That means it's going to start pouring any second."

"I don't want to let you go."

"I know." Neither one said anything for a few moments. "I love you," he said.

"I love you too." Heavy raindrops began to fall. "I'll call you again soon."

"Soon as you can, and definitely the moment you hear anything about the visa coming through."

"I will."

8

Jason had done a pretty good job staying out of sight since the fight at the party just over a week ago. Neither one of them had run into Rob, the guy Jason had fought, although Doug had seen him once across the dining hall on Tuesday. He was sitting with a group of guys, laughing up a storm. Doug figured they were the same guys standing around watching the fight last week. None of them had recognized Doug. How could they? He had rushed out of the dark when he'd tackled Rob and left in a hurry, walking through the shadows.

Doug had only seen Jason twice since the fight. The last time was two days ago. Jason still looked banged up but not as bruised or swollen as he had last weekend. Right now, Doug was sitting in his red Mazda, parked on the curb in front of the men's dorm on Cedar Street. Jason was supposed to be down any moment. Doug had moved out of the dorms last year to an apartment a few streets away, still within easy walking distance to the campus.

Jason had called Doug that Sunday morning, all excited, saying he had a surprise. The only catch was it would cost Doug about twenty-five bucks. Doug checked his allowance account and figured he could swing it.

The front door of the dorm opened. Doug looked up and saw Jason heading his way. He opened the car door and hopped in the front seat.

"Face is looking a little better," Doug said.

"Yeah, the swelling's almost completely gone. It's still tender on the left side, but I'm getting used to it. Should be like new in a couple more days."

"So what's up? What's the big surprise?"

"Start driving and I'll tell you."

Doug pulled out of the parking lot and turned right, down the one-way street bordering the dorm building. When he got to the stop sign, he said, "Okay, which way do I go?"

"Go right, then head down to King Street and go left. Then left at US-1 to 207. All the way up to I-95 and head south."

"Where we going? Should I have packed a bag?" Doug turned onto the road.

"No, we'll be back tonight. Late tonight, but tonight."

"So, how long will I have to wait before you tell me what's up?"

"I'll tell you now. There's a Comic-Con going on in Orlando."

Doug knew that. "That's where we're headed?"

"Thought it might be fun. Maybe give us some fresh inspiration and ideas for our graphic novel. Today's the last day of the event."

Doug smiled as he turned left on King Street. "You surprise me sometimes, Jason. I actually like this idea."

"Figured you would."

"Is that where the twenty-five bucks comes in?"

"Yep. That's for a day pass."

"You know, with gas and food, it's going to be more than that."

"Since when does that matter?" Jason said. "Got my dad's credit card, so don't sweat it. I'll cover the rest."

Jason spent money like the government. And he never seemed to get in trouble for it. Doug had to live on a pretty tight budget. "Well, you better get the card out. I'm going to need some gas if we're driving all the way to Orlando and back."

"Not a problem. There's plenty of gas stations between here and the highway."

A few blocks down the road they passed a Methodist church. Jason didn't even glance in that direction. Doug noticed all the nicely dressed people coming down the sidewalk and walking up the front steps. They were doing the right thing, what people were supposed to do on a Sunday morning. A feeling surfaced. Like the church itself was condemning him. His eyes shot back to the road.

He was glad they didn't get stuck at the light.

Jason reached over and turned on some music. A few blocks farther, Doug crossed the San Sebastian River, a narrow waterway at this point. He turned left on US-1 and saw a discount gas station up ahead. "We'll stop there."

"Okay, you fill it up. I didn't have any breakfast. I'm gonna get something to eat. You want anything?"

"No, I'm good," Doug said.

"Got a long drive. How about some snacks for the road?"

"All right. A bag of cashews and a Diet Coke."

"Diet Coke? First thing in the morning?"

Doug pulled into the gas station parking

lot. "All right, a bottle of water."

Nearly two hours later, Doug got off I-4 on International Drive in Orlando. It was a madhouse. Cars everywhere. But he was glad for the distraction. A while back they had driven past the exit they would have taken to River Oaks. Doug had involuntarily looked at the clock on his dashboard. His parents would be leaving the house for church about then. Christina too. If he'd have been home, he would have been with them. They'd have met Tom, Jean, and their kids in the church lobby. Allan and Michele too. Everyone would have sat together, or at least tried.

And everyone would be happy to be there. Except him.

The Orange County Convention Center was in sight, just up ahead. "Almost forgot how crazy the traffic is around here," Doug said.

"Not as crazy as some of the people. Look at that guy in the Spiderman getup. Guess Spidey's let himself go since his last adventure."

Doug laughed as they drove past. The guy really had no business wearing tights. Jason rolled down the window. "Jason, don't."

Jason hung his head out. "Hey, Spidey.

Three or four times a week on the treadmill, and I'll bet you'll be swinging from buildings again in no time."

"Jason, stop." Doug pulled him back in. Spiderman responded with a familiar hand gesture. A few yards ahead, Doug spotted a rather large girl dressed as Wonder Woman.

"Not seeing the wonder, darlin'," Jason yelled out the window.

Doug sped ahead, raised Jason's window, and locked it.

"Just having a little fun."

"I know, but you better start practicing some restraint. You keep this going when we get in the convention center, and you'll get in another fight."

"You're being paranoid," Jason said. "I know how to handle these situations."

"I'm being paranoid? I'm not the one who's been hiding out all week so his face could heal up." That shut him up. "Which building is it?"

"I'm not sure."

"Look it up on your phone."

"The main intersection's right up ahead. I'll just ask somebody." He tried rolling down his window. "Would you unlock this?" Doug did, and Jason asked the next person in a costume. Turning back to Doug, he said, "Turn right at the light and just follow the weirdos."

"That's not what the guy said." Doug rolled Jason's window up and hit the lock button again.

"No, he said it's in the West Building, which is huge. And just follow all the cosplayers." The insider term for people who love dressing up in costumes.

Doug waited for his turn to turn right at the light. "So do you, like, totally despise these people?" Of the two of them, Doug was the one more into comic books. Jason read them occasionally. But he more enjoyed all the indie artists and writers, not the mainstream comic world that usually dominated events like these.

"I don't despise them. Not all of them. Like that young lady there dressed as Cat Woman, I don't despise her. Actually, I'd like her phone number."

"But you gotta watch your attitude. These are the people we hope will buy our graphic novel. We could potentially make some solid connections at this convention. Some of the people who could help make this deal happen might be dressed in some of these crazy costumes you're mocking."

"I'll behave. As soon as I walk through that door, I'll be a total fan."

The traffic slowed to bumper-to-bumper

as they neared the massive parking lot behind the West Building. There were plenty of sights to see on the sidewalks and surrounding cars. A full-on circus, almost surreal. Everywhere you looked, people dressed in the most outlandish costumes, walking, talking, sipping lattes as if it was the most normal thing in the world.

Doug was beginning to have doubts about his partnership with Jason on this project. They had talked about their differences before. Doug was not a fanatic, but he did enjoy this world and its inhabitants. It was just good fun. But Jason felt nothing but contempt for the cosplayers, the ones who completely bought into the fantasy lifestyle, whose entire lives were wrapped around this alternative world.

How could Jason write a credible fantasy story that connected well with their target audience if he viewed them as nothing more than pathetic losers?

9

Doug and Jason followed the long trail of Comic-Con devotees from the parking lot through the massive lobby area of the convention center. The organizers had set up temporary barriers to corral people in a Disney line toward the ticket booths. Although the main events were beyond the entrance, it was clear the show had already begun in line. Everywhere you looked, life-sized versions of comic book, cartoon, and video game characters walked about, occasionally stopping to take pictures or to pose for someone else.

"This is so crazy," Jason whispered, his eyes darting all over the place. "These people are nuts. Some of them have to be spending serious money on these costumes."

Jason almost sounded like he was genuinely impressed. They moved forward in line a few more yards.

"Look at Thor over there," Jason

continued, "and that Iron Man next to him. Looks just like the movie characters." He leaned closer, talked even quieter. "Of course, that guy dressed up like Wolverine. He's got the hairdo down, but man, he needs to put on a shirt. Nobody wants to see that."

Doug nodded, smiled, and whispered back, "I'm seeing quite a few people with a little too much self-esteem." About half the people in costume were pulling it off. A smaller group looked absolutely amazing. But another block of cosplayers were way too out of shape to be showing so much skin. Some were almost revolting. Doug tried not to stare at one guy wearing a full Superman outfit. He wasn't obese, just flabby. Dressed in jeans and a loose-fitting shirt, he might have looked half-decent. But he was no Superman. Doug had to look away.

They rounded a turn in line and were now on the final stretch to the ticket booths. The guy directly in front of them wore a long black wig. His clothes were all torn and hung like rags. When the guy turned, his face startled Doug. His sickening greenish-gray skin looked like it was falling off his face. The front of his outfit was covered in fake blood.

"That's a great zombie getup," Jason said. "You do all that makeup?"

"Most of it," the guy said. "My mom did the parts I couldn't reach."

Doug couldn't fathom it. His mom would freak out if he dressed up like that.

"I wish this line would speed up," the zombie said. "I don't want to miss the walk."

"The walk?" Doug said.

"The Zombie Walk. Starts in twenty minutes. Everyone in the building dressed like zombies is supposed to walk together — totally in character — like a zombie parade."

"I've got to see that," Jason said.

"I want to be in it," the zombie said.

They moved forward some more. There were about a dozen people left in front of them. A guy dressed like Captain Jack Sparrow walked past. Doug turned and watched him until he blended in with the crowd. He was spot on, even had the drunken walk down.

"If that guy was just a little shorter," Jason said, "I might have believed Johnny Depp just walked by."

"Make you wish we were into this a little more?" Doug asked, quiet enough so zombie man wouldn't hear.

"Maybe just a little. Something about being here surrounded by it all doesn't seem as crazy as it did outside."

"If you were going to dress up," Doug asked, "who would you be?"

Jason thought a minute, took a few steps forward to close the gap. An emaciated, shirtless teenager walked by dressed in a Captain America outfit, complete with a mini red-white-and-blue shield. "I'm not sure," Jason said. "But I can tell you one thing, whoever it was, it'd definitely be a character who wore a shirt."

For the next three hours, Doug and Jason walked around the convention center, taking in all the sights and sounds. They strolled slowly down Artists' Alley, where a number of well-known and some wannabe graphic artists had their latest artwork on display. Doug loved looking at them all and wanted to stay longer, but Jason kept nagging him to move on. Doug wanted to buy a dozen things, but he couldn't think of a way to get them on his school debit card without his dad finding out.

They spent time browsing through the hundreds of comic books on sale. Some of the vintage ones dated back to the 1950s and '60s. Doug was surprised at the prices. A lot less than he'd expected. Someone in line had said the prices really dropped the last few years, so Doug picked up a few.

They walked past a big display of Legos. Jason was like a little kid. There were Lego sets featuring every comic book character you could think of. Superman, Iron Man, Batman. Lego kits for Star Wars and Lord of the Rings. Before they were done, Jason had spent over two hundred dollars.

Of course, he'd just pulled out Daddy's credit card.

Now they stood in a fairly long line to meet and greet a well-known comic book author and artist named Chris Ware. Jason was holding one of Ware's bestselling graphic novels, which he'd just purchased when he found out Ware was here. Doug wanted to meet him too. But Jason *really* wanted to meet him and hoped to get his autograph. The Boy Robin stood in front of them. Behind them, a fierce-looking Klingon.

Robin turned around. "You guys like Ware's stuff?"

"Definitely," Jason said. " 'Course, we're working on a graphic novel of our own right now."

"Really?" Robin said. "I am too." He looked at Doug. "Who's doing what?"

"Doug here's doing the artwork. I'm doing most of the writing. We're both working on the story line."

"Wish I had a partner. It's taking me forever with school and work. How far along are you guys?"

The line had moved ahead, but the Boy Robin was facing them. The Klingon, remaining in character, let out a deep growl and said, "You guys mind?"

"Sorry," Robin said and closed the gap.

"We're still at the rough sketch level," Jason said. "Still hammering out the main concepts."

"What's your story about?"

"It's called *The Prodigal,*" Doug said. "We're sort of borrowing from the biblical story, but just as a metaphor. It's not a religious theme in our book."

"I've heard of it," Robin said. "We read it in Sunday school when I was a kid. About a guy who leaves his home, right? Goes out seeking his fortune so he can marry some girl."

"Not quite," Doug said. "You got the first part right. But he leaves home *with* a fortune he got from his dad, got his inheritance early. He turns his back on everything he's known growing up. That's what the hero does in our story. It's on a planet kind of like Earth, but unlike here, there's only two

70

main groups of people. The main group, the majority, have taken over the world. They've got all the money and the power, all the resources. But they've turned their back on all the values their civilization started with centuries ago. The smaller group live out in the country off the land and scorn material things. The majority group persecutes them because they practice all the old traditions, including some that involve supernatural powers, things that take years to master. The hero in our story is tired of having nothing all the time, so he leaves his family and sets out for this big city —"

Doug felt something kick his foot. He looked down. It was Jason's foot.

"The line's moving," Jason said. "Don't want to get this Klingon mad."

"Oh."

"That sounds pretty cool," Robin said as he caught up to the rest of the line.

Doug was about to join him, but Jason held on to his arm. "What are you doing, man?" Jason whispered. "You're giving our whole story away. You don't tell some stranger all that. People are treacherous. For all you know, that guy could go home and steal what we're doing. Or someone else'll overhear you and do the same thing. You need to work on giving out shorter answers."

"All right," Doug said. "Let go of my arm."

10

After walking all day, it felt good to sit down awhile. Doug and Jason along with several hundred other people sat in a side auditorium, listening to a number of celebrities from the SyFy channel. The stars were up front behind a long table, answering questions into microphones. Behind them, hanging on a black curtain, display posters revealed what the actors looked like on their shows. Necessary for most of them or you'd never make the connection, since their characters' costume and makeup completely changed their looks. It was interesting to hear all the behind-the-scenes stories the actors shared, but Doug didn't watch any of the shows they were on.

Jason leaned over. "That would be kind of a drag, don't you think? Imagine being a star in a hit TV show and the whole time your face looks like a big green lizard with horns. No one would ever recognize you."

Doug was thinking the same thing. "Some of the questions these people are asking are so lame."

A guy dressed like the Riddler was handed a mike and asked one of the actors, "Do you ever wish your show was real and you could, like, be your character in real life?"

"You want to go get something to eat?" Jason said.

"Yeah, let's get out of here."

Fortunately, they were sitting at the end of the aisle. As they walked toward the exit into the main area of the show, Jason froze.

"What's the matter?" Doug asked.

"Quick, over here." Jason turned and walked quickly the other way, nervously looking over his shoulder.

"Where are we going?"

"I'll tell you in a minute. C'mon."

Doug followed. "Just tell me. What's going on?"

Jason ducked into a side room off the main hall, a large area filled with vendors selling comic costumes and paraphernalia. He leaned against the wall. "That was close."

"What was close? What's going on?"

Jason leaned forward and looked through the doorway. "You're never going to believe who I saw."

"Who?"

"Rob. You know, the guy I got in a fight with at the party? He was up ahead in the corridor with his friends, coming this way."

"You're kidding."

"No, I'm not. We gotta get outta here."

Doug didn't want to leave. He looked around, saw something at one of the vendor tables that gave him an idea. "C'mon. We don't have to go. Not until we're good and ready."

"Look, Doug, my face is almost healed up, I don't want to —"

"Trust me. You'll be fine. But you're just gonna have to get out your daddy's credit card again." Jason followed him to a vendor three booths away. "Look. Problem solved." The vendor sold all kinds of masks and hats and colorful wigs. Jason smiled. He got the idea. "Pick something out, and we're back in business."

There was a mirror at the end of the table. Jason tried on a number of things and settled on a Batman mask with a matching cape. He looked ridiculous, especially considering he wasn't wearing the rest of the costume. But in this crowd, he'd blend right in.

"Great idea, Doug. Don't you need to get something?"

"They never saw what I looked like."

"Okay, then, let's go get something to eat."

As they made their way out to the main hall, Doug's phone buzzed. The tone told him it was a text.

"Is that Courtney again?" Jason asked.

Doug looked. It was. She had texted him three times since noon. He'd given her short, evasive answers each time.

"Why don't you just pick it up and call her?" Jason said. "You've got nothing to hide. Just tell her we're at a comic book convention. Meeting all kinds of fun people. Batman, Superman, Wolverine. And look, there goes Bart Simpson."

Doug knew that Courtney liked the comic book world even less than Jason did. She didn't consider it a legitimate art form. More like a waste of art. "You've got so much talent, Doug," she had finally said when he'd pressed for her opinion. "Why are you drawing stuff like *that*?" Doug looked down at the phone again as they continued to walk, trying to decide what to do.

"C'mon," Jason said. "We're going the wrong way. The food court's at the other end, remember?"

Doug turned and followed, put his cell phone back in his pocket.

"You're going to ignore her? If I had a girl that looked like that, I definitely wouldn't ignore her."

"I'm not going to ignore her. I can't text and walk at the same time, not with all these people. I'll respond when we're sitting down."

A few minutes later, they were sitting at a round table with glasses of soda and slices of pizza. Jason laughed. "You know what this reminds me of? That bar scene in the first Star Wars movie. You know, when Obi-Wan Kenobi and Han Solo are sitting there talking, surrounded by all these wild-looking alien creatures. And everybody acts like it's perfectly normal."

Doug looked around. It kinda did. He stood up.

"Where are you going?"

"Over by that partition wall. Away from the noise. I'm going to call Courtney instead. Texting will take too long. I'll say something, then she'll say something. Then I'll say something back. I'm just going to talk to her, get it over with."

"You sound like you're getting a tooth pulled."

Doug smiled and turned to walk away.

"You going to eat this pizza?"

"Yeah, I'm going to eat it. I'm only gonna

be a couple of minutes."

"We'll see."

Doug found a relatively quiet place and called her.

"Hey, Doug. Where've you been all day?"

That was the question, wasn't it? Should he lie? They weren't that close yet, so she probably wouldn't be able to tell if he lied to her. He could say something partly true. He and Jason had gone out of town for the day. He'd just need to think up something better than a Comic-Con. Then he remembered, Jason had already uploaded a bunch of pictures from his phone to Instagram. "I'm in Orlando with Jason."

"Orlando? Guess that answers my next question."

"What were you going to ask?"

"Whether I should come over."

"Oh. Yeah, guess that wouldn't work out."

"How long till you get home?"

"It'll be late tonight."

"That's too bad."

"I know," he said.

"So, what are you guys doing in Orlando?"

He paused. "I'd tell you, but you're not going to like it."

"Why?"

"Because we're at a comic book convention, a Comic-Con. It was Jason's idea. He's been shut up in the dorm all week letting his face heal up from that fight."

"How's it looking, his face?"

That wasn't so bad. He was expecting a stronger reaction. "A lot better. The swelling's mostly gone. You can still see a little bruising. Of course, around here it doesn't matter. Half his face could be falling off and no one would pay any attention."

"Why?"

"Because of the zombies." Doug was looking at three of them walking by right now.

"Zombies?"

He laughed. "You know, everybody's into zombies now. All the video games and movies. And TV shows like *The Walking Dead*. There's at least a hundred people here made up like zombies, walking around in character. They're even having a zombie costume contest in about an hour. But it's not just zombies. Half the people at this convention — and there's thousands of 'em — are dressed up as something. Comic book characters mostly, but lots of other things. Characters from fantasy and sci-fi shows. All kinds of celebrities too."

"Wow. Anyone I'd know?"

Doug thought a moment. Was she just pretending to be interested? "I'm not sure.

79

Maybe."

There was a long, awkward pause.

"Well, I better get back with Jason. There's an event we're supposed to get to in a few minutes."

"Okay."

"I'll see you at school tomorrow," he said. "Meet you at the café outside of Kenan Hall."

"All right." She sounded a little happier.

They said a few more things, then hung up. He put his phone away and headed back to Jason, who was just finishing his pizza.

"How'd it go?"

"Fine. I told her where we were, that we wouldn't be home till late, and that I'd meet her at school tomorrow morning."

"She say anything insulting?"

"Surprisingly . . . no." Doug bit off the end of his pizza.

"See? She's not so bad. A little old school," Jason said. "You know, her taste for artistic things."

"That's one way to say it."

"But hey," Jason said, "with looks like that, I could put up with even worse faults."

Doug took another bite. *Looks*. That was certainly the primary attraction with Courtney, wasn't it? He was sure there were other things.

Nothing else came to mind just now.

11

Just after 10:00 p.m., Doug and Jason headed back to St. Augustine. They had just driven through downtown Orlando and were now headed toward the I-95 junction. The traffic on Sundays was always lighter than during the week.

The Comic-Con had ended on a high note for two reasons. First, they had walked right past Rob and his friends two more times without being recognized. But even better, just before they left, Doug had walked past a booth and read about a graphic novel contest. First prize was seventy-five thousand dollars and a guarantee that your work would be published. They immediately signed up. Now it was all Jason could talk about.

"I know we can win this thing," Jason said. "It's a slam dunk."

"It's not a slam dunk," Doug said. "Did you hear what the guy said? They had already given out almost three hundred applications, just at this event. I'm sure they'll receive thousands more over the internet before the deadline."

"Maybe, but nobody draws like you, and nobody writes like me. And we've got a totally unique story. I'm more confident now than ever after walking through all those exhibits."

Doug couldn't understand how. "What are you talking about, Jason? I was seeing all kinds of impressive graphics in there. Some of the most gifted artists in the business. I don't even play in their league."

"I'm not talking about the established guys. I'm talking about all the newbies, the wannabes. Like most of the people we saw in that Artist Alley area. Your stuff was way better than what I saw in there."

Doug shifted into the middle lane. A busy exit was just up ahead.

"I see you smiling," Jason said. "You know I'm right."

Doug did think his drawings were better than most of what he saw from the up-and-coming artists, and as good as some of the more talented ones.

"And our story idea," Jason continued, "it's totally original. Put all that together, and we're sure to win."

"Totally original? We borrowed it straight out of the Bible."

"I'm talking about in comic book land and as a graphic novel."

"I hope so."

"What do you mean, you hope so?"

Doug looked in his rearview mirror. A pickup truck was way too close; its headlights glared in Doug's eyes. "I wish that guy would pass."

"Tap the brakes," Jason said. "That's what I always do. He'll get the message."

"Or he'll slam right into me."

"Or that. So, what do you mean? You're saying our story isn't original?"

"It's different enough, for the most part. But I told you it reminded me of something I read in one of my old comic books, remember? That's why I drove home last week, to go through some of my old boxes. I found what I was looking for. It was an old Batman series from '94. They even called it the Prodigal series. I started reading it again this week, and it's not that similar to what we're doing. I think we're in the clear. And it came out ten years ago, so that's a plus."

Jason got a concerned expression.

"What's the matter?"

"I just remembered something. I saw a

Wolverine graphic novel called *The Prodigal Son* on one of the tables this afternoon. I checked the date. It came out about four or five years ago."

"You need to check it out on the internet," Doug said, "see what you can find out about it. Maybe somebody's selling it for cheap, and you can buy it."

"Don't you think you're being a little paranoid? Our story takes place on a totally different planet than Earth. The only thing they have in common is they both draw from the Bible story."

"I know. But I still think you should read these things before you write our story, make sure you don't accidentally say things people will think we stole from an existing work."

"I can do that. Give me your Batman comic books when we get back, and I'll look up the Wolverine one this week."

Neither of them spoke for a few minutes. Jason turned on some music. They were finally getting farther out from the Orlando area. The highway shrank from three lanes down to two. There was still a good bit of traffic, but at least there was plenty of space between the cars. Doug began to play back some of the things he'd seen today when he noticed Jason fidgeting beside him. He pulled something out of his pocket. A moment later, Doug heard the click of a lighter. Jason held the flame up to the cigarette he'd just popped into his mouth.

Only it wasn't a cigarette; it was a joint.

"What are you doing?"

"What does it look like I'm doing? Lighting this baby up." That fast, and the joint was lit. "You know I only do this for medicinal purposes. It relieves my stress." Jason took a deep inhale and held it.

"Have you been carrying that around all day?"

He exhaled. A familiar smell filled the car. "No, I hid it under the car seat."

"Great, so it's been in my car all day."

"You *are* paranoid. What, you think they got pot-sniffing dogs out patrolling the convention center parking lot, hoping to find a loose joint? No one cares about this stuff anymore. It's even legal in some states."

"My parents care." Doug reached for the joint. Jason pulled away.

"Stop. You're going to make me drop it. How would your parents even know? How would they find out?" He took another deep inhale.

"Because I don't have leather seats. Because the smell gets stuck in the cushions."

"Then we'll open the windows a little." Jason reached across the seat toward Doug's door.

"What are you doing?" Doug pushed Jason's arm away.

"Pushing the unlock button. You locked the windows, remember? Because I was making fun of all those people on the way in."

"I already unlocked it. Here." Doug lowered all four windows a few inches each. "Do me a favor and exhale out the window."

"You sure you don't want any? It's some good stuff."

Doug had tried pot a few times in high school and didn't like it. "I'm fine with my Big Gulp."

"Suit yourself."

"Oh, shoot." Doug looked up in his rearview mirror. "Put that out, quick."

"What? What's the matter?"

Doug quickly lowered all the windows. A ton of air rushed in. Blue and red flashing lights filled the space behind them and were now flooding the car.

"Are you speeding?" Jason mashed the joint out in the ashtray.

"No, maybe three or four miles over."

"Maybe he's on another call. Maybe he's

going to pass us."

"He hasn't yet. He's still behind us."

Jason double-checked to make sure the joint was completely out, then tossed it out the window.

"You have any more pot on you?"

"Just the one."

"I hope that joint didn't just land on his windshield," Doug said. "Because he's definitely doing this for us. I need to pull over."

Jason sat up straight. He lowered the visor and looked in the little mirror. "How are my eyes?"

"I can't tell. I've got to pull over."

12

Doug's heart pounded as he watched the silhouette of the highway patrolman through his rearview mirror. He was heading this way. Turning to Jason, he said, "Let me do the talking. Don't say a word."

"I won't. Just be cool."

The officer walked up along the driver's side. A moment later, he was standing just outside Doug's door. "Can I see your license and registration, please?"

"Sure, Officer," Doug said. "Is there a problem? I don't think I was speeding."

"License and registration."

"Right." Doug reached across Jason's lap and opened the glove compartment. A little light came on, and he quickly found what the policeman wanted. "Here you go." He handed it out the window. The officer shined a flashlight on it, took a look at Doug through the window, then headed back toward his car.

"He's checking you out, bro," Jason said. "He's not going to find anything, right?"

"No, why would he?" Doug had never gotten a speeding ticket before. Whenever possible, he used cruise control to keep that from happening. But he suddenly wondered if the policeman might find something Doug didn't know about.

Doug waited through a few anxious minutes with neither of them saying a word. Finally, the officer returned.

"Could you step out of the car, Mr. Anderson?" the officer said.

Doug opened the door. "Is there a problem? Did I do something wrong?"

"I didn't pull you over for speeding. But you probably didn't notice me driving behind you back there. I followed you for almost a mile and noticed you swerved out of your lane several times."

"I did?" Doug thought a moment as he got out of the car, wondering how that was possible.

"You and your friend been drinking?"

"Drinking? No, just this Big Gulp here. I don't even drink alcohol. I'm not old enough to drink."

"That hasn't stopped thousands of young people your age," the officer said. "I see 'em out here every night."

"Well, that's not what's going on here. I promise you. You can ask my friend, I don't even like to drink."

"How would you know you don't like it," the officer said with a slight smirk, "if you're too young to drink?"

Doug didn't know what to say. "Guess I'll just have to plead the fifth on that one."

The officer smiled slightly. "Good answer. But tonight I won't be taking your word on that, the way your car was swerving. I'd like you to step over here. We're going to do something called a field sobriety test. First, I'd like you to walk a straight line, toe to toe like this." He demonstrated the maneuver. "Do it for nine steps."

"Sure, Officer. No problem." Doug did it, without a misstep, then turned around. "Want me to come back?"

"Please."

Doug did it again, perfectly.

He held a pen up in front of Doug's face. "I want you to look at this pen as I move it from side to side, following it with your eyes only. Don't turn your head."

Doug did this easily.

"Now I'm going to lift the pen up and down. Again, follow it with your eyes only."

Again, Doug did what he asked.

"Okay, now spread your arms and extend

your index finger. Close your eyes and touch the tip of your nose, like this."

Again, Doug obeyed and was able to do what he was asked. "See Officer, I told you. I haven't been drinking."

"I'll be right back. Don't get back in your car."

The patrolman reached into his car and picked up something, then headed back toward Doug. As he got closer, Doug saw a small electronic device in his hand with a clear plastic tube sticking out. "You know what this is?"

"A Breathalyzer?"

"That's right. I'm starting to believe you might be telling the truth. But I need to make sure. I want you to take a deep breath and blow into this tube, nice and steady, until it beeps."

Doug inhaled and blew into the tube. After it beeped, the patrolman pulled it out and looked at the display. Doug had never been more glad that he didn't like beer than at that moment. He had absolutely no fear of the result. He just hoped the officer didn't want to engage Jason next. He didn't think Breathalyzers could detect pot, but he wasn't sure.

"Okay," the officer said. "You're in the clear."

"I think the swerving was us just goofing off a little," Doug said. He thought back to him and Jason wrestling a bit in the car earlier. Him trying to grab Jason's joint and Jason trying to unlock the power windows.

"Well, your goofing off could have caused an accident. If there had been a car in the other lane, you could have easily sideswiped him."

"I'm sorry. I didn't realize I had swerved at all."

The patrolman stared at him a few moments. Doug tried to read his eyes, hoping to see mercy. He knew any kind of ticket would set him back over two hundred dollars, maybe even increase his car insurance. That happened, and his dad would definitely know about it.

"I'm going to let you off with a warning this time. But cut out the roughhousing in the car. Even if your friend starts goofing off, you're the driver. You need to take control."

"I understand. I appreciate you cutting me some slack. I'll be more careful."

"Where you two headed?"

"Back to St. Augustine. We're students at Flagler College."

"Well, you have a safe trip back."

Doug said thanks once more and good-bye, then got back in his car. The patrolman headed back toward his.

"Man, that was close," Jason said. "He didn't say a thing about the pot."

"Would you shut up? The windows are still open."

Jason looked over his shoulder. "He's already back to his car." He pretended to take a drag from an imaginary joint. "Geez, I'm the one supposed to be paranoid."

Doug turned on the car and closed the windows. "If I'm paranoid, I have good reason to be. Do you know how close we came to you getting us arrested?"

"What are you talking about, arrested? It was one joint."

"And what if that one joint had landed on his windshield? What if he was part of a K-9 unit and his dog came out with him, and he smelled drugs on you?"

"They can't arrest you for smells. Even if they searched the car, they wouldn't have found anything."

Doug watched the patrolman drive off. "Jason, they might have detained you because of the residue. I don't know. The point is, we could've gotten in enough trouble that my father would have found out that you smoke pot."

"I don't care if he finds out. My folks

wouldn't care. I'm pretty sure my dad still does."

Doug pulled onto the highway. "Well, I care. And I'm pretty sure my dad would care if he knew you did. He'd insist I not hang around you anymore. Is that what you want?"

"Your dad still treats you like such a little kid."

"He's just got standards. And he expects me to follow them. I don't half the time, but he still thinks I do. And he's the one paying the bills. So unless you want him to jerk my chain all the way back to River Oaks, which means I'd have to leave Flagler and go to UCF, you need to respect a few standards. Starting with no more pot in this car."

Jason didn't say anything for a minute.

"Well?"

"Okay, no more pot in the car." Jason reached over and turned the music back on.

Doug wasn't really listening to the music. He didn't pray anymore, hadn't for a long time. But he was certainly grateful God had spared him from getting a ticket back there, or worse. He didn't want to see the look on his father's face, in his eyes. The disappointment. The hurt.

His father still trusted him, as fragile as

that trust was. Doug knew he didn't deserve it anymore, but still, he'd do just about anything not to lose it.

13

Jim walked his coffee mug out through the patio door onto the veranda. Marilyn was already seated at the white wrought-iron table.

"You're limping a little," Marilyn said.

He set the mug down on the glass tabletop. "It's my hip. From our tennis match yesterday afternoon." He pulled a chair out and took a seat. "That's why I play golf."

"I'm sorry you're hurting, but I am glad we played tennis. I can't golf with you. And it was fun being with Tom and Jean."

Jim did enjoy that part. He wasn't golfing as often, precisely so they could spend more time doing outdoor things together. Getting to hang out with his eldest son, Tom, and his wife was a plus. "Guess I just used some muscles I hardly ever use."

"Maybe you should've taken a hot bath this morning," Marilyn said. "Used the whirlpool jets in the tub instead of a shower."

They ate in silence a couple of minutes.

"Oh, I forgot to tell you," Marilyn said, "at church yesterday Allan told me Michele had posted some new pictures on Facebook of her and Ayana. When you were getting cleaned up after our tennis match, I looked them up on my iPad."

"Any word on when they're going to let her bring Ayana home?"

"He said it's getting real close now. It could be in a week or two."

"Really? How are they doing?"

"Sounds like they're doing great. Michele says Ayana is picking up lots of new words in English. She uploaded a little video of her saying hi to us and the rest of the family. I've got it ready to go." Marilyn set up her iPad in front of his plate. "You just keep eating and I'll play it."

Jim watched as his daughter, Michele, appeared on screen. He recognized the backdrop from an earlier video. She was at the dining room table in the orphanage. Next to her sat little Ayana, her face full of smiles.

"Hi, Mom and Dad. Ayana and I wanted to say hi all the way from the other side of the world. I miss you guys so much, and

98

Ayana can't wait to meet you. Right?" Ayana nodded enthusiastically. Jim wondered if she understood everything Michele had said. "Ayana's been learning lots of new words. But I thought you'd particularly enjoy a few of her newest ones." Michele looked down. "Okay, Ayana, you can say it."

Ayana looked straight into the camera and said, "Hi, Grandma and Grandpa. It's me, Ayana. I see you soon in . . ." She looked at Michele. Michele whispered something to her. "America."

Marilyn pushed the pause button. "Isn't that the cutest thing? That's the first time she called us Grandma and Grandpa." She looked into the screen. "We love you too, Ayana."

"You know that's not live, right? She can't hear you."

"I know. But still." She hit the play button again and they both listened as Michele gave little updates about her day-to-day experiences in Addis Ababa.

Jim kept eating. When Michele finished, he said to Marilyn, "Can you ask her or Allan to let us know the minute they book the flights home? I think we should have some kind of welcome-home party. Something really special."

"That's a great idea," Marilyn said. "We

can decorate the house, and I can order a big banner to put across the dining room with Ayana's name on it. Tom and Jean will come. I'll invite Uncle Henry and Aunt Myra over. Maybe even Pastor Ray and Julie can come with their kids."

"And if we're real lucky," Jim said, "and give him plenty of notice, maybe we can even persuade Doug to be here." Saying that instantly dampened the mood. "I'm sorry. I spent most of my shower thinking about it. Another weekend without a peep from him."

Marilyn picked up her iPad. "I know. I'm discouraged too. But I don't think we'll have to twist his elbow to get him to come home for something like this, do you?"

"I'd like to be able to say yes, but I'm just not sure." Jim took another sip of coffee. "Did you get a chance to look at his Facebook page yesterday?"

"I did. But he hasn't posted anything since the last time I looked. I spoke briefly with Christina last night before she went upstairs to her apartment."

"And . . . ?"

"Well, she didn't want to say anything, I could tell. But finally she tapped on her phone to Instagram and showed me a photo taken by Jason."

"Is that like Facebook?"

"Sort of. But it's more about posting pictures from your phone. The kids use it a lot."

"So what did Jason put on Instagram?" Jim asked.

Marilyn hesitated.

"What's wrong? Another drinking party?"

"No. This time it looked like just some innocent fun."

"So what's the problem? You seem like you're holding back something."

She sighed. "It's just . . . it looks like they spent the whole day yesterday going to a comic book convention."

"By *whole* day, I'm assuming that means he must've skipped out on church." Which wasn't really big news; they were both pretty sure he hardly went anymore when he was back at school.

"Yes, but that's not the part I thought you'd struggle with."

"What else is there?"

"The convention was in Orlando, at the Orange County Convention Center."

Jim knew what she was getting at. That meant Doug had driven right past their exit on the way there and the way home. And he'd never said a word.

"I probably shouldn't have told you," she said. "It's going to bug you all day."

Now Jim sighed. "Well, at least we know he considers some things worth the drive."

14

Christina peeked out the living room window of her apartment above Jim and Marilyn's garage. They were still sitting at the table on the veranda. It looked like they had finished eating. Marilyn had said several times that Christina was always welcome to join them if she ever saw them eating on the veranda. But like most mornings, she didn't have an appetite for breakfast. At the moment, she was forcing down an orange.

But she did want to speak with them. And she noticed the silver coffee carafe at the center of the table. For some reason, Marilyn's coffee always tasted better than hers.

She walked back to the dinette table, looked down at the half-eaten orange, her empty coffee cup, and the mini iPad the Andersons had bought her for her birthday a few months ago. She'd never been given such an extravagant gift. She decided to do one last thing before going downstairs, though she probably shouldn't.

Sitting down, she lifted the iPad and tapped the screen. It opened to what she'd been doing a few moments ago — looking at Doug's Facebook page. She knew that coming here every day — sometimes several times a day — kept her emotions engaged in a way that was probably unhealthy, but she couldn't help it. He'd posted something this morning about some new contest he and Jason had signed up for over the weekend. First prize was seventy-five thousand dollars, but Doug said they had no chance of winning. She didn't know why he talked like that. He was an amazing artist. She had learned from looking at some of Jason's photos on Instagram last night that they'd found out about the contest at a Comic-Con convention in Orlando yesterday.

Doug didn't mention that in his FB post. She thought she knew why. He didn't want his folks to know — or maybe her either — that he'd come so close to River Oaks without stopping in to say hi. She didn't understand why he was shutting all of them out of his life like this but decided not to let it bother her. She hammered out a brief reply to his post:

Saw Jason's pics from the Comic-Con taken yesterday. I've never been to one before but sounds like you guys had a blast. Some of those costumes were amazing (some, not so much ☺). Can't wait to see your drawings for the new graphic novel you're working on. Hope you guys win!

One thing she was glad about, although it probably didn't mean very much. Doug didn't mention Courtney, and Christina didn't see any pictures of her at the convention center. She got up from the table and was just about to turn off her iPad when a little red 1 appeared over her Facebook message button.

Please don't be Ted.

But of course it was. He was the only one sending her messages these days. She didn't want to open it, because Ted would get a little check mark indicating the time she'd read the message, and then he'd wonder why she didn't reply.

She double-checked to make sure Jim and Marilyn were still downstairs, then hurried down to join them.

Jim had just finished his last sip of coffee and was about to pour another when he saw

Christina come out the garage doorway. She was headed this way. "How much coffee is left?" he asked Marilyn quietly.

"At least two cups. You can have another."

"What about you?"

"I'm fine. Go ahead."

Just as he began to pour, Christina reached the table. "Good morning, Christina."

"Good morning to both of you."

"Do you work today?" Marilyn asked.

"I do, but I don't go in until twelve-thirty."

Jim set the carafe down. "There's just about enough for another cup, if you want one."

"I'd love that. Are you sure?"

"You know where the mugs are," Marilyn said.

"I'll be right back."

As she left, Jim looked at his watch. "I've got maybe ten minutes, then I've got to scoot."

"Wonder if she just wants some company," Marilyn said, "or if she's got something on her mind."

"Guess we'll find out."

A few moments later she returned and sat where she normally did. "You look dressed for work," she said to Jim.

"I am. I have to leave in a few minutes. How's the car holding up?"

"Funny you should ask. That's part of the reason I came down here. That and Marilyn's amazing coffee." She poured the final cup into her mug.

"I asked," Jim said, "because I came in a little before you yesterday and heard you turn it off as I left the garage."

"You mean, try to turn it off. It wouldn't shut off. It just kept chugging and sputtering. It's getting much worse. It's super embarrassing when it does that in parking lots."

"You want the name of my mechanic?"

Christina nodded.

"Here, I'll text it to you with his phone number." Jim pulled out his phone. "You'll like him. He'll be totally straight with you."

"Thanks," she said. "I hope it's something he can fix."

"Well, he'll tell you either way. He won't just start experimenting and running up the bill." Jim took another sip of coffee. "Marilyn told me about Doug's little excursion yesterday to the comic book convention with Jason." He hoped he didn't sound sarcastic in his tone.

"I saw some of Jason's pictures," she said.

107

"It looked like they were having a great time."

"Did he mention anything to you about it, that he was going?"

She shook her head no. "But I wouldn't really expect him to. We don't keep up with each other like we used to."

Jim detected a sadness in her eyes as she said it. He wanted to ask her for more information but wasn't sure he should. He looked at Marilyn, wondering what she'd think if he opened up to Christina this way. Marilyn and Christina probably talked on a personal level all the time, but it would be breaking new ground for him.

He decided to take a chance. "Christina, I want to ask you something, but tell me right up front if you don't want to answer it, or if it makes you feel even a little uncomfortable."

"Okay, but you know it takes a lot to rattle my cage."

Jim smiled, glanced at Marilyn. Her eyebrows reflected mild concern. "When you and Doug were . . . a little closer, did he ever talk to you about me? About any problems he might be having with me? You can tell me if he did, I won't be upset. I'm just trying to figure out why Doug and I aren't connecting. Really, on almost any level. I'm wondering if I've done something wrong or treated him in a way that made him pull away like this."

"Wow, that is kind of a heavy topic."

"I know. You don't have to answer if —"

"No, I don't mind. First of all, the answer I guess is yes *and* no. He did occasionally talk about you, but no, I don't recall him ever saying anything negative. I mean, he did mention how hard-line you used to be. He said you were legalistic, you didn't listen very well, and you were kind of impossible to please."

Christina could be surprisingly blunt.

"But I've heard you talk about that too. I've never seen you act that way, though. With him or with anyone."

That was a relief to hear.

"He talked about that too. How much you've changed. How much, well, nicer you are to be around."

"See, Jim," Marilyn said, "I told you he could see how much you've changed."

She said it tenderly and reached for his hand. All this was somewhat encouraging to hear, but it didn't really improve his mood. This thing with Doug was really starting to get to him. "It's just . . . I've been trying ever since then to reconnect with Doug. I've made all kinds of progress with Tom and

109

Michele, but nothing I do seems to work with Doug."

"Whatever it is," Christina said, "I don't think it's something on your end. At least nothing I can see."

15

Two hours later, Christina sat in the waiting room at Carlos's Auto Service. She closed the Facebook app on her cell phone. So far, Doug hadn't responded to the post she'd sent him earlier. Why should that surprise her? She should be used to it by now. If she had any sense, she'd stop looking. And stop hoping.

She got up and peeked through the glass door into the garage area, saw her car on the lift. A younger mechanic who worked with Carlos stood under it, pointing something out to him. Whatever it was, she hoped it wasn't expensive. The look on their faces gave her doubt.

At least Jim trusted him. She could take some comfort in that. This was the first car she had ever owned. She knew from day one it was a piece of junk. Just something to get you from point A to point B. She'd had it for two years, and so far it had only cost her five hundred dollars in repairs. But five hundred dollars was a lot of money when you worked retail. And she knew every time she turned on the ignition could be its last.

Ever since the Andersons had invited her to move into the garage apartment, Christina had been saving money toward a new one. Well, new to her. That was only possible because they barely charged her anything for rent. But so far, she'd only been able to save twenty-five hundred dollars. That could buy her a wonderful vacation, an entire closet full of new clothes, but, sadly, not a decent car. Really, one only marginally better than the one Carlos was working on now.

She dreaded the thought of going back to riding the city bus, even for a season. Every time she rode past a bus stop, she remembered what it was like. How much longer it took to get everywhere. All the waiting and walking. Sometimes in the rain. Some of the creepy people she had to deal with. She especially hated riding the bus at night.

The glass door opened. Carlos walked through, wiping his hands on a blue rag.

"I've got good news and bad news for you. Which you want first?" With his accent, it sounded like he said "noose."

"I guess the good news."

"I can get your car to stop running after you turn it off for about two hundred dollars."

That's the good news?

"The bad news is, this is really only a Band-Aid. We were checking your engine out, looking at the big picture. You're not far away from some big-ticket items breaking loose, starting with your transmission. Some of these bigger things start to go, and you're looking at a few thousand dollars in repairs, not a few hundred."

That was much worse news. Those kinds of repairs would eat up everything she had saved. "So you think the car isn't worth fixing?"

"I wouldn't say that. If you're not ready to get a more reliable car now, it may be worth it to have us do this Band-Aid thing. Buy you a little time. But I'd recommend you start making plans to replace the car soon. Getting those other repairs isn't really worth it. You'd be spending way more than the car's worth."

She stood there looking at him for a moment. "How much time do you think this Band-Aid will get me?"

"A few months," he said. "Maybe longer. Hard to tell for sure with things like this."

"Well, I guess go ahead and do the fix. Because I need the car for right now. I'll talk to Mr. Anderson about the big picture thing. I have no idea what to do about that. But at least what you're doing will buy me some time. Will it take long to fix?"

"Maybe thirty minutes. We can do it now. Didn't you say you had to be at work in a little while?"

"I do, but thirty minutes will work." She was pretty much all ready for work.

"Then we'll get right on it." He headed back into the garage.

She heard him yell something to the younger man as the door closed. As she sat back in her chair, she felt relieved this temporary fix would only set her back two hundred dollars. That was something to be thankful for. What if she had to pick out a mechanic on her own? How much more would that have cost? She doubted she'd find one who'd give her the kind of advice Carlos just did, someone who cared more about her welfare than making money for himself.

The next time she talked to Jim, she'd have to thank him and see what he thought she should do about — as Carlos put it — the big picture with her car.

As she stared out the plate-glass window,

she thought about how this car situation seemed to confirm something she'd been thinking about the last several weeks about the "big picture" of her life. Wondering if it might be time for her fairy tale existence in the apartment above the Anderson garage to come to an end.

It had been a wonderful experience, especially compared to the harsh life she'd led before getting pregnant over a year ago. And it had been a safe place for her emotions to heal after releasing her baby to that adoptive couple. It wasn't just the place itself that helped but all the love and care she'd received from the Andersons and others at her church.

In a way, the job at Odds-n-Ends was also part of the fairy tale. Getting to work with Marilyn and her boss, Harriet, who treated her more like family than an employee. Soft, Christian music playing continuously in the background. Being surrounded by beautiful crafts and gifts. Every person visiting the store seeming happy the moment they stepped inside. The problem was, she couldn't earn enough money at the store to even think about getting a decent car. And where else in the world could she live paying so little rent?

The road to reality seemed to be pointing

toward going back to school.

Well, maybe *back* wasn't the right word, since she had never gone to college. She didn't even know where to start or what school she should attend. One thing she did know, in the past she didn't like school, and her grades had barely been above average. She wondered if it might be different now, since her life had been an absolute mess back then. She was older, more mature. And this time she wouldn't be distracted by peer pressure. She wouldn't be going to school because she had to; she'd be going for herself, to improve her own life.

Of course, none of this meant she'd be any smarter.

Christina pulled into the employee parking lot behind Odds-n-Ends and turned off her car. How about that? It stayed off. First in the Andersons' garage and now here. Carlos really knew his stuff. She looked at her watch. Her shift didn't officially start for ten minutes, but she was seriously thinking about sitting in her car right up until the last moment.

Normally she didn't mind going in early. But this wasn't a normal time. To get here, she had driven past the front of the store. Right past Ted's car. He was in there now.

Maybe if she waited until the last minute, he'd leave.

She thought about it some more. That's not what he'd do. He'd ask Marilyn or Harriet what time she began her shift, then he'd wait in the store until she arrived. Christina opened the car door, let out a sigh, and walked ever so slowly toward the back entrance of the store.

16

"Hi, Ted." Christina walked past him on her way to the cash register. She had no choice; he was standing in the main aisle, chatting with Harriet.

"Oh, hey Christina. I was hoping I wouldn't miss you. I've got to head back to school in a few minutes."

At least there was that. He followed her toward the counter in the center of the store. She stepped behind it to log on to the register. A moment later, he was standing right in front of her. And of course, he was smiling.

"I was gonna tell you yesterday at church," he said, "but I didn't see you."

"That's because it was my week to watch the kids in the nursery."

"It's nice of you to do that. I bet you're great with kids."

"I don't know about that, but I do enjoy being around them. Most of the time." She

118

looked around the store to make sure there weren't customers standing around, waiting to check out. Sadly, there were not. "So, what were you wanting to tell me at church yesterday?"

"I just wanted to thank you for recommending that ornament and stand for my sister last week. We had her birthday party over the weekend, and she totally loved it. In fact, she told me after it was her favorite present."

"I'm glad she liked it."

"You really have a gift for this kind of thing."

Over-the-top compliment number two. She didn't know how to reply. "Thanks." Just past Ted's left shoulder, she noticed Marilyn straightening some knickknacks on a shelf. Marilyn smiled, looked at Ted, and made some kind of face. If Christina guessed right, Marilyn was suggesting that Ted flirting with her like this was a good thing. She couldn't make an appropriate negative face back, or Ted would see it.

He looked at his watch.

"Have to get back to class?"

"I've got a few minutes," he said.

Her mind fumbled around, trying to think of something in the store she needed to do, but there wasn't anything. Harriet had asked her to spend the first few hours of her shift on the cash register. Lunchtime was supposed to be one of the busiest times of the day. There were a few people in the store, but none of them seemed ready to buy. "So, what's your next class?"

"Just an English class. It's the only class I have left today."

"I was never any good at English."

"I could help you with it," he said.

"I'm not in school. I'm working here."

"Oh. I just assumed you were part-time."

"Nope. Full-time. Although I have been thinking about going back to school." Why did she tell him that? She hadn't told anyone yet. She looked up to see if Marilyn had overheard. Thankfully, she had moved farther down the aisle to help a customer.

"Really? What school? UCF? You said going *back* to school . . . have you gone to college already?"

"Uh, which question do you want me to answer?"

"I'm sorry. I don't know why, I always get nervous talking to you." He smiled. "Did I say that out loud?"

She laughed. She wasn't sure why, but what he had just said, the way he said it, and the smile that followed were almost charming. "Well, anyway, I can answer all your questions with this: I have no idea where I'm going yet, or even if I am going back to school. And by 'back to school' I don't mean to say I've ever been to college, because I haven't. It's just an expression. I do have an idea about what I might study. Well, a few different ideas. But I want to talk it over with Jim and Marilyn first and hear what they have to say."

Ted looked over his shoulder, saw Marilyn at the far end of the store. "Are they kind of like your folks?"

"I guess so."

"They seem like really nice people."

"They're the best people I know." She was about to say she wouldn't be the person she was today if it weren't for them, but that was a little over the top.

He looked at his watch again. "Well, I better get going, or I'll be late."

"Thanks for stopping by."

"Thanks again for giving me a reason. Wait, that didn't come out quite right."

She laughed.

"I mean about my sister, about the gift you recommended."

"I know. You better go."

He took a few steps toward the front door. "Do you get a break later? A coffee break or something?"

"I do get a ten-minute break in about two hours." Did she really want to tell him that? Her answer was almost an invitation.

"Well, maybe I'll stop by after class, see if I get lucky. Wait, that didn't come out right either."

She smiled. "You better go."

He waved and hurried out the door.

Christina followed him with her eyes until he disappeared down the sidewalk, unsure of what she was feeling. When she looked back into the store, she saw that Marilyn had just finished up with her customer and was heading her way.

"How'd it go?" she asked.

"How did what go?" Christina said.

"You know . . ."

"It went fine, I guess. What are you getting at?" Although Christina knew.

"He likes you, you know."

"I think I knew that."

"He's a very nice boy. Jim and I know his parents. They're really nice people."

"Everyone's nice . . . how nice."

"So you don't like him?"

"No, I'm not saying that. I don't, but I'm not saying that." Marilyn looked confused. "I don't know what I'm saying."

"So . . . you don't like Ted *that* way, you mean?"

"Yes, I guess I'm saying that. At least I don't think so. He is nice, and he seems very kind."

"And he's nice looking, don't you think?"

"In a way. No, I guess he is. It's just, I'm not sure Ted is my type."

"What kind of boy is your type? I don't really know, because I've never seen you interested in anyone since we've met. Except maybe . . ."

Marilyn didn't finish her sentence, but they both knew she meant Doug. And Doug would have been her answer to Marilyn's question. Doug was her type. Or was he? Did she even have a type? The only thing she knew was that she wished he was, and she wasn't at all sure she was ready to let someone like Ted become her type. "I don't really know, Marilyn."

"Well, you know how I feel. I wish you and Doug were more than friends."

"But we're not," Christina said. And that was something else she knew, which made all the difference in the world. Because it didn't matter if Doug was her type; she was definitely not his.

17

Doug sat in the student dining hall of Flagler College, picking at his lunch. His thoughts were more focused on the sketch pad beside him than anything on his plate. The class he normally took just before lunch had been canceled, so he'd come here to work on some preliminary drawings for the graphic novel he and Jason were working on. One of the challenges was that the entire story — which both of them hoped would be volume one of many more volumes to come — took place in a totally different world.

World-building was the challenge for any sci-fi or fantasy story. You had to create a world similar enough to this one for your audience to relate to it, but different and exotic enough to stimulate people's imaginations. At the same time, as a world, it needed to be relatively unique so that critics didn't compare it to the better-known fantasy worlds such as Middle Earth, Hogwarts, or the sci-fi worlds of *Star Trek* and *Star Wars.*

Sitting in this ornately decorated dining hall wasn't helping. Everywhere Doug looked, not just here but throughout the campus, were intricate examples of Spanish Renaissance architecture. When the dining hall was first built in the late 1800s, it was known as Hotel Ponce de Leon and was considered to be one of the most luxurious and exclusive resorts of its day. Now it was the centerpiece of St. Augustine's charming historic district. Every day Doug passed tourists on the sidewalks stopping to take pictures or videos of the magnificent Mediterranean buildings.

Being surrounded by all this historic architecture did little to help fuel Doug's imagination or help him visualize the world he needed to create for their graphic novel.

Unless . . .

Maybe that was it. Maybe he shouldn't try to come up with something completely different. It only had to be different enough so that it wasn't like the popular worlds people were already used to. Maybe he could model the capital city of their New World using the Spanish Renaissance architecture found all over historic St.

Augustine.

Hey, that might just —

"Man, you're deep in thought. Mind if we sit down?"

"What?" Doug looked up. It was Jason holding a tray of food. Drew was right behind him. "No, have a seat. I was just daydreaming about what the world in our graphic novel should look like. And I just got an idea. Maybe we could model the capital city after this town."

Jason sat across from Doug. Drew sat next to him. By now, Jason's face was all healed up, so he moved about the campus freely. "Make it just like St. Augustine?"

"Not exactly like it," Doug said. "Just the style. You and I have talked about the amazing craftsmanship around here, how nobody builds stuff this way anymore. Everything now is so metallic and square and cheap. We could make one of the groups in our story a whole race of master craftsmen."

Jason took a bite of his meatloaf. "Yeah, I guess that could work."

"I think that would be cool, Doug," Drew said. "I haven't seen any comic books that look like this town."

"By the way," Jason said, "I've been working on my assignment."

"What assignment?" Doug asked.

126

"You know, checking out those Batman comic books you gave me last night, the ones with 'the Prodigal' in the title. I spent all morning on it and also checking out that Wolverine issue I saw at Comic-Con. From everything I've read, we're in the clear. Our story is totally different. I don't think anybody's going to say we stole anything from either one of those story lines."

"Whoa," Drew said. "There's Courtney standing in line with some of her friends. Looking mighty fine, Doug, if you don't mind me saying."

Doug looked over his shoulder, just long enough to see her. She hadn't seen him yet.

"But I guess we'll need to change the subject if she comes over here to join us," Drew said. "What's she got against comic books, anyway?"

"We're not doing a comic book," Jason said. "It's a graphic novel."

"Whatever. What's she got against them?"

"She's not against them," Doug said. "Not completely. It's just not her kind of art. Anyway, she might be softening up a little on that."

"What kind of art's she into?" Drew asked.

"We haven't talked that much about it," Doug said. "But I know she likes the more classic stuff, like Impressionism."

"I like Impressionist stuff," Drew said. "But I don't know why she can't like more than one style. I like all kinds of art."

"I don't know."

"Seems like it's gonna hinder your relationship," Drew continued. "I mean, how far can this thing between you two go if she can't get behind something that's so important to you?"

"What are you, Dr. Phil?" Jason said. "Who cares if she doesn't like our kind of art? Doug's not gonna marry her. Right, Doug?"

Doug looked back to see where Courtney was in line. She still hadn't seen them. "Right. We're not even that serious yet."

"Well, that's my point. How can you even get serious with someone who doesn't like comic books? Excuse me . . . graphic novels."

"You don't get it, Drew," Jason said. "Doug's not in some kind of long-term relationship with Courtney. She's a party girl. A very hot party girl. You get with someone like Courtney for a few months at the most, to increase your stock value."

"Stock value?" Doug said. "What are you talking about?" Drew also looked confused.

"I mean, being with someone that hot increases your desirability factor with the ladies. They figure if you can get someone like her, you must be a catch. All kinds of beauties who never noticed you before see you differently now."

"That's crazy," Doug said.

"It is not. You don't see it, Doug. But I see it. You stick with Courtney a few more months and you can take your pick from almost anyone on campus. Drew and I couldn't get someone like Courtney. That's not the league we play in."

Drew took a swig of his soda. "He might have something there, Doug. But maybe . . . maybe there's some kind of rub-off factor in play. You think our stock's going up some 'cause we're friends with Doug?"

"I wouldn't be at all surprised," Jason said. He looked over at Courtney, who was now starting to get her food. "See those two friends of hers? They might just follow her over here and sit right down beside us."

"Because we're sitting here with Doug," Drew said.

"If they do," Jason said, "you let me do most of the talking."

"You guys are nuts," Doug said. They were right about Courtney's looks, and Jason might even be right about Doug's "stock value" going up because of her. At the moment, though, he was thinking about how shallow all this sounded.

Courtney turned to him and waved; he smiled and waved back. She made a signal suggesting she and her friends could come over there and join them. Doug nodded and pointed to three empty chairs nearby.

"That's what I'm talking about," Jason said quietly.

Doug smiled, but there was nothing behind it. He started to think about the time he'd spent with Courtney so far. Their whole relationship was based on physical attraction. And the physical attraction was substantial. But he couldn't think of a single conversation with her that was more than a quarter-inch deep. A memory flashed into his mind, a conversation with Christina back in December when he was on his Christmas break. He was waxing the hood of his car. She had come down the steps of the apartment to do some laundry. She'd set the basket down on the dryer, walked over, and they had just chatted for twenty minutes or more.

That had been just one of many such conversations with Christina on that visit home. She was so easy to talk to. So easy to be with. Not just that time, but most of the time. He looked up. Courtney was walking toward them. He turned his sketch pad over and stood up for the coming embrace.

18

Christina was just finishing a Chick-fil-A salad at her little dinette table. She hadn't worked a full shift today at Odds-n-Ends, only six hours. Harriet didn't like them to work overtime, and Christina had put in two extra hours on Saturday. Getting off early tonight evened things out.

As she ate, she continued exploring the internet for college ideas. She was starting to get a little excited because some things were beginning to gel. One idea in particular had grown a little taller than the rest. Jim had given her some good advice about making big decisions. He'd suggested she give the ideas she liked their own page, then divide the page into two columns to keep track of the pros and cons. Sometimes, he'd said, sorting out the facts this way helped strengthen an idea or else rule it out altogether.

So far she had created four idea pages,

but this one idea had the longest list of pros and the shortest list of cons. She was eager to run it by Jim and Marilyn, see what they thought. Turning in her chair, she peeked out the window at the big house. Good, it looked like they were having coffee and dessert out on the veranda. She put the rest of her salad in the fridge, picked up her iPad, and hurried down the stairs.

Marilyn greeted her before she'd crossed the sidewalk connecting both parts of the house. "Are you going to join us?"

"Is that okay?"

"Of course. Set your iPad down and go get a plate of this delicious crumb cake. You'll see it right there on the counter."

"And there's at least one more cup of coffee in the pot," Jim said. "Just made it after dinner."

"It's decaf," Marilyn added.

Christina left and came back to the table with a small square of cake and coffee. She noticed Marilyn seemed a little too excited to see her. She couldn't begin to guess why.

"So," Marilyn said, "how'd it go?"

"How'd what go? Work? It picked up a little after you left but nothing crazy."

"No, silly. I'm talking about your time with Ted."

"Oh . . ." Her time with Ted. Now she

133

understood. That afternoon, Ted had "gotten lucky." After his English class, he'd come back to the store just a few minutes before her afternoon break. "It was fine."

"That was very thoughtful, what he did," Marilyn said.

"What did he do?" Jim asked.

"He figured with Christina's break only being ten minutes, she wouldn't have time to meet him for coffee, so he bought coffee from Starbucks for both of them, along with some creamer, sugar, and Splenda packets, since he didn't know how she liked it."

"So are you two . . . becoming an item?" Jim said.

"No, we're not."

"Sounds like Ted wants you to be," he said, taking a forkful of crumb cake.

"Well, it takes two to make . . . an item," Christina said. "Right now, there's only one."

"So your time with him didn't go well?" Marilyn asked.

"No, it was fine. But it was only ten minutes. It's really the first conversation we've had that was more than a few sentences. I barely know him. But I agree, that was thoughtful of him to get my coffee."

"See, you're smiling." Marilyn set her fork

down on the edge of her plate. "It's nice having someone treat you so special, isn't it? And I'll bet Ted will remember how you fix your coffee for the next time."

"You think there'll be a next time?" Jim said.

"Maybe," Christina said. "It wasn't a bad time. He was fairly easy to talk to. But no bells went off in my heart. No tingly feelings." What she really meant was, her time with Ted didn't even begin to scratch the surface of the feelings she had for Doug. Feelings she wished she didn't have.

"Well, they could still come," Marilyn said. "In time." She patted Jim's forearm. "It wasn't love at first sight for me, right, Jim?" Jim smiled, continued chewing. "For him it was. But I was dating someone else when we first met. Eventually my heart changed. Sometimes these things take time."

Christina wondered why Marilyn seemed to be working so hard to push her in Ted's direction. The only thing that made sense was that she must really believe there was absolutely no chance for her and Doug.

"If you'd like to spend a little more time with Ted, Christina, maybe get to know him a little better without it being a date, I could always invite him to dinner."

"Now, Marilyn," Jim said, "maybe you

should slow down a little." He turned to Christina. "Is any of this making you uncomfortable? Marilyn playing the matchmaker?"

"Not really." But Christina was feeling a little uncomfortable, though not about Ted. She wished she had the courage to ask Marilyn straight out: *Do you feel like I should give up on Doug completely, like we have absolutely no chance of ever being together?* But what she said was, "I guess you could invite Ted over for dinner some night. But I'm a little concerned that with his level of enthusiasm, it might still register as a date in his mind."

Jim nodded. "She has a point. Most guys can be pretty dull about these things. Remember that first time you let me drive you home from school? I was certain that was my big moment, that your heart had finally turned the corner. Every time you looked at me on that car ride home, I saw love in your eyes." He turned and looked at Christina. "But I was dead wrong. Whatever it was, it wasn't love. I was clueless. Before she got out of the car, I asked Marilyn for a date . . . again." He looked back at Marilyn. "You turned me down flat."

Marilyn smiled. "I'm sorry. What can I say? I wasn't there yet."

"Well, Christina's not there yet. Right?"

"Not yet." Not even close, Christina thought.

Marilyn looked at her. "You want me to just let it go? Because I'm fine with that."

"Maybe not let it go, just put it on pause. Ted sent me a Facebook friend request a little while ago. That might be a safer way to get to know him a little better. I'll try that route for little while. If he starts to grow on me, I'll let you know. *Then* you can invite him to dinner."

"Sounds like a plan," Marilyn said. "You brought your iPad down. Is there something you want to show us?"

"Yes. I've been creating a list of pro and con pages like we talked about."

"Got some new ideas cooking, huh?"

She nodded. "A pretty big one. The pages are all the different ideas that have come out of it. But before I show you, let me take just a few minutes to explain it."

19

"We're all ears, Christina." Jim set his fork down, picked up his coffee cup.

Start with the headline, she reminded herself. "Okay, the big idea is me going back to school. I've been thinking about it a lot lately. Oddly enough, my car troubles are what clinched it for me. I really need to get a better car. Carlos told me it's on its last legs. With what I make at the store, I'm afraid I won't save enough before it dies completely."

"If that happens," Marilyn said, "we'll help you."

"I appreciate that. He got it going again for now. The point is, it made me realize I've been kind of hiding out here, just enjoying the apartment, my job, the church, being around you guys. But I should be making plans to do something more. All I have is a high school diploma, some waitress experience, and now some retail. I've been looking into it, and with a degree from some of the college programs I was looking at, I can make almost twice as much per hour as I do now."

"I think going to college is a great idea," Jim said.

"Would you have to leave here?" Marilyn asked.

"It depends on what I wind up taking and what college is the best place to go to get the training."

"Do you have a goal yet?" Jim asked. "A degree in mind?"

She picked up her iPad. "It's an Associate of Science degree, not a bachelor's. I'm thinking about something in the medical field, like radiology. I'm not totally sure yet, but that's the general direction."

"Anything in medical is a great idea in Florida," Jim said. "It's a great idea anywhere, but Florida has a much greater share of seniors living here. They often need medical care a lot more than younger people."

"I agree, Christina. I think a medical program is a great idea. Have you looked into any of the local colleges to see if they offer the program you're looking for?"

"I started looking tonight. A few of them do."

"I hope there's one close enough so you don't have to move."

"UCF does, and both Seminole and Valencia have a radiology program."

"See?" Marilyn said. "If you picked one of those, you could still live here and just commute."

Christina hadn't looked into things close enough to tell which school had the best program, but she loved seeing Marilyn so eager to have her continue living here. "My idea didn't exactly come at the best time. We're in the middle of the semester. But I thought I could use my spare time to do a little more research into each of the schools." She looked at Jim. "Don't you think I should try to find out which school is considered the highest rated in the area I'm wanting to study? Take radiology, for example. All the colleges have the same degree, but maybe one college is more respected by people who hire radiology techs."

"That makes sense to me," Jim said. "Since you have some time, the more info you can get, the better. If you're serious about radiology, you might even want to visit some labs, see if you can talk to the supervisor. Maybe they could tell you which college is the best, or if they're all basically the same."

"That's a great idea." This conversation was going wonderfully. She took a big bite of crumb cake.

"Could I look at some of your pro and con pages while you eat?" Jim asked.

"Sure." She opened her iPad to the file with all of the information. "Here. Just keep swiping until you get to the end."

A few minutes later, he looked up and said, "I'm proud of you, Christina. You've mapped this out very well. I'm really impressed."

"Thank you." Coming from him, that meant a lot.

"Another idea just came to me," Jim said. "Something else you can do to check these schools out while you're waiting for the next semester to begin. You could visit the campuses. They're not that far away. Measure things like the distance, the gas, the traffic. Even any thoughts you have about the campus itself. Put everything down as either a pro or con."

"That's a great idea," she said.

"Maybe if we both have the day off," Marilyn said, "I could go with you."

"I'd love that. I just remembered another school I wanted to check out. This one's a little farther away. St. John's River State

College. The campus for their radiology program is just outside of St. Augustine."

"Near Doug," Marilyn said.

"Maybe fifteen minutes from his school," Christina said. "If I went there, it's too far to drive back and forth every day. But I could definitely come home on the weekends." She thought about Doug's broken promise on this score and quickly added, "And I definitely would come home every weekend."

"Is that the school you're leaning toward?" Jim asked. "I notice on your iPad here you have it highlighted and underlined."

Christina was suddenly embarrassed. She only did that thinking about how close it was to Doug, not whether it was the best school for radiology. So far, that was its only major selling point. But how could she say that? She wasn't even sure Jim knew of her interest in Doug.

Marilyn seemed to sense the moment. "Maybe that's because it's the only one out of town."

"I haven't really decided about anything just yet. Tonight I just wanted to introduce the idea, lay out the big picture."

"Well, I like what you've done," Jim said. "And if you did wind up going here, to this" — he looked down at the iPad — "St. John's

River State College, maybe you could reconnect with Doug. I'd like it if you and he were good friends again."

Good friends. She knew what he meant. But would something like that be good for her, being that close to Doug? What if she went to St. John's and he knew she was going there, and he remained just as distant and aloof as he was now? That would be even more painful. At least now she had the distance for an excuse.

"I have an idea," Marilyn said. She looked at Jim then at Christina. "We're both wanting to know how Doug's really doing in St. Augustine. Maybe Christina and I can use the next day we both have off to go visit this school. If it's only fifteen minutes away from Doug, after we tour the school we can stop in and see him, maybe have lunch together?"

"That's a great idea," Christina said. At least she hoped it was.

"I'll look on the schedule tomorrow," Marilyn said, "find out the next day we both have off."

Later that night, Jim was getting ready for bed. He had just finished brushing his teeth when Marilyn came in to their master bath suite.

"Before I forget," she said, "I wanted to mention something to you about Christina."

"About her college idea?"

"No, about her and Doug."

"Her and Doug?"

"About their friendship."

"What about it?"

"Remember when you noticed how she had the college near St. Augustine in bold and underlined? And you mentioned how you thought it would be good if they reconnected as friends?"

Jim set his toothbrush back in the holder. "Yeah."

"I realized then we haven't talked about something I should have mentioned before."

Jim suddenly understood. "She likes Doug . . . as more than a friend?"

Marilyn nodded. "I'd say way more."

"Really?"

"Really."

"How long's that been going on?"

"For her, I think it goes back to when she first moved into the apartment."

"You're kidding."

"Back then, I'd say it was more of a crush. I thought there might have been something brewing on his end too. Remember when he was coming home a lot more often during the weekends, right around the time she

144

came into the picture?"

"Not really. Well, maybe."

"Well, he was. And I started thinking maybe it was because of Christina, that maybe he was starting to like her."

"But he wasn't."

"No. I talked to him about it once on the front porch, just as he was leaving. He made it pretty clear he didn't like Christina that way. Just as a friend. This was back when she was still pregnant. In fact, that was part of the reason he gave. It was pretty disappointing, what he said. He made it sound like, I don't know, like he saw her as damaged goods."

"Really?" Jim said. "Like she wasn't good enough for him?"

"That's what it sounded like. I didn't press him, but either way, he made it clear he just saw her as a friend, and he asked me to give up on the idea. So I did."

"Does Christina know anything about this?"

"No. I didn't have the heart to tell her. When it comes up, I've just tried to ignore it or gently shift her focus in another direction. That's kind of why you heard me talking up this new guy, Ted."

Hmm. The dots were starting to connect. "Thanks for telling me this. I'll be a little more careful with Christina when I talk about Doug."

Jim understood why Marilyn had felt disappointed with Doug back when they'd had this conversation. Jim was feeling that way now. Not because he thought Doug and Christina should be together but because Doug had completely dismissed the idea because of Christina's past mistakes. He and Doug weren't on the same page about a lot of things, but he'd never figured Doug to be the self-righteous type.

20

As Christina ascended the carpeted stairs to her apartment, she felt pretty encouraged. Jim and Marilyn both really liked her back-to-school plans, including the radiology tech idea. Even though there were still a lot of details to work out, it felt good to finally be heading in a direction that might lead to something better.

She flicked on the living room lamp and set her iPad on the end table, then sat on the couch. She had recorded a Hallmark movie on her DVR and was just about to turn it on when she got curious about her Facebook post to Doug. It was stupid, but she couldn't help it. He rarely responded anymore. She reached for her iPad and clicked on the Facebook app. Before she forgot, she clicked on the buttons to accept Ted's Facebook friend request. Then she checked on Doug's earlier post.

To her surprise, Doug had replied. Looking down at the time, she saw that he had responded less than five minutes ago. He might even be online now. *Calm down, girl, you're getting way too excited about nothing.* She grabbed a pillow next to her and laid it across her lap as a makeshift desk and read his reply:

Doug: It really was fun, Christina. But really strange to see so many people in so many different costumes. One of Jason's pics you didn't see (because he wouldn't let me take one) was him wearing a Batman mask and cape. It was hilarious. I can't explain here why he wore it, but he really had no choice. Maybe I'll tell you why sometime.

She smiled, and typed back:

Christina: I'm having a hard time picturing that. Was he wearing the whole costume or just the mask and cape?

As soon as she hit the enter button, she wondered if that was a mistake, asking a direct question like that. Obviously, she'd like to get a conversation going, but how would she feel if her reply sat there unanswered for the next several days? She stared at the screen, wondering if she should delete it. But what if he was still online and had already read it? Then she would look insecure.

She was being ridiculous. Totally over-thinking this.

She was just about to shift her focus to Ted's friendship request when a little red 1 appeared by her notification button. Someone had sent her a Facebook message. Clicking on it, she was delighted to discover it was Doug. She clicked on his message and read:

Doug: Hey Christina, how are you? I was just about to reply to your reply to my reply when I noticed you were online now. Figured I might as well message you instead. That way I won't have to worry about everything I said being read by everybody in the world.

Christina: I'm doing great, Doug. Great to hear from you. Just came from eating dessert with your folks out on the veranda. Definitely would have enjoyed seeing a pic of Jason in a Batman mask. You said you couldn't explain why he had to wear it in a Facebook post, but can you do it here in a FB message?

She waited a few moments. A little message appeared saying, *Doug is typing . . .* This was kind of exciting.

Doug: Sure, it's not top secret. You'll understand why I'm being a little secretive after I explain. The weekend before last we were at a party and Jason got into a fight with a girl's ex-boyfriend. It wasn't his fault, but he was getting creamed. I had to step in and stop it, but after the fight, he did something stupid in revenge. Really stupid. We had to flee the scene in a hurry. The guy and his fairly big friends came after us, but we got away.

Christina: Oh no, that's terrible. Was he badly hurt? Were you hurt?

Doug: I'm fine, not a scratch. But Jason's face was all black and blue. He stayed in his dorm all week to let it heal. The guy and his friends didn't get a good look at him that night because it was dark. But we figured he had to know that whoever it was, their face would have been a mess. It was healed up some at the Comic-Con, but towards the end we saw the guy and all his friends coming right toward us. We didn't want to take a chance he would recognize Jason, so that's why he had to wear the Batman mask.

Christina: What a wild story. Maybe you can use it in your graphic novel. How's that coming along? Have you started to do any drawings?

Doug: Just some preliminary sketches at this point. Trying to "build the world" our story will take place in. Playing with some fun ideas. Trying to come up with something that hasn't been done before in these kinds of books.

Christina: I'd love to see them. Maybe you could bring some with you the next time you come home.

Doug: They're nothing special. Not now anyway.

Christina: I don't care. I'd still love to see them. While I look at them, you can tell me the story you have in mind. Do you have it worked out yet?

Doug: We have the main concepts and some of the big plot points figured out, but not the details yet.

Christina: Sounds exciting. Guess with this big contest, you'll really have to stay focused on it, right?

Doug: Yep. Taking up most of my spare time. But I'm loving it. Don't think we have a serious chance of winning, but it's definitely helping us get it in gear.

Christina liked the sound of that . . . that this was taking up most of his spare time. That meant less time to be with Courtney.

Christina: I wouldn't say that about your chances of winning. I don't know anything about Jason's writing, but I've seen your artwork. It definitely seems to be up to par with the comic books I've read.

Doug: Wait . . . you read comic books?

Christina: Some girls like comic books. I'm not as big a fan as you are, but I've definitely read my share. I've seen most of the movies about comic book heroes too.

Doug: That's wild. How come you never told me that before?

Christina: I don't know. Guess it never

came up. Anyway, don't forget to bring your sketch pad the next time you come down. Have any idea when that might be? Not pushing, just asking.

Doug: No plans at the moment, but I'm guessing Michele's supposed to be coming back from Africa soon with Ayana? I'm sure I'll be back when that happens. My parents will probably throw a big party.

Christina: I don't think they have an exact date set yet, but it could be in a week or ten days. You're right about the party. Your parents were talking about it again tonight. I'll text you or message you as soon as I know when.

Doug: Great. Well, it's been nice chatting with you. I better get some studying done before it gets too late.

Christina: Nice chatting with you too.

Should she say it? Would it come across as nagging?

Christina: I miss the way we used to talk.

She waited for what felt like the longest time for his reply. Finally, it came.

Doug: I miss that too. Let's do this again soon.

He signed off.

Well, that was unexpected. Pleasant, but unexpected. Her eyes drifted to the beginning of the conversation, and she started reading it again. Then she stopped. She knew what came next. If she wasn't careful, she'd reread it a dozen times. Each time imagining it meant more to Doug than it really did. It was just a pleasant conversation. It wasn't the beginning of something more. Maybe he would follow through on what he said at the end, and they'd start reconnecting again.

Or maybe nothing would happen and this was just a nice distraction.

She clicked on the little *x* and backed out of the box that contained their conversation. When she returned to the home page, lo and behold, Ted — nice and kind and thoughtful Ted — had already responded to her friend request by posting on her wall:

Ted: Thanks for friending me, Christina. Enjoyed our time together this afternoon. The only problem was, it was too short. Look forward to seeing you again.

After reading it, she sighed.

A sigh probably didn't bode well for their future as a couple. But then, would she have sighed if she hadn't just had such a nice chat with Doug? Probably not. She might have even been slightly glad to hear from him.

Then another thought . . . wouldn't Doug be able to see what Ted had just posted on her wall, since they were Facebook friends? Was that a good thing?

21

Michele sat on the edge of the sofa in the orphanage, staring at the driveway through the window. Henok, the orphanage director, was due to arrive any moment. Adina had already started dinner. Ayana was playing with the other children in the backyard.

This was the moment they had waited for for so many months.

Last week, the two things that had been holding up Ayana's visa had finally come: her birth certificate and passport. An hour ago, Henok had called sounding very excited. He said he'd be arriving soon with a big surprise. She tried to dig it out of him, but he said she'd just have to wait, and that the wait would be worth it.

There was a low rumbling sound outside, followed by the crunching of stones. A car pulling into the gravel driveway. Michele shot up and ran to the window. It was Henok. She watched as he turned off the car and got out. There was that smile. He didn't smile often, but when he did it filled his face. She saw a manila folder in his hand. As he neared the front door, she said through the open window, "Is that it? Is that Ayana's visa?"

"It is. It finally came."

She opened the door and he stepped through. She couldn't help it, she threw her arms around him. "I can't believe it! We're going home!"

"Yes, you are," he said as she released her hug. "It's official. Our orphanage has successfully placed its first child in an American home."

Adina came hurrying around the kitchen counter. "I'm so happy for you." She held out her arms, and they hugged.

Henok walked into the living room and sat on the sofa, laid the folder on the coffee table. "It's all in here. I want to make copies for our files, but after that, it's all yours."

"When can I make travel plans?" Michele asked. She walked around the table and sat beside him.

"Right away. You and Ayana can go home to America as soon as you're ready."

"It's like a dream. We've been waiting so long, then just like that, and we're free to go." She looked at her watch, trying to calculate where Allan would be right now. "It's a little after four-thirty." She counted back nine hours. "So it's just a little after seven-thirty back home. Allan should just be heading out the door for work. I've got to try and call him." She stood up. "Please don't tell Ayana yet. I'll tell her as soon as I'm done with Allan."

"We wouldn't dare," Adina said. "She's having fun outside. She'll be fine until you're done."

Michele hurried out to the spot in the front yard where she seemed to get the best reception. For the next fifteen minutes, she tried but couldn't connect with him. She was just about to come into the house and give up when she heard the phone ringing on his end. *Please, Lord, let it go through. Let him pick up.*

"Hello? Michele?"

He was coming through nice and strong. "Allan, I finally got you."

"Is everything okay? I'm on my way to work. You never call me this early."

"Everything is more than okay. How would you like me to bring your daughter home?"

"Really? Are you serious? The visa came through?"

"I'm serious. We just got it a few minutes ago."

"I thought it was gonna take at least another week or so."

"Me too. Henok called an hour ago, said he had a great surprise and was coming right over. He just got here and showed it to me. I asked him when we could leave and he said right away. We have everything we need right now."

"Oh Michele . . ."

He started getting choked up, which of course made her start to cry. "You better pull over before you get in an accident."

"I already did. I pulled into a convenience store parking lot. This is wonderful. I've missed you so much. I'm so glad the waiting is finally over."

"I know. If I could, I'd leave right now. But I guess that's the next thing, making the flight arrangements . . . for one adult and one little girl."

"Our little girl."

She loved hearing him say it. "I've been with her long enough over here, I feel like that already. I can't wait until you get to have that feeling."

"Have you told Ayana yet?"

"No. I just found out moments before I called, and I ran outside hoping to get you."

159

She got an idea. "Do you have a few minutes, or do you need to start driving to work?"

"I'm already going to be a few minutes late. What's a few minutes more? When they hear why, they're not going to care. Why?"

Michele walked to the front door. "Why don't you tell her?"

"Me? Over the phone?"

"Sure. Why not? You're her daddy. She loves it when she gets to talk to you. I'd love for her to have the memory of hearing it first from you."

"Okay. Where is she?"

"She's out back playing with the other kids. I'll go get her." She stepped inside and closed the front door. Henok and Adina were looking right at her. Then she got another idea. She pulled the phone away from her face. "Adina, would you mind getting my iPad? It should be right there on my bed."

"I'd be happy to."

"Henok, could you bring Ayana inside? Say her daddy's on the phone and he wants to talk to her."

"That'll get her in quick," he said.

"What do you want with your iPad?" Allan asked.

"You'll see." She looked at Adina, who

160

was coming out of the bedroom. "I'm going to let Allan tell Ayana the good news first, over the phone. Would you mind getting it on video?" Michele had taught Adina how to use the camera features last week, so she could be in some of the pictures with Ayana.

"It would be my pleasure." Adina got right to it.

"That way we can upload it so our family can see it back home."

"And Ayana will watch it at least a hundred times," Adina said, smiling.

Michele heard the back door open.

Ayana came running through, all excited. "Daddy's on phone?"

"He certainly is. And he wants to talk to you." Michele handed her the phone. "He has some exciting news."

Ayana's eyes lit up. She held the phone against her ear. "Daddy? It's me, Ayana."

Michele bent down, close enough to hear.

"Hi, sweetie, it's Daddy."

"Are you here?"

"No. I'm still in America. But guess where you're going to be in just a few more days?"

"Where?"

"Right here, with me, in America. Mommy's going to bring you home."

"In an air-o-plane?"

"Yes. In an air-o-plane. In just a few days.

You see Mr. Henok standing there?"

Ayana looked and nodded.

"He said you can come home with us. As soon as we hang up, I'm going to buy the airplane tickets."

"Should I hang up now?"

"No!" He laughed. "Give the phone back to Mommy. I need to talk to her a minute. But as soon as she hangs up, I'm going to buy those tickets so you two can come home, and we can be a family all together. Would you like that?"

Michele's eyes teared up again.

Ayana nodded and handed Michele the phone. "You need to hang up so Daddy can buy tickets."

Michele hugged Ayana. "I will, honey. I will hang up very soon." She looked up into the iPad, realizing this was being filmed, and waved to everyone back home.

"Can I go play?"

"You most certainly can." Ayana ran back outside. Michele turned her attention back to Allan. "Did I hear you tell her you were going to book the flights?"

"Figured I should. You're going to have your hands full getting ready for the trip. Besides, your internet reception is always iffy over there. The only thing I need to know is, how much time do you need, so I

162

know which day to book the flights?"

"I haven't even thought about it. I want to say just make it tomorrow, but I know that won't work. How about I talk it over with Henok and text you what day?"

"That'll work."

"Speaking of work, you better get back on the road. Can't wait to see you."

22

"Okay, Michele, I'll spread the word," Marilyn said. "It's so exciting! I'm so happy for you, and for us. Can't wait to see you both."

Christina was standing right next to Marilyn as she hung up her phone. They were at Odds-n-Ends. The store had just opened, and only a couple of customers were milling about. Christina had jumped when she first heard Marilyn answer the phone, three aisles over, thinking something must be wrong. A moment later, she could tell Marilyn's reaction was a happy one.

Marilyn turned and gave Christina a hug. "It's happened, Christina. It finally came through, all the paperwork for Ayana. She's officially Michele and Allan's little girl. They're coming home Saturday night. Can you believe it?"

"That's such great news. I am so happy for Michele." Thanks to all of Michele's

Facebook posts, pictures, and YouTube videos, Christina felt completely connected to Allan and Michele's journey. Over the last year, she had really come to see Michele as a big sister. "I thought she wasn't coming home, though, for another week or two."

"I know," Marilyn said, "isn't it wonderful? Something must've happened, Michele didn't say what, but everything came through." She looked at her watch. "She called Allan when she first got the news a few hours ago and waited to call me until he'd called back a little later after booking the flights. But it's all set. They'll be here Saturday night."

Christina looked around the store. "Look, I'll go take care of those customers. Why don't you go into the back room so you can call Jim and Tom and Jean. After I'm done with the customers, I'll text Doug and let him know."

"Thanks. I won't be long. I sure hope Doug will come."

"I'm sure he will. We were on Facebook a few days ago, and I asked him when he thought he might be coming home again. He said probably when Michele got back from Africa."

"He said that? I'm so glad. I'll mention that to Jim." Marilyn started walking down

165

the aisle toward the back.

"Wait," Christina said. "Will we be having the welcome home party Saturday night?"

"I think they'll be too tired. It'll be a long flight and a nine-hour time difference between there and here. Maybe we'll have it Sunday afternoon, after church."

"Great, that's what I'll tell Doug." Christina headed the other way to greet the customers already in the store.

Jim was out in his office's little reception lobby, reviewing some office procedures with Marie, his new secretary/ receptionist. She had just started a week ago. His former secretary had left on pregnancy leave three weeks ago, but she'd made it clear she wanted to stay home with her baby for good. That was the third secretary he had lost in three years for the same reason. Marie was a nice lady from their church. She held out more hope for permanence, since her children were grown and she had smiling photos of three grandchildren in picture frames on the corner of her desk.

"I think I hear your phone," Marie said.

Jim looked at the phone sitting on the other corner of her desk. None of the lights were flashing.

"I mean your cell phone. I think I hear it

ringing from your office."

"Oh." He listened and could just barely hear it in the distance. "I can't believe you heard that."

"I hear like a bat," she said.

"I'll be right back." He hurried down the hall. As he reached his desk, he saw Marilyn's face on the screen and picked it up.

"I'm so glad," she said. "I thought I was going to have to leave a message."

"I was in the front office with Marie. Is everything all right?"

"It's official — we're grandparents again!"

Jim thought a minute. Was Jean pregnant again?

"It's Michele, the paperwork came through. Ayana is officially adopted. She's their little girl. Well, they still have to do things on this end, but everything is legal in Ethiopia. She got the green light to come home."

"When?"

"Saturday night. They'll be flying into Orlando. I'm sure Allan will want to pick them up, but we'll —"

"Oh, we're definitely going to be there."

"I was hoping you'd say that."

"Do you know what time?"

"Not yet. I think she said seven, but she's

167

going to email me all the details. But isn't it wonderful?"

"Thank you, Lord. I'm so glad the wait is over. I know you wanted to have a big welcome home party . . ." Jim walked around his desk and sat.

"They'll be too tired on Saturday. I thought we'd do it Sunday after church."

"That'll work. Have you told anyone else yet?"

"Just you. Christina knows. She was standing next to me when I got the call."

"You gonna call Jean next?"

"Yes."

"I'll call Uncle Henry and Aunt Myra," he said. "I'm sure they'll want to come."

"Christina said she'd contact Doug."

"You think that'll do any good? Maybe I should do it. I thought you said they weren't that close anymore."

"Let's wait and see what she hears back from him. She said they were going back and forth on Facebook a few days ago and Doug said he planned to come home whenever Michele got back from Africa."

"Really? Maybe it'll happen then." Jim wondered if he shouldn't contact Doug anyway, for a little extra push. But he decided against it. Maybe this was one of those times for silence and trust. Both concepts were still so hard to master.

Doug was brushing his teeth, trying to wake up after staying out way too late last night at a party. His first class wasn't until eleven, which was the excuse Jason and Courtney had used last night when trying to get him to stay out longer. Staring at his puffy eyes in the mirror, he regretted not acting on his first instinct.

His cell phone started to ring, but he didn't hear it at first. Maybe it was the bathroom door being closed or the noise of the water running as he rinsed out his mouth. But he was glad he finally did hear it, because when he stepped out of the bathroom, Courtney — in his bed and still half asleep — reached for it on the nightstand.

"I'll get it," he yelled.

"Okay, okay. You don't have to yell." She rolled back under the covers, pulled the pillow over her head.

She was probably nursing one heavy-duty hangover. Picking up his phone, he saw it was Christina. Now he was *really* glad he got there before Courtney. He quickly walked back into the bathroom and closed the door. "Hey, Christina."

"Hi, Doug. Hope I'm not calling too early."

"Not at all. It's already, what, a little after ten?" He was talking quietly and hoped it didn't come off as a whisper.

"I can only talk a minute, 'cause I'm at work. But I thought you'd want to know. Your mom just got that call from Michele, the one we've been waiting for."

Doug couldn't imagine what she was talking about. Then he remembered, Michele was in Africa.

"When we chatted on Facebook a few days ago, you said the next time you'd probably be coming home was when Michele came home with Ayana. Well, she's coming home Saturday night, and your mom's putting together a welcome home party for Sunday after church."

Sunday, Sunday, he thought. He didn't think he had anything happening then. "Well, so soon. I don't know why, but I thought it would be a few more weeks."

"We all did. But something happened, and it came through now." She paused. "I told your mom I'd let you know."

"That's good. I'm happy for Michele. I know that's something they've wanted to happen for a long time."

"Think you can make it? I know it's short notice."

"I should be able to. I don't have any classes that day, obviously. I can't think of any plans I made at the moment, but even if I did, they're nothing I can't change."

"Good. Your mom will be so happy. You think you'll be coming Saturday night or Sunday morning? If you're coming Saturday night, she'll want to get your bed ready."

"Hmm. Not sure. Let me think about it. Can I get back to you in a little while on that? I'll text you."

"Sure, no problem."

A banging on the door. "Doug, I need to get in there. Like, right away." It was Courtney.

He put his hand over the phone. "Hold on, Courtney. I'll be right out."

"No, I mean, like, right away."

"What's the matter?" Christina asked.

"Nothing. Someone's at the door." Technically, that wasn't a lie. "I've gotta go, but I'll text you on that Saturday or Sunday thing real soon."

He hung up and opened the bathroom door. A very disheveled-looking Courtney pushed him out of the way.

"Please close the door," she said.

Which he did, right away.

23

It was late Sunday morning. Doug and Jason were just finishing a big breakfast buffet at Golden Corral. They had slept in after another late night out with their friends. When Jason learned Doug was going home today, he'd asked to tag along. It had been several months since he'd been home to see his folks. "Might as well remind them what I look like."

Doug was eating cheese grits when Jason came back to the table holding a plate stacked high with blueberry pancakes. "I can't believe how much you eat," Doug said. "And you're still so skinny."

Jason sat. "It's my metabolism. Burns everything up. It's hereditary, what can I say? You watch, I'll be hungry two hours from now. Just about the time we get to River Oaks. My parents will be eating lunch, and I'll join right in."

Doug finished his last bite of grits. Should

he go up again?

"What's the matter?" Jason asked.

"What do you mean? Nothing's the matter."

"You seem all mopey." He began layering his pancakes with whipped butter.

"I'm just tired."

"You sure? Because I know your tired look. You look more mopey."

"Maybe I'm both. What difference does it make?"

"Because we've got almost a two-hour drive, and I'm in a good mood. I don't want you bringing me down. That's my parents' job. I wanna stay in a good mood till then." He poured maple syrup over his pancakes until a moat formed around the base. "Look at this. I just ate half a plate of cheesy eggs, about ten sausage links, and a dozen strips of bacon. Now I've got this plate of blueberry pancakes. After this, who knows? They've already started putting cake and pie out for the lunch crowd. I might get a slice for the road. Be happy, bro."

Doug laughed. Was he being mopey? Maybe he was. "I'm an artist. Artists get mopey sometimes. We don't need a reason."

"If you say so," Jason said through a mouthful of pancakes. "But if there is a reason, I'm here if you want to talk about

173

it." Still chewing, he said, "You worried about getting with your family? I know they can be a little uptight, all their religious stuff."

"They're not uptight."

"You're kidding, right? How many times have you complained to me about all the pressure you get from them and what a hypocrite your dad is? And now because I mention it, you're going to defend them?"

Was this Jason's idea of trying to help improve his mood? "First of all, you and I haven't talked about my dad in a while. He used to be that way a few years ago. Remember when I told you I thought my folks were splitting up? And my mom moved out for a while? Something happened back then that changed him. Kind of changed the whole family." Really, everyone but me, he thought.

Jason stabbed his fork through another oversized bite. "Like how? They still seem pretty religious to me. Way overboard sometimes. Like right now . . . they're probably in church again, am I right?"

"Jason, c'mon, it's Sunday morning. Not exactly overboard for people to go to church on Sunday."

"See, you're defending them again."

"I am not."

"Uh . . . yeah, you are."

Jason was right, he was. Then he realized what was bugging him. It was Sunday morning, and *he* wasn't in church . . . again. He'd gone to church every Sunday of his life before coming to school here. Now he hardly ever went. It wasn't as if he really missed it. He'd pretty much hated the church his parents took him to before they split up. Got absolutely nothing out of it. He only went to the new church for a few months after they got back together, then his focus shifted to going off to school.

"They're probably going to hassle you when you get home. Ask you how church was this morning. Am I right?"

"That could happen," Doug said.

"How about this? Before we head out of town, we can stop in at some church. Just for a minute or two. We don't even have to go all the way in. That way, when your folks ask you how was church, you can say fine. And it won't be a lie."

"I'm going to get some more to eat."

"That's right, change the subject," Jason said as he walked off.

Jason was a decent friend but a lousy confidant. He rarely gave advice, but one thing you could count on when he did: it would be worthless.

After walking slowly around, eyeing the different buffet selections, Doug settled on a big cinnamon bun with lots of icing. He carried that and a cup of coffee back to the table.

"Think you just made my mind up," Jason said. "Forget the chocolate cake, I'm getting me one of those."

Doug took a sip of coffee. "This stuff's awful." He pushed it aside. "I'm going back to grab one of those milk cartons."

"While you're up, get me one of those buns? One with at least as much icing as that one."

Doug got the milk and Jason's cinnamon bun, then came back.

Jason was eating the last of his pancakes. He set the plate with the cinnamon bun on top of the empty pancake plate. "Thanks, man." He sliced off a corner of the bun. "You know, maybe I can use all this parental angst you're experiencing in our story. Our main character's having all kinds of parent problems. So maybe it's a good thing we're talking about this."

"Guess you'll have to use my story. Certainly can't use yours. You never seem to be going through any . . . *angst* with your parents."

"That's 'cause my parents are liberals.

They don't have any rules. At least not ones they impose on anyone. They're all about live and let live. You know? But your folks . . ." He paused.

"What?"

"Nothing."

"It's not nothing. Just say it."

"You're gonna get defensive."

"No, I won't, just say it. What about my folks?"

"Rules, bro. Lots of rules. Moral codes. Everything's black or white, right or wrong. And all these expectations about how they want you to live."

Doug lifted a big gooey bite of cinnamon bun from his plate. "If your parents are so 'live and let live,' why did you say you expect them to bring down your good mood?"

"Okay, good point. But they get on me for lightweight stuff, like why I'm such a slob or not taking out the trash when I'm home. Crap like that. Your folks want to tell you how to live, how you should spend your time, who you should spend it with. I'll bet they don't even know about Courtney yet, do they?"

Doug looked away.

"They don't. Look at you. You haven't told them about Courtney? You two've been going out for what, two months now? See? Proves my point. You haven't told them because you know they wouldn't approve. Am I right or am I right?"

Of course he was right. Everything he was saying was right. That was how Doug's parents were. The problem was, and this was the thing eating at him, he didn't know for sure what he believed about all this. Who was right and who was wrong?

All he knew was, he hated how it felt being stuck in the middle.

24

An hour after the Andersons got home from church, the house was filled with excitement. Allan and Michele, along with little Ayana, were on their way. Jim and Marilyn were there, so were Tom and Jean, their kids, Uncle Henry and Aunt Myra. Even Marilyn's friend Charlotte. Christina was grateful to be included in this family event. But beneath this festive mood, she detected a slight undercurrent of tension.

Everyone was here except Doug.

While the rest of the family looked out the front windows for Allan and Michele's car, Christina sent Doug a text: *They're almost here. Are you close?*

A few moments later, Doug texted back: *Around the corner, just dropped Jason off at his house.*

Christina gave Marilyn the news, loud enough for Jim to hear.

"Thanks, Christina," she said.

A few minutes later, Jean said, "There's Doug's little red Mazda."

"And there's Allan and Michele," Tom said, "right behind him."

As both cars pulled up to the front curb, everyone hurried out on the front porch to greet them. Marilyn led the way down the steps. Christina watched as Allan came around behind the car to open the door for Ayana. She took one look at the crowd of people rushing toward her and reached up for Allan.

"It's okay, Ayana," he said. "You know all these people. Here's Grandma and Grandpa. They were at the airport last night, remember? And you've seen almost everyone else's picture."

Ayana looked at each person, even Christina. Her expression softened, and a little smile appeared. Christina wondered if they had shown Ayana pictures of her too. She glanced to the right, in time to catch Doug stepping out of his car. He joined the throng on the sidewalk.

"Sorry I'm late," he said quietly to his mom. "Ran into bumper-to-bumper traffic on I-4."

"On a Sunday?" Jim said.

"There was an accident."

Marilyn hugged him. "Glad you could

180

make it."

"Me too, Doug," Jim said.

People were already hugging Allan and Michele, welcoming them home. Ayana seemed more at ease. Jean walked their three children up to her and introduced them. Tommy and Carly were so cute, repeating an obviously rehearsed greeting, "Very nice to meet you, Ayana."

Marilyn looked at Michele. "Can I hold her?"

Michele turned to Ayana. "What do you think? Can Grandma hold you a minute?"

Ayana nodded then reached out her hands. Marilyn took her and squeezed her tight. "We're so glad you're finally home with us. We've been waiting so long. Are you hungry?"

Ayana nodded and said something in a different language.

"That means a little," Michele said. "That's Amharic, her native tongue. But she's learning English, aren't you, Ayana?" Ayana nodded. Michele encouraged Ayana to repeat the phrase "a little" in English, which she did.

Marilyn turned toward Christina with Ayana in her arms. "Ayana, this is Christina. She lives with us."

"You remember Christina," Michele said.

"From her picture."

Ayana smiled. "Chris-teen-a."

"That's very good," Christina said.

Michele looked around. "I think the only ones here she hasn't seen, in pictures, I mean, are Doug and Charlotte."

"Even us?" Uncle Henry said.

"Even you guys," Michele said. "Must've been one of those weekends you visited a few weeks back. There were several pictures of you guys here at the house."

Marilyn walked Ayana over and introduced her to Charlotte. Charlotte gave her a big smile and a kiss on the cheek. "She's adorable," she said in her strong Bostonian accent.

Doug stepped up to greet her. "Hi, Ayana, I'm Doug. I'm your mommy's little brother."

A confused expression came over her face. She said something to Michele in Amharic. Michele laughed.

"What's the matter?" Doug said.

"I don't understand everything she said," Michele said, "but I think she's wondering how you can be my little brother when you're bigger than me. She didn't have any siblings."

"Well, now that everybody's met everybody," Jim said, "why don't we head into the dining room and eat some of this delicious food?"

"A great idea," Allan said, and began walking toward the house.

Everyone followed. Christina waited till the others had passed. Doug waited too, so they wound up walking in together. "Good to see you, Doug."

"You too, Christina." They climbed the porch steps. "You're looking very well."

"Thank you." He was too, very much so. But should she say it? And what did he mean by what he said? It wasn't quite a compliment, more like something you say to someone who was just getting over being sick. Was he referring to her weight? She glanced down at her stomach, which was almost flat again. She tried to remember, had she done something different with her hair since the last time they were together?

Doug grabbed the front door from Tom, who'd been holding it open, and held it open for her. "After you."

The atmosphere at the dinner table was light and easy. For the most part, Michele told stories about her adventures in Ethiopia and answered questions about the life Ayana was leaving behind. Clearly, on some answers Michele was choosing her words

183

carefully, for Ayana's sake. It was hard to fathom how radically different her life had just become. Christina had some sense of what the little girl was experiencing, from the culture shock she'd gone through when she first began to hang out with the Anderson family.

But as she listened to Michele, Christina knew that in her former life she had lived in the lap of luxury compared to what Ayana had known up until this moment.

Michele described the home Ayana had lived in with her grandmother before moving into the orphanage as about half the size of Jim and Marilyn's walk-in closet. All the homes she'd seen in Ayana's village had dirt floors. Most had no windows or running water.

Several times as Michele talked, Ayana appeared distracted. Her eyes roamed all over the place. She seemed mesmerized by the height of the cathedral ceiling and the loft upstairs. It was also fun to watch Ayana's first bite of Italian food. Marilyn had made a big tray of baked ziti with a side dish of meatballs in marinara sauce.

At first, Ayana stared at the food on her plate with great concern. Her first bite was really just a bit of sauce on the tip of her fork. Her expression instantly changed when she tasted it. In no time at all, she was eating away.

Another enjoyable aspect of this dinner for Christina was the seating arrangement at the table. She didn't know if it was by accident, but the last two available seats were together, so here she was, sitting next to Doug. They weren't getting to spend any real time together, since everyone's attention was centered on Michele, Allan, and Ayana, as it should be. But still, it was nice.

There was only one truly tense moment during the meal for Christina. She wasn't sure anyone else even picked up on it. Possibly Jim and Marilyn. Certainly Doug. About halfway through, Marilyn's friend Charlotte asked, "So Doug, how's things going at your school? You got a girlfriend yet? Anyone special?"

Doug looked startled but quickly recovered his composure. "Uh, no, Charlotte. They keep us pretty busy up there. No special girlfriends. Not yet."

"A nice-looking boy like you? I'd be thinking the girls would be gobbling you up."

Doug's face showed some serious embarrassment. Marilyn looked annoyed. "Charlotte," she said, "I think you're making Doug feel uncomfortable."

"I am? Sorry, Doug, you know me. So are

you liking it up there? What do you think of the school?"

Doug clearly appreciated the shift to a new topic and answered freely. The rest of the conversation remained safe and neutral. But it left Christina wondering if Doug's answer to Charlotte was an outright lie or if he simply didn't consider Courtney as "someone special."

When everyone had finished eating, during a lull in the conversation Marilyn said, "There's a fresh pot of coffee in the kitchen. I'm guessing we're all a little too full to eat dessert just yet . . ."

Everyone agreed, except Tommy and Carly. Jean told them, "Sorry, guys, you don't get a vote."

"Well," Jim said, "I know I'm stuffed. But coffee still sounds good."

A few minutes later, Christina was standing next to Doug by the coffee pot. He poured himself a cup and said, "Would you like some?"

"I would." He poured hers. "By the way, did you remember to bring your sketch pad home?"

"I did," he said. "It's in the car. But you weren't really serious about wanting to look at my drawings."

"Of course I was. Why don't you go get it?

We can sit out on the veranda and drink our coffee. It's so nice out there now. Your mom and I have planted a bunch of new flowers in the beds. While I look at the drawings, you can tell me a little bit about the story."

25

After everyone who'd wanted coffee had gotten some, Michele, Jean, Aunt Myra, and Marilyn went upstairs with the kids. Marilyn had converted one of the bedrooms into a playroom for the grandkids, which now included Ayana. Normally at family events, the kids played upstairs by themselves. The ladies had joined them today because, understandably, Michele didn't want to leave Ayana alone on her first full day home.

Allan and Tom were watching an NBA game in the living room. Christina sat outside in the shade under the veranda with her coffee, waiting for Doug. She had brought his mug out with her while he went out front to get his sketch pad from the car. Judging by the scene she was looking at through the patio door, she figured he had been stopped on his way back in by his father and Uncle Henry.

They didn't appear to be talking about

188

anything serious. A few moments later she understood what was going on. They must've seen him carrying his sketch pad and stopped to ask about it. Doug was now flipping through the first several pages. The look on both men's faces indicated they approved. Even Doug was smiling now.

She waited a few minutes longer, thinking she should at least get up and bring Doug his coffee before it got cold. Just as she reached for the mug, the patio door opened and Doug walked out.

"Sorry about that," he said. "My dad and Uncle Henry wanted to see my latest drawings."

"You don't need to apologize. Looks like they liked them."

"They did. I was a little nervous at first. Not so much about Uncle Henry. He'd say something nice no matter how bad they were. But I was afraid my dad would start wondering if he was getting his money's worth out of my college education."

"Did he say anything negative?"

Doug pulled out a chair and sat, set the sketch pad between them on the table. "Not really negative. He definitely seemed impressed by the drawings themselves, which was nice. But of course, at the end he had to slip in the fatherly advice. 'These are good, Doug, but remember, this is just a hobby. You can't let it interfere with your schoolwork.' And of course I said, 'I won't, Dad.' " Doug said the first part in a low voice, trying to mimic his dad.

Christina sipped her coffee. "I'm sure that kind of thing bugs you. But that's only because you've always had it."

"What do you mean?"

"Parents who care about what happens to you. Who don't want to see you make big mistakes, so they give you little warnings all the time about the potential potholes in the road."

"Yeah, I guess." He reached for his coffee then slid the sketch pad all the way in front of her. "You can start looking at them, and I'll kind of describe what you're seeing."

She flipped open to the first page. "Wow. This is really good." In the center of the page stood a large, ornate Spanish-looking building with multiple stories on various levels and different roof lines. On each end were bell towers set at different heights. One side of the building bordered a jungle, the other a wide river. In the background, rolling hills led up to a snow-capped mountain. "I guess the two suns in the sky make it clear this is a different world, right?"

"That's the idea. We're not totally sure

how many suns our world has just yet. Isaac Asimov wrote a story about a world that had six suns. I think that's a bit much. Since you don't use as many words in a graphic novel, you're always looking for visual ways to communicate things to the reader. We think having two suns gets you there."

"I like the look of this place. It seems too big to be a home, unless it's some kind of palace."

"You're close. My main character falls in love with a girl whose father is like . . . a powerful senator. A ruler but not a king. She lives here. She kind of helps him decide that he wants this kind of life, not the simple life his parents and his people have chosen."

She flipped to the next page. It looked like the same scene but much closer to the palace, looking up at it from the side. "I can't believe how realistic this looks. You do a great job with perspective."

"Thanks. This one's a view from a boat tied up at the dock. Right here." He flipped back to the first page and pointed to a little boat dock she must have missed, then flipped back to page two.

"The building looks a little familiar," she said. "Is it based on anything real?"

"Have you been to St. Augustine?"

"No, but I hope to soon."

"All the buildings at Flagler College look like this, and quite a few other buildings around the historic area. We decided to use the Mediterranean look as the foundation for our main city. We haven't seen many comic books use that look. You know, the big ones, the ones everybody knows."

"You mean like Batman and Superman, the DC and Marvel superheroes," she said.

"Yeah." He took another sip of coffee. "I think that's wild that you like comic books. Not many girls do."

"Really? I may not be in the majority, but I don't think I'm that strange. What was the ratio of girls to guys at that Comic-Con you and Jason went to last weekend?"

Doug thought about it. "Now that you mention it, I guess it was more like one out of three."

"See? I'm not that strange. When I saw *The Avengers* at the movies — which was the last superhero movie I saw, or was it *Thor 2* — I'd say the ratio of guys to girls was about fifty-fifty."

Doug smiled.

"What?"

"Nothing," he said. "You're right. It's not that strange."

"You mean, *I'm* not that strange."

"Okay, *you're* not that strange."

192

"And I'll bet," she said, "that there were thousands of people at that Comic-Con."

He nodded. "It was huge."

"And these superhero movies, coming out one right after the other, most of them making a fortune. Have you ever thought about why?"

"What?"

"Have you ever thought about why all these superhero movies are so popular?"

Doug reached for his mug. "I guess because they're great stories. Most of them. Great-looking characters. Incredible special effects, some romance, some humor."

"Yeah, they've got all that. But I don't think that's the main reason they're so popular, especially with our generation."

"You don't, huh? You've given this some thought?"

"I have," she said. "I think they're so popular because they give us hope that all the bad, crummy things going on all around us, and all the evil people making them happen, can be stopped. The real-life people in charge don't seem to be able to do anything about it. Things just keep getting worse and worse. They promise things, and then they don't deliver. In real life, we don't have any heroes. No one to step up who has the moral goodness to do the right thing just because it's right, or the power to pull it off. In these comic books and movies, we get to root for people who are like that."

"Wow," Doug said. "You have thought a lot about this. And I think you might be on to something."

She looked down at the page. "And you know something else? I know this is gonna sound strange, but that's one of the things I like about Jesus so much, the more I get to know him and read about him in the Gospels. It's like, Jesus was a superhero, but for real. He stood up for the people no one paid attention to or cared about. He defied all the power brokers of his day, all the greedy people, all the users and the takers. And he said things about life and love and relationships that no one had ever said before. And if that wasn't enough, he had the power to pull it off. He could heal the sick with a word, walk on water, calm a raging storm, even raise the dead back to life. But then he didn't use all that power to get things for himself. Instead, he gave it all away, even his own life . . . just so we'd have a chance to get close to his Father."

She looked up. Doug was just staring at her. She couldn't read the look on his face. Maybe she had said too much. She looked down, turned the page. There were two different characters, a guy and a girl, in several different poses. They were very well done, like they could already be in a first-rate comic book. "These are great, Doug. They've got kind of a Middle Earth look to them, don't you think?"

"What?"

"These characters. I really like them. Is this the main guy and the main girl in your story?"

"Uh . . . yeah." He looked down at the page. "That's what we're thinking now anyway. But we haven't firmed anything up yet."

"Well, I think these drawings are amazing. I can't wait to hear more about the story."

26

"So, what do you think, Uncle Henry?" Jim said. "You up for a walk?"

"Sure, it's such a nice day out. Why not?"

Jim and Uncle Henry had been drinking their coffee, sitting at the dinette table in the kitchen. Doug had just stepped out onto the veranda a few minutes ago, after showing them some preliminary drawings he'd made for his graphic novel. Jim could see him sitting out there now with Christina. It was nice having him home, if only for the day. But ironically, having him so close reminded Jim of how far away he was. That was what he wanted to talk to Uncle Henry about. "Let me just go upstairs for a minute and talk with Marilyn. Make sure we have time before she wants to serve dessert."

Uncle Henry set his cup down. "I'm fine either way."

Jim walked through the living room and up the stairs, stopping near the top. The ladies were hanging out in the loft to his right. He could hear the grandkids in the playroom a few doors down. He said to Marilyn, "Do I have time to take a short walk with Uncle Henry?"

She looked at her watch. "I guess so. About twenty minutes?"

"That should be fine. See you in a few."

She smiled, made a look with her eyebrows that told him she understood what he was up to. That morning before church, he'd mentioned the possibility of talking about Doug with Uncle Henry, if the opportunity arose. Jim headed down the stairs, motioning to Uncle Henry that the walk was on. He got up and met Jim by the front door.

When the door opened, Tom looked up from the couch. "Where you guys headed?"

"Just a short walk. We'll be back in twenty minutes for dessert." Tom nodded and shifted his focus back to the basketball game. Jim and Uncle Henry stepped out onto the porch and headed for the sidewalk.

As they stepped away from the house, Jim felt the cool breeze blowing through the trees. "Won't get too many more days like this." Both men were experienced Floridians. The month of May, considered the first month of summer, was just around the corner.

"The Jim I used to know would have been out playing golf in weather this nice."

Jim shook his head. "You know what's sad? I wouldn't have thought twice about it. The whole family would be here, and I'd be out there."

"It's been a wonderful thing for Aunt Myra and me to see, all the changes in your family over the last couple of years. Used to be all kinds of tension in the air when we'd visit."

It did Jim some good to hear Uncle Henry's perspective. Jim usually focused on the one place where the tension still remained. "You two have definitely played a role in the way things have turned around."

"Maybe a small one," Uncle Henry said. "But you and Marilyn carried the heavier load. I know it was really hard at times. Maybe even a little scary. But God has really honored your humility and all your hard work."

"Well, we're not out of the woods just yet. It may look like we are on a day like today with everyone together. That's really why I wanted to take this walk. I need your help. This time with Doug."

"Doug? What kind of problem is he having?"

They reached the corner and turned left

on the sidewalk. "We're not exactly in a crisis, not yet anyway. But I'm concerned we could be heading for one."

"What's going on?"

"I guess you could say that Doug's something of a casualty from the way I used to be, before Marilyn and I almost split up. We've seen some restoration with everyone else in the family. But so far, nothing with Doug. He and I weren't close before, and, if anything, we're even farther apart now. It's not just me, Marilyn feels the same way. There's no hostility going on between us, no big disagreements or heated arguments. Of course, that could be because we're keeping our mouths shut most of the time. If I had a dime for every time I wanted to say something to him . . . well, I'd have a truckload of dimes."

Uncle Henry laughed. "Believe it or not, knowing when *not* to speak was one of the hardest lessons I had to learn with my boys. If you've got that one down, you're halfway there. Most fathers either check out completely or they're always in lecture mode. What are the main issues with Doug?"

"Guess the main one is . . . I feel like we're losing him. He hardly ever comes home on weekends anymore. Today was a rare treat.

He never interacts with us during the week. When we do talk, it's totally surface level. We never feel like we're hearing what he's really thinking. If I try to ask him questions that could lead to a deeper conversation, he gets very vague, shuts down, and quickly changes the subject. We're pretty sure he never goes to church anymore. Christina and Doug interact on Facebook sometimes. She's expressed some real concerns about the crowd he's starting to hang with at school. Lots of parties. Lots of kids drinking in the background of his pictures."

"You think Doug is?"

"Not sure. Marilyn went on Facebook. She said she didn't see any evidence of it. But you know what the Bible says about the company we keep, and the effect it can have on us. If Doug's not drinking now, that could change in time. But it's not just the drinking I'm worried about. It's the lack of any interest in a relationship with the Lord."

"And maybe where that path might lead from here?" Uncle Henry asked.

Jim nodded. They walked in silence a few moments. "I'm guessing you probably can't relate to this very much, with the kind of relationship you had with your boys. The kind of father you were."

"Actually, I can."

"You can?"

"A lot more than you might think. Ever heard that verse in Ecclesiastes? There's nothing new under the sun?"

"You and Aunt Myra had troubles with your boys?"

"Had? We not only had troubles with our boys — with one of them in particular — but we still have troubles sometimes. And both of them are older than your Tom. Remember that RV trip we took last year to see them? A part of it was to help them reconcile with each other. They had gotten into some big disagreement and were hardly talking to each other anymore. Turned out to be something of a working vacation for us."

"You're kidding."

"I wish I was. It took a lot of prayer, a lot of patience, a lot of listening, and some carefully timed suggestions, but I think we made some real progress. They seem to be doing a lot better now. But Jim, sometimes relationships with your kids, even when they become adults, are hard work. Even if you and Marilyn are doing everything right."

Jim didn't know if he felt more encouraged or discouraged to hear this. If someone who *had* done everything right with their kids — like Uncle Henry and Aunt Myra —

201

had serious problems . . . what hope did Jim have of turning this situation with Doug around?

"Let me guess," Uncle Henry said, "you're feeling pretty hopeless about your relationship with Doug right about now."

"Yeah. It seems like you're saying that what we do as parents, even when our kids get older, doesn't really matter. It doesn't make any difference. They're gonna do what they're gonna do anyway."

Uncle Henry looked at his watch. "Maybe we should turn around and start heading back." They spun around, and he continued. "I think what we do as parents matters a great deal in how our kids turn out, and in how they deal with the mistakes they make when they're on their own. But being a parent isn't about pushing all the right buttons or saying all the right words. Sometimes it's about being the kind of person they'll want to turn to, maybe even listen to, when they've made a total mess of things. Sometimes all the hard things and all the right things God wants us to do now — when they're drifting away from us — are just the building blocks to a bridge they can cross over on their way back."

That really hit home. "Uncle Henry, I wish I could write that down, what you just said. I need to let that one simmer. Marilyn would want to hear it too."

They reached the corner again. "Well, if we talk again, I probably won't remember the exact words I just said. You're the one with the younger memory. But I won't forget the idea. It was one of the hardest lessons Myra and I had to learn as our kids got older."

They kept walking. Neither one said anything till they reached the walkway leading to the house.

Uncle Henry stopped. "As this thing with Doug goes on from here, and I know it will, you and Marilyn feel free to give me a call, anytime you like. Aunt Myra and I will help you any way we can."

"I will, Uncle Henry." Jim had a feeling that he'd be taking up Uncle Henry's offer before long.

27

Everyone was sitting around the Anderson family table, eating a slice of Marilyn's homemade chocolate cake. Once again, Christina was sitting next to Doug. It probably didn't mean a thing. No, she was sure it didn't mean a thing. But there was this: he'd sat next to her on purpose. She had deliberately picked a different chair from where she had eaten the Sunday meal, and Doug had deliberately sat in the chair beside her. Unlike last time, there were several chairs he could've picked from.

The rest of their conversation out on the veranda had been pleasant. She was sad to see it end. Even for chocolate cake. Although she couldn't detect any romantic sparks from the exchange, it was an easy conversation and flowed smoothly. Just the way they used to talk a few months ago, before Doug had started pulling away.

Before . . . Courtney.

At the very least, she held out hope that their time this afternoon might spark a renewed connection online. Maybe he would begin to respond to her posts more often and more quickly on Facebook. And maybe something would happen between him and Courtney that would bring an end to . . . whatever it was they had going on. From what she saw on Facebook, she was certain they were a couple on some level. But he hadn't mentioned her name one time in the entire conversation. What did that mean?

"Look at her face," Doug said. "I've never seen anyone enjoy a piece of cake so much." He was looking at Ayana.

Christina looked, and it was wonderful to see. Each bite for Ayana was like opening a present.

"I knew she'd like it," Michele said. "She loves chocolate. And Mom, you make the best chocolate cake ever."

"I agree," Jim said, putting another large bite into his mouth.

"She must be experiencing sensory overload," Doug said, looking at Michele. "Don't you think? All these new things she's seeing and hearing and tasting all at once."

"I'm sure she is," Allan said. "Happens to me every time I come home after being over there. Michele knows what that's like now too. Don't you?"

"I do. And I'm sure this is all very strange for her. Probably feels like some kind of fairy tale. But I'm hoping her age will work to her advantage. I don't remember hardly anything from when I was her age."

"How did she like her new room?" Christina asked. "You guys got home last night, right?"

"We did, but she was sound asleep. Allan carried her in. But I was there this morning when she woke up. I wish you all could've been there. Her eyes were just like they are now. Only she was looking all around. She couldn't believe it when I told her it was her room."

"What did she say?"

"All this? For me?" Michele said it, mimicking Ayana's accent.

Hearing that, Ayana looked up at Michele and smiled. It didn't appear she was paying attention to what everyone was saying until now.

"I'm telling everyone about what it was like for you waking up in your room this morning."

"It was so big and so pretty," Ayana said.

"She said that very well," Jim said. "I understood every word."

"Kids pick up languages so easily," Allan said.

For the next ten minutes, everyone continued chatting and enjoying their cake. When Doug finished his, he set his fork down on the plate, slid his chair out, and stood. "Well, I hate to do this, but I really have to go."

"So soon?" Marilyn said.

"Yeah. I've got a test first thing in the morning."

"You're really going to miss out," Tom said.

"On what?"

"Around six or seven o'clock, I'm going to make my famous Reuben on rye sandwiches."

"I really am gonna hate missing that. But I haven't had a chance to study all weekend. If I don't get back and hit the books, I'm sunk."

"That's too bad," his father said. "We'll miss you. But I'm glad you came, Doug, even for a little while."

"Me too," Michele said. "I'm so glad we were all here for Ayana's first family dinner."

Jim and Marilyn stood.

"Don't get up," Doug said.

"The least we could do is walk you to the

door," Marilyn said.

"No. You guys are still eating. I'll come over there." He walked to their end of the table and gave them both hugs, then he hugged Michele. Bending down, he said, "Can I give her a little hug?"

"Sure," Michele said. "Ayana loves hugs."

After giving Ayana a hug, Doug walked around the table and gave Uncle Henry and Aunt Myra one too. He started walking toward the front door, waving and nodding to the others. He looked at Christina and said, "Really enjoyed our chat. We'll talk some more on Facebook."

"I look forward to it," she replied.

It wasn't much, but it was something.

He waved to everyone again by the front door, then he was gone. "His sketch pad," Christina said aloud. "He forgot it."

She ran out to the veranda and picked it up off the glass table, then headed to the front door. By the time she was out on the porch, he was already in his car. She ran down the steps, waving it as she hurried across the walkway. The car turned on and began to pull away. Fortunately, they lived in a cul-de-sac so he had to turn the car around and head the other way. She ran out into the street, still waving the sketch pad.

He finally saw it and stopped the car. As

she walked toward him, he rolled down the window. "I can't believe I did that. Thank you so much. I would have had to drive all the way back here."

Panting, she handed it to him.

"I really am sorry I have to go so soon. And I really did enjoy our talk on the veranda. It was . . . refreshing."

"Refreshing is good." She didn't know quite what to make of that.

"I'm just not used to having such an in-depth conversation about comic book stuff with . . ."

"A girl?"

"Well, yeah. But it was fun. If you're okay with it, I'd like to keep you in the loop. Bounce some ideas off you from time to time. Maybe take some jpegs of my drawings, see what you think."

This was exciting. "I'd love that."

"There's just one condition."

"What?"

"You can't just tell me what you like. If you see anything that bugs you, anything you think doesn't work, I need you to tell me."

"I will."

"Promise me."

She laughed. "Okay, I promise."

"Starting now."

"What do you mean?"

He picked the scratch pad up from the seat. "Was there anything on these drawings that you didn't like but were afraid to tell me because you didn't want to hurt my feelings?"

"No."

"Really? There isn't one thing you thought about, then talked yourself out of bringing up?"

"No. Really. You don't have to worry about me being straight with you. I'm from New York."

Doug laughed. "That's right, I forgot. Your accent isn't as strong as it used to be."

She'd been working on that. "But really, I loved them. I thought they were perfect. And I know other people will think so too."

"Speaking of being straight with me, what's going on with you and this guy . . . Ted? I'm starting to see him post a lot more often on your wall. Are you two, like . . ."

"We're just friends," she said, perhaps a little too strongly. "From church. We know each other at church."

"So you're not going out?"

"We had coffee once, but that's all. He's a nice guy, but we're just friends."

"You want a little . . . friendly advice? Or

maybe friendly observation is a better word."

"Sure."

"I think Ted likes you as more than a friend. Just from little clues I'm seeing on his Facebook posts. If you're not thinking of him as more than that, you might want to be careful there."

"Thanks. I will be." Of course, this wasn't news to her. What she really wanted to know was how much Doug cared about this. Was he asking friend-to-friend, or was there anything more behind his concern?

28

The house was quiet once again. Jim was helping Marilyn tidy up the kitchen, loading the dishwasher at the moment. Marilyn was washing pots and pans by hand. "I'm exhausted," she said, "but that was a lot of fun."

"It was," Jim said. "I think the most fun was just watching Ayana's eyes trying to take in one thing after another."

Marilyn turned off the faucet a moment. "Allan and Michele looked so happy. I love it when my kids are happy."

Jim did too. For some reason, what she said made him think of Doug, but he didn't want to bring the subject up and kill the mood.

Marilyn dried a large pot and set it upside down on a towel. "So how'd your talk with Uncle Henry go?"

Guess she's thinking about Doug too. "Pretty well. I shared our struggle with him, thinking he probably couldn't relate. I was shocked by what he said when I finished."

"Shocked? By what?"

"Wouldn't you have thought, with how they are and everything they've taught us, that their experience with their boys growing up would've gone pretty smooth?"

"I always assumed it did. Of course, we weren't all that close back when their boys lived at home. We only saw each other a couple times a year. But I never heard anything about them having any real problems."

Jim dropped a handful of dirty spoons into the plastic holder. "Well, he says they did. He didn't go into it, but he said that with one of his boys in particular they had some real trouble."

"Really? That's hard to believe."

"Isn't it? He said even if you do everything right as parents, it doesn't guarantee your kids won't have troubles as they get older. It's not like you push the right buttons and everything works out the way you planned. Even now that they're grown, he said they've had challenges. You know that trip he and Aunt Myra took out west last year? Part of it was to help the boys reconcile some big conflict they were working through. They hadn't even been talking to each other for a while."

Marilyn leaned against the counter. "In a way, hearing this makes me feel a little better about our situation. I don't know why."

Jim stopped working a minute. "I think I do, because I felt the same way. At first I was feeling discouraged, thinking if they had problems with all they know and how differently they raised their boys, what hope do I have? But he said something toward the end of our conversation that helped me a lot. I wish I could remember it exactly. Something about being a bridge for our kids to cross back over when they make a mess of things. It was the idea that the way we talk and the way we treat them does matter, but it's more about setting a tone with them, now that they're adults, that'll keep the lines of communication open. We can't tell them what to do anymore. If anything, doing that makes things worse."

She turned the faucet back on. "I know that one already."

"I wish we'd had more time to talk," Jim said. "But Uncle Henry made it clear, there isn't any one thing I can do or say to fix this thing with Doug. It's going to be a process, maybe a long one. The nice thing is, Uncle Henry's made himself available,

214

and talking to him definitely helps me. He said call anytime. Him or Aunt Myra. And he didn't just mean me — you too."

Christina wanted to get on Facebook, see if Doug had said anything about this afternoon, but she couldn't find her iPad anywhere. She looked all over the apartment, but it didn't turn up. Then an image flashed in her mind: she saw herself putting it down on the little table behind the couch as everyone was leaving to say good-bye.

She hurried down the stairs and across the walkway. The light was on in the kitchen; she could see Jim and Marilyn through the window. After tapping gently on the patio door, she stepped in. They were in the middle of a conversation. "Sorry, don't mean to interrupt. Forgot my iPad in the living room." She scooted across the tile floor.

"No problem," Jim said. "We weren't discussing anything heavy."

There was her iPad, right where she left it. As she walked past them, Marilyn asked, "How did your time go with Doug? Seemed like you guys were talking like old friends."

"Felt like that for me too," she said. "Not sure what's going on with him, but even over the last few days, we've been interacting on Facebook like we used to."

"Saw you guys out there on the veranda looking at his drawings," Jim said.

"I liked them. And he told me about this new graphic novel he and Jason are working on. They signed up for some big contest at that convention last week. The deadline is not that far off, so they're really getting serious about it."

"Hope not too serious," Jim said.

"I'm sure it's just a hobby, Jim," Marilyn said.

"Maybe so, but for guys, it doesn't take much to get obsessed over something like that. His grades could start to slide."

"Did he seem obsessed to you, Christina?" Marilyn said.

"Not obsessed. Not right now anyway. Just excited. But I think he really is talented. His drawings are as good as anything I've seen in comic books." Christina could see what she said puzzled them. "I used to read them a few years ago. I was going out with a guy who was totally into them. Now *that* guy was obsessed. I started reading them a little, then found several that I liked a lot."

"That's great, Christina," Marilyn said. "Maybe that'll open a window for you guys to stay more connected."

"In a way, it already has. Before he left, he

asked me if I would be willing to critique his graphic novel as they develop it."

"Well," Jim said, "I'm for anything that keeps you more involved in Doug's life."

After saying that, his expression changed. He glanced at Marilyn, who was looking at him a certain way. Christina didn't get it, but if she had to guess, Jim was acting like he had just "stepped in it." Christina figured Marilyn must have told him about her feelings for Doug and advised him not to push it.

"Speaking of connecting with Doug," Marilyn said, "I wanted to tell you before I forget, we both have this Thursday off. If you want, we could drive up in the morning, tour that school you want to check out, and meet with the guidance counselor. Then maybe we could drive into town, pop in on Doug, and treat him to lunch."

"I'd love that," Christina said. "Let's definitely do it."

"Why don't you contact the school tomorrow, see if you need to set up an appointment."

"I will. It'll be so much fun," Christina said. "Well, I'll leave you two alone. Good night." She walked out to the patio with a big smile on her face. Now she had something new to talk to Doug about on

Facebook.

As she opened the door leading to her apartment, she changed her mind. It would be much more fun to make their visit a surprise.

29

Christina was getting excited. She and Marilyn were driving from River Oaks to St. Augustine and had just gotten off the highway and turned onto the final road of their journey. Up ahead she saw the sign for St. John's River State College. She wasn't sure if she was more excited about visiting the school or their plan to pop in on Doug for a visit after.

Marilyn began to slow the car for the left turn into the college campus parking lot. "How far did you say Doug's school is from here?"

"I think about fifteen minutes," Christina said. She remembered what she'd read about Doug's college, located downtown, right in the center of the historic district. St. John's was situated on the outskirts of town. "I got the address of Doug's school. We can put it into the GPS after we're done here." She surveyed St. John's campus.

"We're supposed to meet in the administration building. I looked at the campus map online. It's the little building over there." She pointed, and Marilyn steered the car in that direction. They pulled into an open parking space right along the curb.

"It's a pretty place," Marilyn said. "Very Spanish looking."

"I think that's the theme of the whole area around St. Augustine. Did you know it's the oldest city in the US? It was settled by the Spanish back in the 1500s."

Marilyn turned the car off. "I think I'd heard that. It's a beautiful little town. Jim and I came up and spent a few days in the historic area, just to check it out before Doug enrolled. You're going to love it. All kinds of quaint little shops and restaurants, old churches, and cemeteries. And lots of history. And wait till you see Flagler College, where Doug goes. The buildings are magnificent."

Christina thought she had a good idea of what to expect, since Doug said he'd based the drawings she had looked at on his campus. They got out of the car and started walking on the sidewalk toward the administration building.

Marilyn looked around. "I really like the look of this place, but I guess it's kind of a small school."

"Actually, this is just a branch campus; the main one's in Palatka." A student was coming out of the office door and held it open for them. "Thank you."

Both women walked up to the reception desk. A girl about Christina's age looked up. "Hi, my name's Christina Sampson. I have an appointment with Elizabeth Manzetti, the guidance counselor."

"Christina," she repeated. "That name rings a bell." She started flipping through some papers on her desk. "Here it is. A note from Mrs. Manzetti. You just missed her by ten minutes. She was very sorry. You were supposed to be her first appointment of the day, but her son's school called. I guess he was feeling sick. She had to leave to pick him up. But she said her mother can watch him, so she plans to come back in a little while. She said if you can make it, she should be back by eleven."

Christina looked at Marilyn, wondering what they should do.

"I think we can do that," Marilyn said. "We were planning to stop in and surprise Doug after and take him to lunch. Maybe we can go visit him now, take him to breakfast, and be back here in time for your appointment."

221

Christina liked that idea. She turned to the receptionist. "Okay, we'll be back at eleven." They said good-bye and headed for the front door. "But what if Doug had an early class today? Maybe I better call him first, make sure he's there." They walked over to a bench under a shady tree. She dialed the number and waited through several rings until his voice mail picked up, but she didn't leave a message. "I don't know what we should do. He might be asleep or maybe he has his phone turned off because he's in class."

"Let's just go to his apartment and see," Marilyn said. "If he's not there, we'll leave a note and walk around St. Augustine for a couple of hours and enjoy the sights."

Doug was shaving in front of his bathroom mirror, wearing the bottom half of the pajamas his mother had given him last Christmas.

Courtney walked in wearing the top half. She wrapped her arms around his waist. "Maybe you shouldn't do that."

"Do what? Shave?"

"Yeah."

"You want me to grow a beard?"

"Not a thick one like a lumberjack. Maybe just, you know, the way some guys do. Leave a few days' growth. I kind of like that look."

Doug looked at his face. "Not sure I can pull off 'that look' with half my face already shaved."

"Well, start tomorrow then." She grabbed her brush and walked back out.

Courtney had been inviting herself to spend the night several times a week now. Doug was preparing himself for her to suggest that maybe she should move in for good. He wasn't keen on that idea. There was a knock at the door. "That's probably Drew," Doug said. "I left the textbook I need this morning in his car last night. He said he'd drop it off on his way to class."

"I'll get it," she said.

"Well, put a robe on or something."

"Drew's seen me in my bathing suit. I'm wearing more than that now."

Doug glanced at her through the open bathroom door, saw her peeking through the curtains.

"Oh great," she said. "Looks like some Jehovah's Witnesses."

"Don't answer it. They'll go away."

"No, I know how to get rid of them."

He heard the door open. Then a gasp, followed by a horrible sound.

His mother's voice.

■ ■ ■ ■

"Uh . . . who are you?" Marilyn said.

She and Christina were standing in front of an open door. An attractive blonde had just opened it, dressed in what appeared to be a man's pajama top. She looked familiar. It took Christina a moment to make the connection. When it did, her heart sank.

It was Courtney.

Christina watched as Marilyn looked at the apartment room number to make sure she had knocked on the right door.

"What do you mean, who am I? What kind of thing is that to say to someone when they open the door?"

"I beg your pardon," Marilyn said. "It's the kind of question a mother asks a young woman who answers the door of her son's apartment first thing in the morning wearing the pajama top she bought him last Christmas. Now where's Doug?"

"Oh," the girl said, a significantly changed expression on her face. She stepped back a few feet.

"Who are you?" Marilyn asked.

"Her name's Courtney," Christina said. She felt dead inside. The full implication of seeing Courtney standing there at this moment, dressed like that, was sinking in.

"How do you know my name?"

Christina didn't answer.

"Would you please get my son? Is he here?"

"Yes, I'm here." The door opened the rest of the way. There stood Doug, wearing the matching bottom half of the pajamas, a look of fierce anger on his face. "Hello, Mom." He looked over her shoulder, saw Christina. His eyes shot back to his mother's face.

Christina wanted to turn and walk away. But she didn't. Not yet. She saw Courtney step behind the door, out of sight.

"Doug, who is this girl?" Marilyn asked. "What is she doing here?"

"What is *she* doing here?" Doug said. "What are *you* doing here? Are you checking up on me?"

"What? Checking up on you? No, but maybe we should be. I'm not stupid. I know why she's here. Guess your father and I were right to be concerned."

"What are you talking about?"

"Never mind. We just came up here to check out a school Christina is thinking about attending, out by the highway. But the appointment got postponed, so we thought we'd pop in and surprise you, take you out to breakfast."

"Well, I can't go out to breakfast anyway. I've got a class in thirty minutes."

Marilyn stepped away from the door. "That's hardly the point now, is it?" She turned to face Christina. "I guess we better go."

Christina looked up for just a moment. Doug was looking right at her. Their eyes locked.

Then he closed the door.

30

Marilyn and Christina walked back to the car in silence. After they got in, they sat in silence. Marilyn's hands were gripped on the steering wheel as she looked straight ahead. Christina saw tears welling up in Marilyn's eyes. Her own were not far behind.

Finally Marilyn said, "I knew he wasn't doing well, but I had no idea things were this bad. Jim is going to be furious."

Christina had had her suspicions that things might be "this bad." She knew how casually her generation treated the idea of sleeping around. Sadly, much the way she did until coming to Christ last year. She'd held on to a slim ray of hope that Doug's strong moral upbringing might have given him the strength to resist the gravitational pull in that direction.

Obviously not.

"I don't know what to do," Marilyn said,

hands still on the wheel. "I'm just numb."

Christina didn't know what to say.

"If he's doing this, maybe he's taking drugs too. And getting drunk. Who knows?" She turned the car on and backed up. "I don't even know where I'm going. But I don't want to sit here and take the chance Doug will come down and try to explain. I'm afraid of what I'd say if he did." She stopped before pulling out into the road and looked at Christina. "I'm not really in the mood for shopping anymore, are you?" A tear rolled down her cheek.

Christina shook her head no.

"And now I don't have an appetite for a big sit-down breakfast."

"Me either," Christina said. "Maybe we can just go through a drive through, get a breakfast wrap or something. I saw several fast food places on the way here."

Marilyn started driving back the way they came. "That's what we'll do then."

A few more minutes in silence. Then just as Marilyn turned the car onto a main road, she said, "Did you have any idea Doug was . . . living like this?"

"Not really. More of a two-plus-two-equals-four kind of thing."

"What do you mean?"

Christina had to be careful here. She

needed to restrain a little of her New York. They were talking about Marilyn's youngest son, not just some guy. "I know what kids my age are into. At college. Really, anywhere. People just sleep around like it's no big thing. Even with people they're not all that serious about. I'm sure you know that already, counseling all the girls down at the Resource Center."

Marilyn sighed. "I do, but it's still so sad. I also see it on almost every TV show and movie with young people in it. Jim and I don't watch most of them, but it's almost the norm now." They stopped at a light. "I guess we just hoped Doug wasn't your typical college kid. We knew his walk with the Lord wasn't very strong, but I was hoping maybe he had a stronger moral code."

"I was kind of hoping the same thing," Christina said.

"Obviously, we were wrong." Marilyn turned left, back toward the highway and St. John's. "There's a McDonald's up on the right." She looked at the clock on the dashboard. "We might as well go in and eat. We've got lots of time to kill before we head back to the school for that appointment at eleven."

"I don't know, Marilyn. I'm not sure I want to keep that appointment now." She was sure St. John's was a fine school, but the primary reason she was considering it was its close proximity to Doug. There seemed no point in that now.

"You sure? We're so close."

"I think so. Besides, there's no hurry. I've already missed the deadline for the start of the summer semester. I was just checking it out for the semester that begins at the end of August. I can always come back later if I decide I want to go there."

Marilyn turned into the McDonald's parking lot. "I'm kind of glad you want to cancel. I think I'd rather just go home."

"Me too," Christina said. *Go home and have a good cry.*

Doug was furious. Furious and humiliated. After his mom and Christina had left, he'd gone back into the bathroom and closed the door. He'd told Courtney he needed to use the bathroom and to finish getting ready for class. She had a horrified look on her face, but he wasn't in any condition to help her sort out her emotions just now.

After he finished getting ready, he sat down on the edge of the tub, holding his head in his hands. He could hear her out there, but he didn't care. He wished she would just leave.

It felt like his life was over.

He'd worked so hard to keep this relationship quiet. Even on the internet. He'd never mentioned Courtney, made sure none of his friends did, either. Made sure none of them uploaded a picture of the two of them together, in any way that looked boyfriend/girlfriend. Jason was right about Doug's parents. Of course, they wouldn't have approved of her. She wasn't a Christian. So now they could probably guess their son wasn't just going out with a nonbeliever, he was also "sleeping around."

And they'd discovered this news in the worst possible way. If his dad didn't know yet, he'd find out about it before lunchtime. Before the end of the day, his siblings and their spouses would know. Maybe the whole family would know, including Uncle Henry and Aunt Myra.

How could he ever go home again?

A knock on the door. "Doug?"

He didn't answer.

"Doug, I'm going now. I wish you'd open the door to talk to me. I feel horrible right now. And a little hurt, to be honest. Please open the door. We have to talk."

Doug knew he couldn't ignore her, not unless he was willing to end the relationship right now. Part of him wanted to. But even

231

if he did, it shouldn't be this way. He stood and opened the door. To his surprise, there were tears in Courtney's eyes. She was completely dressed, even had her purse over her shoulder.

"Guess it's safe to say you never told your folks about us. About me."

He shook his head no. "I didn't."

"Are you ashamed of me?"

"It's complicated, Courtney."

"Well, try to uncomplicate it. At least a little. Unless you want me to walk out that door and never come back. Because I really don't understand what just happened."

Doug walked past her. He sat in an upholstered chair. "This is not your fault, Courtney. It's mine. I've been living two lives for quite a while now. Guess I thought I was pulling it off. What just happened is my two worlds colliding, and you got caught in the middle."

"So, what, are your parents just old-fashioned and uber-conservative?"

"That's one way of putting it. They're devout Christians, and they take the Bible very seriously. I was raised believing premarital sex is wrong, for example. Well, it's more than a belief. The belief is that it's a serious sin. And from their perspective, I've committed that serious sin . . . with

232

you. I'm pretty sure neither my older brother or older sister ever had sex before their wedding night."

"You're kidding. People still think that way in this day and age?"

Doug looked up. "Do I sound like I'm kidding? And yes, people still do think that way. Millions of them. You wouldn't think it, looking at the way things are now in movies and television. But there's a huge conservative world out there, people who pretty much view life in a radically different way. I grew up in that world and, until a few minutes ago, my family thought I was still a part of it. My mom just got the shock of her life, seeing you standing there in my pajama top." He didn't even want to think about how Christina viewed him right now.

"So are you?"

"Am I what?"

"Are you still part of that world? Is that why you've been keeping us a secret? Which is the pretend world, Doug . . . the world with me, here, or the world you came from?" She walked over and sat on the bed across from him. "I mean, I hate what just happened here. The way your mom looked at me made me feel horrible. And that girl, who was she and how did she know my name?"

"Her name's Christina. She's a family friend. She and my mom are real close. She's actually renting the garage apartment back at our house in River Oaks. I guess she knows your name from Facebook and Instagram."

"Well, as bad as it was, maybe it's a good thing they were here this morning. Because now you have to choose. Which world do you want to live in, Doug? Because I don't think you can live in between anymore."

31

Jim drove down the little one-lane road that ran behind his house on Elderberry Lane, saw his three-car garage up ahead. He was feeling tense. A short while ago, he'd received a text from Marilyn asking if he could please come home for lunch. She said the visit with Doug hadn't gone well, and she really needed to talk to him about it. In person, not on the phone.

He'd wanted to stop what he was doing and drive home immediately, but he was in the middle of contract negotiations with a promising customer. It didn't sound like an emergency, seeing as how it could wait till lunch. But now that he was here, he felt his apprehension growing by the second.

The garage door couldn't go up fast enough. He was tempted to jog across the walkway connecting the garage to the main house. When he walked in, he saw Marilyn across the room, sitting on the couch in front of the TV, watching the news. Something she never did unless he was there. She must've been lost in thought; she didn't even move when he closed the patio door.

"Hey, hon," he said when he reached her. She looked up and sighed, her face full of sadness. He walked around and sat beside her, reached for her hand. "So, what's this all about? What's going on?"

"For the last hour, I've been trying to remember what you said Sunday afternoon, after that talk you had with Uncle Henry. About trying to be some kind of bridge your kids can cross back over after they've made a mess of things. Right now, it's not helping."

Jim braced himself for whatever came next. "So you and Christina drove to St. Augustine and, what? I thought you guys were going to have lunch with Doug. Judging by the time of your text, I'm guessing that didn't happen."

"That was the plan, but the guidance counselor we were supposed to see got delayed. She couldn't meet with us until eleven. So we thought, let's surprise Doug and take him out to breakfast instead. When we got there, a cute blonde girl opened the door. Let's just say, it was obvious she had been there all night."

The news hit him like a punch in the gut. "Was Doug there?"

"Yeah, he came to the door a moment later. Pretty much yelled at me as though we had come there to spy on him."

"Wait, he acted mad at you?"

"Yeah. Can you believe it?"

"What did you say?"

"I said we weren't spying on him. We wanted to surprise him and treat him to breakfast. He about slammed the door in our face, and we walked off."

They sat in silence a few moments as Jim tried to process what he'd just heard. One part of him was furious, but an even bigger part of him was just sad. This news wasn't totally unexpected. He'd harbored a growing concern for months now that Doug was in worse shape than he was letting on. This simply confirmed it.

"I thought you'd be more upset than this."

"Oh, I'm plenty upset. Believe me. But for some reason I feel more pain than anger."

"That's the same way I feel," she said. "That and a little numb."

"Have you had any more communication with him since it happened? Did he text you or call?"

"No, and I didn't try to contact him."

"Does anyone else know?"

"Just Christina. She was there with me when it happened."

The poor thing. Seeing a scene like that must've crushed her. "How's she doing?"

"I can tell she's pretty upset. But she's not showing it very much. She mostly looks sad."

"I'm guessing from the feelings you said she has for him, she must be devastated."

Marilyn let go of Jim's hand and stood. "I was kind of devastated myself. I wasn't in any mood to draw her out, and she didn't volunteer very much."

"Where are you going?"

"To get you some lunch. I was going to heat up the leftover beef stew from last night. I'm not really hungry, but I'll get some for you."

Jim stood up and followed her to the kitchen.

"I can't believe how calmly you're taking this," she said as she opened the refrigerator.

It sort of surprised him too. "I've suspected Doug's been living a double life. Knowing it's for real is painful, but I guess I've been waiting for this moment to come for quite a while. But I feel bad for you and

Christina. If I was there seeing it for myself, I might have blown up and lost it."

She set a dish in the microwave. "I did, a little. I walked away before it became a lot."

"Did Christina say anything?"

"No, not then. Well, she did say the girl's name when I asked who she was."

"Who was she? So Christina knew her?"

"They've never met. We talked about it in the car a little. She said her name is Courtney, and she was pretty sure Doug and her have been a couple for some time, a few months anyway."

Jim leaned against the counter. "I wonder why she never told us about her."

"She said she was just guessing by the way the girl looked at Doug in a bunch of online pictures when they were at parties. Nothing blatant or obvious. But she wasn't 100 percent sure, because she never saw Doug looking at the girl that way. And he never talked about her in any of his posts. Even last weekend, remember that awkward moment when Charlotte asked him if he was seeing anybody special? And he said he wasn't. Looking back, Christina said she's pretty sure this girl Courtney is the reason why Doug had started pulling away from her."

"Looks like he was hiding her from us.

Maybe from Christina too." Jim felt a headache coming on.

The microwave pinged; the beef stew was done. Marilyn lifted it out with some pot holders. "Besides being so painful and disappointing, it's also confusing," she said. "I was watching Doug and Christina on Sunday. I could've sworn he was looking at her and treating her *that* way. Like he did have feelings for her."

"I thought the same thing too. I was actually getting a little excited by the time he left, thinking that maybe something was brewing between them. Well, on his end. We already knew about her feelings."

Marilyn dished a big helping of beef stew into a bowl.

"That's why I'm confused," she said. "Could we both have been wrong about something like that?"

They walked over to the dinette table. "Guess it doesn't matter now anyway," Jim said. "If there was anything there, I'm sure Doug smashed it to pieces this morning."

He sat and picked up a fork, his appetite even smaller than it was a few moments before. Where did they go from here? What should he do? One thing was abundantly clear . . . they had lost Doug's heart completely. Jim was pretty sure that had

240

happened a long time ago. But then, why did it hurt so much now?

He set the fork back down beside the bowl.

32

Christina carried a load of laundry up the stairs. It felt twice as heavy as it looked. Getting caught up on laundry was not exactly the way she had thought her day off would end. She walked inside her apartment, set the basket on the coffee table, and plopped down on the sofa.

Why should she feel so hurt by what happened this morning? It really made no sense.

It wasn't as if she and Doug were a couple or anything even close. He hadn't betrayed her, hadn't led her on. If she wasn't so fixated on him, she'd have recognized that all the signals he'd been sending were about friendship and nothing more. Her imagination had formed a pile of crumbs into a cake. Now she could see things as they really were. That was a good thing, wasn't it? Maybe now, once and for all, she could finally put away this silly schoolgirl crush.

Her phone rang. She walked toward the

edge of the counter and saw it was Michele. She should answer it. But what if Michele didn't know about this morning, what if Marilyn hadn't told her? Christina didn't have the energy for pretense right now.

But she and Michele had become good friends, and they really hadn't had a chance to catch up since Michele and Ayana had come back from Ethiopia last weekend. Michele's trip provided plenty of distracting things to chat about. She picked up the phone. "Hey, Michele."

"You sound a lot more upbeat than I expected."

She knew. "I guess you and your mom talked?"

"We did. I wish we hadn't. I was hoping my walk in the clouds would have lasted at least a few days longer."

"When I woke up this morning," Christina said, "I thought I might be right up there with you by now."

"I'm so sorry, my friend."

The softness in Michele's voice brought tears to Christina's eyes. Michele knew, more than anyone, how deep Christina's feelings for Doug had grown. She was the one who'd helped Christina see that she really did love him. She remembered the moment Michele had said it, the moment she saw it for herself. It didn't make her smile, because she knew he didn't feel the same way. It was more a sense of relief, that she could admit it and that someone else knew. Even if it wasn't the one who mattered.

"Are you okay?" Michele said.

"Okay? I'm doing laundry."

Michele laughed. "See how strong you are? If it were me, I'd be sitting in the corner in a fetal position."

"No you wouldn't," Christina said. "You'd be on the sofa watching an old movie and finishing off half a gallon of cappuccino fudge blitz."

Michele laughed again. "You're right. But I really am sorry. I have such loser brothers."

"Tom's not a loser anymore," Christina said.

"You're right. But I remember last year having a similar conversation with Jean, right after she found out Tom had been lying about being out of work for five months."

Christina wished Doug had been hiding something like that. "Well, look where Tom's at now. He and Jean are doing fine. They've got a new baby, even a new house."

"You're right," Michele said. "I shouldn't

give up on Doug so fast."

Then again, Christina thought, Tom and Doug were two totally different people. For some reason, Doug's situation seemed so much darker than Tom's had been.

"Are you thinking it's time to give up on Doug?" Michele asked.

"I'm not going to stop praying for him. But I'm pretty much giving up on him ever returning my feelings."

"I think that's wise," Michele said. "He hasn't given you a lot of reason to hope things will ever change. It's probably better to protect your heart, but I —" She cut herself off.

"What?"

"Nothing."

"No, what were you going to say?"

"It's just, after Mom told me what happened this morning, I told her this whole thing with Doug and this girl is so confusing to me now."

"What's confusing? Doug's got a girlfriend. He's been hiding her for a few months, and this morning we found out why. It's not very complicated to me. Painful maybe, but not complicated."

"You're right," Michele said.

But Christina could still tell she was holding something back. "But . . ."

245

"It's just . . . when I was talking with my mom a little while ago, we both thought the same thing and were just as confused by it. Then she said my dad had the same impression."

Christina walked back toward the couch. "What are you talking about?"

"I don't know. It just seemed that something was happening with you and Doug on Sunday. It wasn't just you — I always see you looking at him — it was him. I was thinking he was looking at you differently. I didn't just think it once, I thought about it several times. And it's not like my mind was on it, because I was mostly focused on Ayana being home and, physically, I was exhausted. But then to hear my mom say the same thing, and my dad too. It just —"

"Your dad thought Doug was acting interested in me?"

"Apparently. That's what my mom said. But you told her you're pretty sure Doug's been seeing this Courtney for a few months now. If that's true, then what you two walked into this morning wasn't some kind of one-night stand."

"It probably wasn't," Christina said, "though I'm not sure." But that wasn't exactly something she wanted to think about now, was it?

"That's why I'm confused. If he was seriously seeing this other girl, why was he looking at you that way?"

Christina needed to change the subject. "So where's Ayana right now?"

"She's sleeping."

"Isn't she a little old to be taking naps?"

"She is. I think it's just a combination of leftover jet lag and all the excitement of so many new things coming at her at once. Today's the first day I feel relatively normal."

This was better. This was the kind of conversation Christina needed to have. To hear all about the new and exciting things going on in her friend's life.

"So," Michele said, "something else Mom mentioned. I guess while I was gone there's been a little something brewing between you and a guy at church? Some guy named Ted?"

Not Ted.

"Mom said he's really nice," Michele continued, "and he's been kind of pursuing you lately. She said you guys went out for coffee once."

Did Michele really think this would help? Changing the topic to Ted?

"Uh-oh," Michele said. "Sounds like

Ayana's awake. When she sleeps during the day, she wakes up kind of confused. Can I call you back in a little while?"

"Sure," Christina said.

As soon as Christina hung up with Michele, Ted, of all people, sent her a text: *Heard you had the day off. Want to grab a cup of coffee?*

Christina looked at the laundry basket, thought about the phone call with Michele, and texted back. *Why not?*

33

Jim sat at his desk, staring at the phone. It was a few hours after lunch. He hadn't been able to get anything done since his talk with Marilyn about her visit with Doug. He'd already made one call, left a voice mail on Uncle Henry's phone. Jim didn't say much but did make it clear something big had come up and that he could really use some advice.

He had another phone call to make . . . to Doug. Was he ready? His emotions felt under control, but you could never really tell with emotions. What if Doug said something outlandish or extremely hurtful? Could Jim keep his composure then, not say something he'd regret?

He had already determined that this wasn't a time to remain silent. But Marilyn warned him to make sure he'd thoroughly calmed down before making the call. He lifted the receiver, pressed the button for his secretary. "Marie, could you hold any calls for me for the next few minutes or so? I'm going to make a personal call, and I'd rather not be interrupted."

"Sure, Mr. Anderson. I can do that. I won't put any calls through until I see your extension light stop blinking."

"Thanks." He stared at the button next to Doug's name. It was the least-used button on his office phone. Better get this over with. He pressed it, said a quick prayer as it rang. Would Doug pick up?

"Hey, Dad."

"Hello, Doug, thanks for picking up."

"I knew you'd keep calling until I did. So . . ."

That was true. Fair enough. "Then I guess you know why I'm calling."

"Yeah."

"Anything you want to say first?"

"Not really. I'm not happy about what happened this morning, but of course, I didn't have any control over the situation."

"You didn't? That girl just forced her way into your room last night, tied you up, and insisted she spend the night?"

Doug didn't immediately reply. "That's not what I mean. I'm saying if Mom had called first, even if Christina had texted me before they came over, I would've said it's

250

not a good time. And we all would have been spared that embarrassing situation."

"That's one way of looking at it, I guess." Jim had to be careful. He felt the sarcasm switch aching to be turned on full blast. "Your mom said you accused her of spying on you."

"I didn't accuse her, I —"

"You didn't say she was spying on you? She was lying about that?"

"No, I did use the word. But I didn't accuse her of it. I *asked* her if she was."

"Doug, you say you asked her. She said you accused her. Okay, so maybe you asked her in an accusing tone. What difference does it make? The point is, they were only there trying to do a nice thing. She wanted to treat you to breakfast, that's all. No sinister plot. They were in the neighborhood anyway, checking out a school Christina might want to attend. Their appointment with the counselor got canceled, so they thought, why not pop in on Doug, take him out to breakfast? Wouldn't that be a nice surprise? It never entered their minds they might be greeted by your girlfriend wearing your pajama top. None of us even knew you had a girlfriend. As I recall, we had a considerably less awkward moment at the dinner table last Sunday, when Charlotte asked you if you were seeing anyone special at school. Remember what you said to her?"

"I said I wasn't."

"Right. So do you still want to blame them for popping in on you this morning, as though they should have known better?"

Doug didn't answer. Jim hated when he did that. Whenever Jim successfully refuted something Doug had said, he'd never acknowledge it. He'd just clam up, or worse, change the subject.

"But Dad, I'm not a kid anymore. Aren't I entitled to a little privacy?"

"Of course you are. But what does that have to do with anything? Didn't your mom knock or ring the doorbell?"

"Yes."

"Then, seems to me, she was respecting your privacy. Someone who didn't would just barge in. Pretty sure she even had a key. You gave us one in case you ever lost yours, remember?"

Again, no answer.

"So what do you want me to do, Dad? Why did you call?"

"I'm not sure. I guess I thought we should just clear the air, stop this pretense we've been living for . . . well, quite a while now."

"It's not been a pretense, it's . . ."

Jim waited, but Doug didn't seem to know

252

what he wanted to say. "Doug, just be honest. It has been a pretense, you just don't like how that sounds. You've been living two lives, son. The pretend one with us and the real one when we're not around. I may be getting old, but I'm not dead. I remember doing the same thing with my parents when I was your age. I just never had a moment when those two worlds collided, like you did this morning."

A long pause. Should Jim continue? No. He needed to keep this conversation from becoming a lecture. He had to be okay with long, awkward pauses. Just let them happen and resist the urge to fill the space with words.

"I guess you're right," Doug finally said. "But it wasn't like I set out to live two lives. I wasn't trying to lie to you guys. I grew up living in your world, I guess you could call it. I knew how, I knew what you guys expected from me. But then I had to learn to fit into another world, outside our home."

"So," Jim said, "are you saying what your mom and Christina walked into this morning was just you . . . fitting in with that world? It's not what you really want, you're just caving in to peer pressure?" Jim instantly regretted using the phrase "caving in."

"No," Doug said, "I'm not caving in to anything. No one's making me do anything I don't want to do."

Well, at least that was honest. Jim forced himself to say the next part in a gentler tone. "So, is that what this morning means? You've chosen which world is the real world for you? The one you really want to live in? You are the guy your mom and Christina met this morning, not the guy at the house Sunday afternoon?"

"I don't know, Dad. Maybe that's what I'm saying. Can't I keep on being both guys? Are you saying I have to choose?"

"It kind of feels like that, Doug. What happened this morning is like the toothpaste getting squeezed out of the tube. Kind of hard to get it back in again."

Neither one said anything for a few moments. Finally Jim said, "You still there?"

"Yeah, I'm here."

"Listen, Doug, you don't sound all that sure of yourself right now. Seems to me you've already made your choice, but maybe I'm wrong. Maybe you need a little time to think this through some more. Figure out what you really want to do here."

"I think you're right."

"To be honest, I'd like to know what you decide by the next time we talk."

Doug didn't reply.

"Well," Jim said, "I better go. I've got an appointment coming up in a few minutes."

"Okay. Well, guess I'll say good-bye."

Jim hesitated a moment. "I love you, Doug." He heard a click. Doug had hung up. Did he hear what Jim had just said?

34

Christina sat at the black wrought-iron table in the outdoor section of the downtown Starbucks in River Oaks. She'd already bought her latte. Ted was inside fixing his. It was probably a silly thing, but she'd ordered and paid for her own before he got a chance to buy it. For Christina, this wasn't an official date. She didn't know what it was, or what she would call it later when Marilyn asked her about it, which she certainly would.

As she watched Ted step out from the glass door to join her, she tried to look at him in a different way. Tried to imagine him as someone she could be interested in. He wasn't unattractive. Some girls would probably think he was downright handsome. But so far, all she thought when she saw him was . . . he was nice. Ted was nice.

"You know I would have bought that for you," he said as he sat beside her.

"Thanks, but I don't mind." She took a sip.

"You picked my favorite table. I love this one in the corner. Got a great view of both sides of the street."

"I just picked it for the shade."

"It is a little warm out here," Ted said. "You can never tell which way it's going to go in April. Some days it's perfect, other days feels like summer's about to begin. I almost got an iced coffee."

Wouldn't that have been something? She took another sip.

"So how's your day off gone so far?" he asked.

Hmm. Well, this morning she'd learned the man she loved not only didn't love her back but was sleeping with his girlfriend. She probably shouldn't open with that. "Fine, I guess. I have made a decision since the last time we talked."

"What is it?"

"I'm definitely going back to school. I think I mentioned something to you about it."

"You did. I think that's a great idea." He slid forward in his chair, rested his elbows on the table. "Any idea what you're going to study?"

"Think I've settled that one too. I want to

be some kind of medical technician, maybe radiology."

"Should be easy to find a job in that area. When you graduate, I mean. Florida's loaded with medical-related jobs because of all the elderly that live here."

"That's what I was thinking," she said. "And I'd finish in less than two years." She took another sip. "How many more years of school do you have?"

"It depends on whether I go for my master's degree or not. I probably will. You almost have to, to get very far in banking or finance. I'm a junior now, so I'll be going at least a few more years. But I don't mind. I'm kind of in a rhythm now. Some of my classes are hard, but it's nothing compared to, say, a degree in computer science or engineering. Some of my friends are going in that direction. They have way more homework than me."

Homework, Christina thought. She hadn't even thought about that. She'd have to start doing homework again. Was she up for that? She had never been very good at school before.

"So what do you like to do?" Ted asked. "For fun, I mean."

"Do? I don't know." He was probably fishing for things they could do together. Most of the things she liked to do, she did alone. Playing Sudoku, solitaire on her iPad, spending time on Facebook or other social media sites. The only thing she did with others was occasionally some gardening with Marilyn or shopping with Michele. She remembered her last conversation with Doug. "I used to like to read comic books."

"Comic books?" Ted said, making a face. "Really?"

You'd think she'd just said she liked playing out in traffic. Obviously, Ted wasn't into comic books. "I used to like to ride bikes."

"I like to ride bikes. You said *used* to. You don't like to do it anymore?"

"I'm sure I do. I don't ride anymore, mainly because I don't have a bike."

"That's not a problem. I've got one, a nice one. And my sister left her bike in the garage when she went off to college. I'm sure she wouldn't mind if you borrowed it. That is, if you'd like to go bike riding sometime."

Did she? She wasn't sure. One thing she did know, if she was going to continue seeing Ted like this, they had to be doing *something*. Sitting around like this with nothing to do but talk was worse than watching paint dry. "Sure," she said, "I'd give that a try."

When Jim got home from work, Marilyn apologized that dinner would be about twenty minutes late. She'd been on the phone counseling a young girl from the resource center and lost track of the time.

"That's okay," Jim said. "I'm not starving."

She flipped the oven light on and peeked at her dish. "How did your phone call go with Doug?"

"Depends on what you're measuring, I guess."

She straightened up. "Okay. Not sure what that means . . ."

He set his brief bag on the dinette table. "If you're wondering whether I kept my cool, I guess I'd give myself a solid B-plus. If you're wondering if I made any progress with Doug, I'd say on that one I probably get an F."

"Since I wouldn't expect Doug to be very receptive right now, I wasn't thinking you'd be making any progress so soon." She flipped off the oven light. "But I am glad you kept your composure. I was a little worried about that, to be honest. Especially if he talked to you with the same tone he used on me this morning."

Jim walked over and reached for her hand. "Since we've got twenty minutes, let's take a little walk. I could use the fresh air."

Marilyn took his hand. "Okay, but let's not lose track of the time. I don't want to burn dinner."

"We won't." They walked through the living room and foyer and out through the front door. "What I'd really like to do is take a walk on the beach." They headed down the porch steps. "I don't know why, but at times like this, a walk on the beach always improves my perspective."

"It does the same for me," she said. "But walking around here with you will still be nice." They turned left onto the sidewalk. "I still love living here."

Jim loved hearing her say that. "I remember when you didn't feel that way two years ago." During that cataclysmic time, Marilyn was so unhappy living in this house with Jim, she'd left. For a while, he'd thought for good.

"I know. That's part of the reason I said it. I've been thinking about that this afternoon. Maybe the Lord even put it back into my mind. I felt so discouraged after my visit with Doug this morning and so hopeless. Then I remembered how I felt almost the same way about us back then. And look, now we're in a healthier and better place."

Jim sighed.

"What's the matter?" she asked.

"I wish I could bottle up some of that hope you feel right now and take a swig. Because I'm not feeling it."

They walked past the next house in silence.

"What are you thinking?"

"A whole mixture of things," Jim said. "I feel angry, for one thing, that I'm basically funding my son's sinful, rebellious lifestyle. I feel like he's taking advantage of me, of us. It's not just because of this new development with this girl, it's the whole way he's been acting since he started going to that school. This is just one more dark moment in a whole string of dark moments. It's like, it totally escapes his notice that he wouldn't even be at that school, buying those schoolbooks, renting that apartment, eating those meals, driving that car, or spending whatever money he's spent on that girl if it weren't for us . . . and all the money we've saved. Even the money we're putting out now. Does that seem right to you?"

"Put that way, no, it doesn't."

"Is there any other way to put it?" Jim said. "I mean, the financial part of it?"

"I don't know. Are you thinking we should yank his funds, pull him out of the school?"

Jim shook his head. "I don't know . . . kind of. If we're spending all that money, and he's totally dependent on us, shouldn't there be some accountability on his end? Should he be allowed to just do as he pleases and never experience any consequences?" Jim could tell, Marilyn didn't really have an answer to this.

"You said you were experiencing a mixture of things. What else?"

"Fear," Jim said. "Fear if I take the kind of stand with Doug that I just blurted out, we'll lose him completely. He'll harden his heart, dig in his heels, and go totally off the deep end. It could ruin our relationship forever. And he could make some of the biggest mistakes of his life trying to prove me wrong. The kind of mistakes a parent can't fix."

Neither one said anything as they reached the end of the cul-de-sac. Marilyn squeezed his hand. "We should probably turn around."

Jim agreed. His phone vibrated in his pocket. He pulled it out. "It's Uncle Henry. Looks like he left a message."

"Have you talked with him about any of this yet?" she asked.

"Not yet. This is him returning my call. I'm hoping he's going to say we can meet tomorrow."

35

The next morning shortly after sunrise, Jim sat at a table staring out at the ocean in a park at the end of Flagler Avenue in New Smyrna Beach. Uncle Henry should be here any minute. When they had talked last night, he had immediately agreed to meet with Jim, even volunteered to drive to River Oaks. Jim had said he'd rather come here.

This view was why.

The ocean had a similar calming effect on his soul as spending time in the mountains. It seemed like whatever problems Jim faced instantly dropped by half just being here. He could already feel the tension about this Doug situation loosening its grip. He watched an older couple walking hand-in-hand down by the water and wished he'd thought to invite Marilyn along.

Beyond the tiny waves lapping against the shore, the ocean was like glass. As he scanned the horizon from left to right, he marveled that men had ever doubted the earth was round. You could clearly see the curve on the horizon with just a cursory glance.

"Hello, Jim."

Jim turned toward the familiar voice. "Hey, Uncle Henry. Thanks for coming." He stood up and they hugged.

"You want to sit here awhile or start walking?"

"Let's walk," Jim said, "if you don't mind."

"No, that's fine. Can always use the exercise." They walked across the paved area of the park and down the sidewalk, which disappeared into the sand. Uncle Henry squinted as he gazed at the ocean. "The sight never ceases to amaze me."

"So, you never get tired of it?" Jim said.

"Nope, never do."

"I wondered if it ever became old hat, since you live so close."

Walking through the soft sand, Uncle Henry said, "We drove all over the place, Aunt Myra and me, on our trip out West. Saw some mighty nice sights. Some places we might've liked as much as this. Nothing we liked better. Of course, living in a small town like this helps. I think the beach would lose half its luster if you had to share it with thousands of noisy people."

They reached the hard-packed sand. Since both wore sneakers, they didn't go all the way down to the water's edge. Jim was tempted to toss his shoes up in the soft sand and wade in, at least up to his ankles.

"As we walk," Uncle Henry said, "why don't you fill me in on where things are with Doug?"

Over the next ten minutes, Jim did. By the time he finished, the sense of peace and joy he'd been enjoying since he arrived here had dropped several notches. Why was that exactly? How did talking about your troubles always seem to magnify them? Sometimes you didn't even need to talk about them; thinking about them was enough. The growing look of concern on Uncle Henry's face as he spoke told Jim he was right to be troubled.

"Brings back some very un-fun memories."

That wasn't what Jim expected him to say. He'd forgotten about Uncle Henry's challenges with his own two sons.

"How are you and Marilyn holding up?"

"It's been a rough couple of days. But this situation wasn't altogether unexpected. I think some of our pain comes from hearing out loud some of the details of Doug's life we've been observing quietly for months."

"I can see that. In fact, I remember that kind of pain. Some of it comes from realizing we can't do anything to fix the situation. One thing we found that did ease some of it was getting to the place where we could entrust our sons completely to God. When we're trusting God for them, we're not focused on all the discouraging things in front of us. We see them. We know they're real. But the negative impact doesn't sink in as deep."

A Bible verse popped into Jim's mind. "Take up the shield of faith, so you can extinguish all the flaming arrows of the evil one."

"That's the idea," Uncle Henry said. "Faith does the job, whether the negative thoughts come from the devil or our own minds. Think about how applying faith to this situation with Doug would look. You'd still be aware of all the negative things going on right now. You wouldn't ignore them or pretend they don't exist. But you'd lift your eyes above the fray and see God still on the throne. The situation is still under his control. And *that's* where you set your hope. Not on Doug and how he's doing at the moment. I'll never forget what one old retired minister said to me years ago: 'Worry is fearing the future without God present.'

I'm confident God will turn this present situation into something good for you and Marilyn." He slowed his pace. "Faith is knowing that God keeps his promises, we just don't always know how he'll do it. Or when."

He stopped walking and looked out at the ocean. Jim stopped too.

Uncle Henry continued. "I think that's why just being out here — seeing the ocean, hearing it, even feeling it — is so therapeutic. It's so massive and timeless. And so completely beyond our control. The waves were coming in way before we got here, and they'll keep coming in long after we leave. The tides come in and go out on a specific schedule, down to the minute. And it does this all by itself, without any help from us. Standing here, with all this going on in front of us, it's not hard to believe that the God who makes all this happen can easily untangle the problems we're dealing with."

That pretty much said it, Jim thought. His uncle had just put into words what he had been feeling since he arrived here. "The thing is, Uncle Henry, while I'm here, I have no trouble believing what you're saying. Right this moment, our situation doesn't seem all that big or scary. But I can't live here on the beach. And from a practical standpoint, I'm not really sure what I'm supposed to do. How we're supposed to treat Doug, what we should say to him. Since you and Aunt Myra have been through this, and lived to tell the tale, you have any ideas?"

Uncle Henry thought a minute and said, "I think so." They started walking again. "The strategy we wound up following is actually in the Bible. I'm sure you've heard the story about the Prodigal Son."

36

Jim arrived back home to River Oaks a little more hopeful after visiting with Uncle Henry. On the way home he called Marilyn, who also didn't have to clock in at Odds-n-Ends until after lunch, suggesting they eat together on the veranda. While they did, he could share with her some of the helpful things gleaned from his time with Uncle Henry.

After pulling the car into the garage, he lowered the door. He got out but had to go back for his iPad, which he'd left on the front seat. "Can't forget you," he said aloud.

Especially now.

As he walked through the door leading to the pool and patio area, he saw Marilyn already sitting at the table outside. She stood and greeted him. "This looks nice," he said, smiling. "I'd forgotten about this." They hugged and gave each other a quick kiss. Marilyn had heated up some leftover macaroni and cheese they had eaten a few nights ago. But not just any macaroni and cheese. Marilyn's version blended five cheeses together. The first time Jim had tasted it, he said it could be served at any five-star restaurant. He sat and set his iPad up in the center of the table between them.

They prayed over the food, then Marilyn said, "I'm going to officially break a rule. You can talk while chewing. I want to hear everything you have to say, but I also want you to eat this while it's still hot."

"Thanks. I'll need to break that rule the first few minutes, when I share the first half of my talk with Uncle Henry. But not for the second part. That's why I brought the iPad. Wish I had it for the whole thing. When he started sharing what he and Aunt Myra learned about the Prodigal Son, that's when I got the idea. I could record it on this rather than try to remember it all when I talked with you."

"Uncle Henry was okay with you making a video of him?"

"It was awkward at first, but I told him to just pretend it wasn't there. Just talk normally, like you would if it wasn't recording. He was fine after a few seconds." Jim looked down at his bowl of macaroni and cheese. "First, a few forkfuls of this." It was so good. "You really need to enter this into some contest." For the next ten minutes, between chewing, Jim shared the things Uncle Henry had talked about on the beach before the Prodigal Son part.

When he finished, Marilyn said, "I would've loved hearing all this with the ocean right there."

"I know. I was wishing you were there too. Not just to hear what he said, but after we could've taken a nice walk, maybe end up having brunch at one of the diners near the beach."

"So did this first part help you?"

"It did. But the second half, the stuff he said from the Prodigal Son parable, really did."

"So, are we ready to turn it on?"

"I think we are," Jim said. "One thing, though. This is really the second time he shared this. The first time we were still walking on the beach. That's when I remembered the iPad in the car. I asked him if he could please say it again while I recorded it. I think the second time, he left out a few things. But you'll get the idea." Jim reached over and turned it on.

Uncle Henry was sitting at a picnic table at the beachfront park under a pavilion. "Is it on? Is it working?"

You could hear but not see Jim respond. "It's recording. Just talk normally, like we were on the beach a few minutes ago. You were telling me all the things you and Aunt Myra learned from the Prodigal Son story back when your sons were younger and things weren't going so well."

"Right . . . well, the Prodigal Son story in the Bible isn't very long, but I think it's pretty familiar, even to people who don't read the Bible very much. I've heard pastors preach on it many times over the years. But the things that helped Myra and me the most with our boys, I think, weren't things I learned listening to messages, and they're not the points everyone usually makes when they teach from this parable. They're more like truths *implied* in the story. I wrote some of them down in a journal back when we were in the thick of it with our boys. Just things God was showing me when we were crying out for wisdom."

Uncle Henry coughed, then continued. "One of the first lessons I got was from something Jesus *didn't* say about this parable. He didn't talk about what a failure this father was for having such messed-up sons. One wants to turn his back on God completely and leave home, and the other is totally self-righteous and legalistic, like the

Pharisees. You can tell by the things the father says to his boys, and what he does, that he's not like either one of them. Or I should say, they aren't anything like him. They're not even trying to follow his example. And Jesus doesn't say anything to blame him for how his sons turned out.

"That's one of the things Aunt Myra and I were really struggling with. We felt so guilty for the poor choices our boys were making, as though somehow it was our fault, like we had failed as parents. We weren't perfect by any means, but we really tried our hardest to raise them right. Brought them to a good church their whole childhood, read them Bible stories, and taught them scriptural truth, disciplined them when they needed it but never in anger. Loved on them all the time, hugged them. My father never once told me he was proud of me, so I told them how proud I was every chance I got. I went to all their games, even coached Little League a few seasons. But here we were, with both of them at different times . . . when they got to a certain age, they just started pulling away from us, doing all kinds of things that could ruin their lives."

Marilyn paused the video. "Was that kind of hard for you to hear?"

"You mean, because I didn't do half of those positive things with Doug?"

She nodded.

"It was, a little. But in one sense, it made me feel, I don't know, hopeful. I screwed up a lot with Doug when he was younger. Really, until my breakthrough with you a couple years ago. Since then, I've been doing everything I can to close the gap. But nothing's worked. Listening to Uncle Henry share all the things he did right with his boys for all those years, then to hear about all the hard times they still had, helped me realize it's not all up to me, or you. Even the best parenting can't change your child's heart or fix everything that's broken inside them. In the end, they still need to experience Christ for themselves."

Marilyn tapped the play button.

"So that was a big help to us," Uncle Henry said, "to Aunt Myra and me. There is no condemnation in Christ. We realized . . . Jesus didn't condemn this father for what his sons did and he wasn't condemning us, either, for the challenges we were facing with ours. The father in this parable loved his boys and showed them remarkable patience and compassion, but still they went astray. You and Marilyn need to hear that truth, Jim, and hold on to it.

We meet so many parents who carry around so much guilt because of their kids. Now, I'm not saying parents who've wronged their kids in some way don't need to feel responsible to make things right. I had to apologize to my boys over the years more times than I can count. But most of the time, that's not the kind of guilt we're dealing with here. I think most of this guilt comes from the devil making us feel blame for things we have no control over."

Jim paused the video. "That *really* helped me. Want to hear the rest?"

Marilyn reached over and tapped the play button again.

On the video, Uncle Henry looked at Jim and said, "Have you ever wondered why you come to us for advice once in a while?"

"Because you and Aunt Myra always seem to know just what to do. Because God's given you guys a lot of wisdom."

"That may be so, but this wisdom didn't come easy. It came through everything we suffered with our sons and through lots of other trials. We kept crying out to God, and eventually we learned to trust him for whatever the outcome was."

37

Christina had stayed busy all day working at Odds-n-Ends, which helped keep her mind off Doug. Marilyn had come in after lunch. She seemed a little more upbeat than she did yesterday. They didn't get to talk much, but she said her mood had something to do with a fruitful conversation Jim had with Uncle Henry that morning. She promised to fill her in when they got the chance.

At the moment, Christina was finishing up a grilled chicken salad from a café a block down from the store, waiting for Ted. She hoped he'd continue to keep her mind off Doug, at least for the next few hours. This was to be her and Ted's first bike ride together. She wasn't sure how he planned to get the bike to her. When they'd talked, she'd offered to drive to his house, but he'd said that wouldn't be necessary. He'd bring the bike here.

A few minutes later, the mystery was solved when Ted arrived at the café with two bikes strapped to a rack behind the trunk of his car. She returned his wave as he pulled up next to the curb.

He got out of the car. "Told you I'd bring the bikes."

"Yes, you did."

"It'll just take me a minute to get them off the rack, and we'll be set to go."

She stood. "I'll go take care of my bill." When she came back, Ted was standing there wearing one of those dumb-looking bike helmets. Even worse, he was holding a pink one in his hand. "You can't be serious."

"What?"

"You expect me to wear that?"

"I do. Legally, you don't have to. But it's a good idea. I've had to wear one my whole life. The law says until you're sixteen. But I've kept wearing mine. Fell three different times when my head made contact with pavement. I decided I could put up with how stupid they look."

He held hers up, clearly expecting her to take it. This was almost a deal breaker. She struggled through a few more moments of indecision but finally gave in. "You better not laugh."

"Why would I? I'm wearing one."

She put the helmet on her head. "I don't even know how it goes."

"You never wore one before? Even as a kid?"

"Never."

"Wasn't it the law in New York?"

"I don't know." It wouldn't have mattered either way. She finally figured out how to snap it on and changed the subject. "Nice bike." He owned a mountain bike; the one she was borrowing was a beach cruiser with three speeds.

"I thought you'd like it. My sister's short, like you. It's only a twenty-four-incher."

"Petite."

"What?"

"I'm petite. Not short. Say . . . petite."

Ted smiled. "That's what I meant, petite." He held the bike out for her.

She took it. "Where would you like to ride?"

"Wherever you want."

"I'd be fine anywhere around here. You lead, I'll follow."

He got on. "I'd feel better if we rode through some of the neighborhoods. Too much traffic around here."

She looked at the level of traffic in front of them, thought about the streets of New

York. Ted was clearly not the adventurous type. "That's fine. I haven't seen a neighborhood around here I didn't like."

They started riding, staying on the bike paths until they reached the first neighborhood, then Ted led them out into the street. As expected, there were almost no cars on the roads.

"I know this whole town like the back of my hand," he said.

"Did you grow up here?"

"Pretty much. We moved here when I was three, but I don't remember anything else."

She couldn't imagine such a thing. Spending your entire childhood in a place like this.

"How long have you lived here?" he asked.

She wondered how much of her story he already knew. "Less than a year." She decided not to hide it, any of it. They went to the same church, and he was there last year when she'd had the baby. She knew people in the church had been praying for her, so her situation wasn't exactly a secret. "I was pretty much living in a dump before that, in a not-so-safe section of Sanford. I met Mrs. Anderson — Marilyn — at the Women's Resource Center. She was my counselor. Well, they call them advocates. Anyway, we hit it off and, to my great surprise, she and Jim invited me to live in the garage apartment."

"Their son Doug was living there then, right?"

"Technically. But he was mostly away at school. He attends Flagler College in St. Augustine, working on a graphic arts degree. But he didn't mind me moving in, either. He said he'd stay in one of the guest bedrooms whenever he came back into town."

They turned a corner and rode past one of River Oaks' beautiful neighborhood parks. "Think I'd heard something about that," he said. "He was back in town last weekend. I bumped into him at a gas station on the outskirts of town."

"Just Sunday afternoon. We had a big party to welcome his sister home. She and her husband have just adopted a little girl from Africa. She's really adorable." They rode past two moms sitting on a bench in front of a handful of toddlers playing on a kiddie swing. The children were about Ayana's age.

"I heard about that too," Ted said. "That's wonderful they could do that. I went on a mission trip to Africa a few summers ago, with our youth group. Not to Ethiopia though. We went to Kenya."

One more reminder of how different her

youth had been from Ted's. A few summers ago she waited tables at a diner in the Bronx Zoo. Well, hey, she thought, they had some jungle plants there, and plenty of jungle animals. After riding past the park, they turned left at a stop sign and began riding through the townhome section of River Oaks. She'd been here several times before, visiting Michele. It took her a minute to get her bearings. "Doug's sister's house is just a few streets over."

"I've met her," Ted said. "She seems really nice."

They rode down a few streets in silence. Then Ted said, "Is Doug dating anyone?"

Great, she thought. So much for getting her mind off Doug.

38

Michele, her mother, and her sister-in-law Jean were sitting together on a park bench in one of the many neighborhood parks scattered throughout River Oaks. Michele's mother had called that afternoon, asking if she and Jean could meet here after dinner. She had some things she wanted to share with them about Doug. Michele had asked if Christina would be there, but apparently she had other plans.

For Michele, this moment was the fulfillment of a dream. Being here, as a mom, with other moms, while her child played with other children in the playground. How many times had she stood off in the distance, anguish in her heart, watching a scene like this unfold, trying to imagine what it might be like to be a part of it?

Now, she was here. A few yards away, Ayana, her little girl, laughed and played with Jean's three children, Ayana's new cousins. The joy of this momentarily overshadowed the tension she had been feeling ever since she'd heard the news about Doug.

"Thanks for coming," her mother said to start things off.

"I'm always happy to get out of the house," Jean said, "especially coming here with the kids."

"Well, you know how much I love to see my grandkids," Marilyn said. "Thought it might be nicer to talk here rather than at the house."

"You said this was going to be about Doug," Michele said. "Is there any news?"

"Not about Doug. But about your dad and me. Dad met with Uncle Henry this morning. He's helped us out so much in the past, your dad wanted to hear what he had to say about this situation with Doug."

"I'm guessing by the look on your face he had some good advice?" Michele said. She glanced over at Ayana, who was doing just fine.

"He did. He said some things we had never thought about before. Since they involve how we're going to respond to Doug, we thought we should share them with you. See if we can all get on the same page."

"Whatever it is," Michele said, "I hope you're not planning to go too easy on him, Mom." She slid back a little on the bench. "Tom and I have talked about this, not about what just happened — although this recent thing kinda proves our point — but we've felt like you and Dad raised Doug in a totally different way than you raised us. I'm not sure you guys see it, but you've really been soft on him. For years. You would've come down hard on us for so many things he got away with."

Jean raised her eyebrows in a way that suggested she agreed.

Her mother didn't respond for a moment. Michele looked at her eyes. She didn't see anger or hurt there.

"You're right, Michele. That's one of our great regrets, spoiling Doug. I don't know why we did. It's certainly not because we loved him more."

"I think you were probably just worn out," Jean added. "It happened with my parents too. You guys were ten years older by the time Doug hit the teen years." She looked at her children on the playground in front of them. "I have to be careful even now, with little Abby. I'm already seeing times I should discipline her, and would have with Tommy or Carly, but I'm tempted to let it slide because I don't have the energy."

"That's definitely part of it, I'm sure," Marilyn said. "And I'm sure the way Jim and I had drifted apart in our marriage didn't help." She looked at Michele. "The problem is, Doug's not a kid anymore, or even a teenager. We can't go back and fix the mistakes we made back then. He's an adult. And even if we don't like what he's doing now, we have to remember that."

Michele wasn't sure she liked the sound of this and braced to hear a strategy she probably wouldn't agree with. But she had to say something. "I know Doug's an adult, but he's still totally dependent on you and Dad. That has to count for something." Again, her mom didn't immediately respond. Michele decided she was probably pushing too hard. "But I'll listen with an open mind."

"I hope so," her mother said. "This has really been hard for all of us, especially your dad. But we felt a glimmer of hope after hearing what Uncle Henry said. Two things stood out for me. First, what he said is right out of the Bible, and second, he and Aunt Myra followed this advice with their boys when they were younger."

Michele didn't even know Uncle Henry's sons had ever been anything but decent

Christian men.

"It's pretty much based on the Prodigal Son parable. I know you both know that story very well. But some of the things Uncle Henry drew out of it weren't things we've ever heard or thought about before."

"Like what?" Jean asked.

"For one thing," Marilyn said, "there's some things about the father in the parable that can help us as parents when our kids go astray. And really, when you think about it, both of this man's sons went astray. The first son, obviously, because he rebelled and left home and turned his back on all the things he knew were right. But the other son's reaction was terrible in its own way. He was harsh and legalistic toward his brother, which wasn't the father's heart at all. He even got angry at his dad after his brother came home, just for being compassionate. Now for the most part in this parable, we connect more with the rebellious son, because of what Doug is going through. But your father and I both felt convicted that our reaction already has more in common with the self-righteous brother than with the father."

Jean chimed in. "And Uncle Henry thinks our goal when dealing with Doug should be more like the father's heart in the parable?"

"Exactly," Marilyn said. "And that's not going to be easy. Because what Doug has done hurts. He's rejected our family, what we believe about the right way to live and the right choices to make. And to be honest — getting to what you said, Michele — he's taken advantage of us. All the money your father and I have spent — and are still spending — all the sacrifices we've made to send him to college. That kind of parallels, though, what the father in the parable did. He gave all that money to his son, which he didn't have to do, knowing what his son would do with it."

"He definitely could've said no," Jean said. "Pretty sure I would." She stood up to get a better look at her kids.

"But he didn't," Marilyn said. "He let his son go. Uncle Henry believes he wasn't giving up on him but was entrusting him to God. Which means the most important thing we can do now, while we're waiting, is to trust God to deal with Doug in his own way and time. Even if things get worse for a while. And they might. Doug may be out of our reach right now, but he's not out of God's. We've got to trust that God's in control and keep praying God will protect him until he changes his heart. Until that happens and he really understands the gospel, all our efforts to talk to him just come off as lectures."

"And if you think about the parable," Jean said, "there were no lectures. The father didn't say a thing to his son between the time he left and the time he came home."

Marilyn nodded. "That reminds me of something else Uncle Henry said. He asked your dad a question. What if the father in the parable kept chasing after his son while he was still on the run and still had money in his pocket? Then he found him and tried to straighten him out. Would the son have listened?"

Both Michele and Jean shook their heads no. For Michele, the message was starting to sink in.

"Excuse me," Jean said. "Speaking of straightening out your kids, I've got to do a little of that myself. Carly just pushed Tommy so she could move ahead of him on the slide. If I don't get over there, Tommy will push her back, or worse. Then things will get very loud." She hurried off toward the children.

Marilyn looked at Michele and said, "There's one more thing Uncle Henry said, but I want Jean to hear this." She looked out toward the children. "So, how are you doing with Ayana? Are you settling in yet?

Getting used to being a mom?"

"Oh Mom, it's been wonderful. I started feeling like her mother a few weeks ago, back in Africa. We were together every day. But it wasn't like being here. Allan wasn't with us. But now . . . we've only been all together for a few days, but I'm already loving it. And Ayana gets so excited when Allan comes home from work. I took a picture last night when he was reading her a bedtime story. Let me show you." She pulled out her phone and swiped until she found it.

"Ah, look at that," Marilyn said. "Look at both their faces. So precious."

Jean came walking back. "Okay, the fire's out. What are you two looking at? Let me see."

Marilyn showed her.

"How cute," Jean said. She looked at Ayana on the playground then back at the phone. "She seems so happy."

"We all are," Michele said.

Jean sat back on the bench.

"Okay, where was I?" Marilyn said. "There was one more thing Uncle Henry said that I wanted to tell you." She thought a moment. "I remember. He said he believed the father in the parable must have prayed every day for his son, which is why God put faith in his heart that one day his son would return. That's why the father's eyes were looking toward the horizon, why he saw his son coming when he was still far away. It was something the father did every day, because he knew God would be faithful to bring his son home where he belonged." She choked up as she said the last part.

"That's what your dad and I are hoping for Doug."

39

Doug sat at one of the outdoor café tables in a courtyard beside Kenan Hall. The sun had begun to set, making it harder to read his textbook. It was hard enough trying to concentrate through the fog of emotions he'd been experiencing since that confrontation with his mother yesterday morning. He and Courtney hadn't spoken to each other since she'd left his apartment shortly after. She had sent him one text that afternoon, just to say she was thinking about him.

All he said was "Thanks" in reply. He wanted to keep the door open, at least for now.

He closed the textbook and looked up to find Jason and Drew heading his way across the West Lawn. He and Jason had already talked yesterday, so he pretty much knew what was going on. Doug was sure Jason had filled Drew in. There was no such thing

293

as keeping secrets in their little group of friends.

"Doug, there you are," Jason said. "Went by your place, but you weren't there. You got your phone off?"

Doug pulled his phone out of his pocket. "Guess so. Had it off since my last afternoon class. Why? What's up?"

"Nothing's up, bro. Figured you were still a little down from that clash with your mom yesterday. Saw Courtney this afternoon, she said she hadn't seen you. You're not thinking of letting that one go, are you?" Jason pulled out a chair and sat at the table. Drew did the same. " 'Cause I think that would be a mistake."

"We're still a couple, I guess."

"You guess? Whatta you mean, you guess?"

Why did Jason care about this? Then Doug remembered his little speech about how a girl like that raises your stock value. And his too. "We're just taking a little breather for a few days. I think she's still into me, but she was a little peeved after what happened. Can't say as I blame her."

"I can see her being majorly embarrassed," Jason said, "but why was she peeved?"

Doug looked at him. "You know the answer to that. Do I have to spell it out?"

Jason thought a moment. "Oh yeah. I get it."

"Well, I don't," Drew said.

Doug sighed.

Jason looked at Drew. "Doug's folks didn't know about Courtney."

"That you guys were shacking up?"

Jason shook his head no.

"They didn't even know the two of you were dating?"

Again, Jason shook his head no.

Doug wanted this conversation to end.

Drew looked at Doug. "Why, man? I had a chick looked like that, I'd want the world to know."

"You don't know Doug's world," Jason said. "Back in River Oaks."

"Could we not get into all this?" Doug said.

"Why not?" Jason said. "I think we need to get it all out, Doug. Bury this thing once and for all. You're missing a golden opportunity."

"What are you talking about?"

"To break free, man. To get a clean slate, a fresh start. You've been wanting that for years. You just didn't know how to pull it off. Looks like fate decided to step in and lend you a hand. I think that episode with your mom yesterday is the best thing that could've happened. The cat's out of the bag. You don't have to hide anymore. Think of all the wasted energy you've put into keeping up this façade. I wouldn't be surprised, now that the hiding's over, if you don't experience a burst of fresh inspiration. Have you even been working on our graphic novel lately?"

"What? No, not for the last few days."

"Then start it up again. I'll bet you'll find all kinds of new ideas floating up." Jason leaned back in his chair, put his hands behind his head. "You've been clogged up, Doug. For so long, you don't even realize it."

"I think he's on to something, Doug," Drew said.

How would he even know? Drew knew nothing about Doug's family or his life back in River Oaks. He looked at Jason. "I don't know. Maybe."

"It's gonna happen," Jason said. "Has to. It's like what I learned in one of my classes today. We were talking about when the Berlin Wall came down. And all those people living behind the Iron Curtain were suddenly freed up from Soviet oppression. Their whole world was turned upside down. All kinds of new things started happening, with their art and music . . . and their economy. It completely turned around. We looked at before and after slides of East Germany. It didn't even look like the same place."

"So you're saying I'm like East Germany before the Berlin Wall came down?"

"That's exactly what I'm saying. Yesterday morning your wall fell down. Now, you're free. You can be anything you want to be, from here on out. Do anything you want to do."

Doug didn't know about that. But maybe, just maybe, Jason was on to something.

"Makes sense to me," Drew said.

Of course, Drew's commendation meant nothing to him. He had become Jason's personal yes man. But still . . . he liked Jason's outlook. It was certainly more hopeful than what he'd been feeling the last two days.

"And what better way to kick off the new freed-up Doug than to have an old-fashioned Xbox tournament, like we used to have all the time at my house. We can go over to our dorm room now. It's all set up. If we play with headphones on, we can play all night."

"What about class in the morning?" Doug said.

"Tomorrow's Saturday, Doug."

Doug laughed. "I don't even know what day I'm in."

Jason stood. "Grab your book and your backpack, and let's go."

Drew stood, looked at Jason, and said, "You got any brews? If we're doing an Xbox tournament, we gotta have brews."

" 'Course I've got brews," Jason said as he started walking toward his dorm.

40

It was Sunday evening, three days since Jim had talked with Doug. Still no word from him. The house was quiet. Everyone who'd come over after church for Sunday dinner had left. Christina was either up in her apartment or out with Ted; Jim had heard her telling Marilyn her plans, but he didn't remember what she'd said. Marilyn was sitting in her favorite spot on the sofa, reading a book. The TV was on.

Jim stood in the doorway of their master bedroom, looking at her, wrestling with himself about calling Doug. Should he ask her advice or just call Doug and fill her in after? The way he and Doug had left it, Doug was supposed to be thinking about which direction he wanted to go, which life he wanted to live. The pretend life he'd lived at home, or the life he'd been hiding from them whenever he was on his own.

Jim picked up his phone from his dresser

and walked out to the living room. Marilyn looked up. "Are you watching that?" he said, pointing to the TV.

"What?" She looked at the TV. "No, one of the kids must've left it on. Are you going somewhere?"

"Not really. Maybe just out to the veranda. I was thinking about calling Doug."

"Why? Has something else come up?"

"No. The silence is starting to get to me. When we talked on Thursday, I'd given him some things to think about. I thought he'd have called me by now, rather than just leave things hanging in midair."

She reset her bookmark and closed the book. "Did you really think he'd call? Doug hates confrontation. He avoids it like the plague."

"Guess you know him better. Maybe I'm the one who hates being in midair. I'd like to call him, see where he's at."

"I think we know where he's at, don't you? The fact that he never called back is pretty much his answer."

Jim inhaled deeply, then sighed. He really did believe the things Uncle Henry had said about the Prodigal Son story, and in that story, the father didn't pester his son once he'd left. But this was a little different. In the parable, the son leaves in pretty dramatic fashion, leaving no doubt about his plans. "You're probably right. This isn't a case where no news is good news. But I'd still like to have things clarified, so we at least know where we stand."

"I think that's fine," she said. "Just as long as you don't get angry when he says things you don't want to hear, which he probably will."

"I'll try hard to keep my cool. And if he still isn't sure what he wants to do, I won't pressure him." He leaned down and kissed her on the cheek.

She reached for the remote and turned off the TV. "Come back after you're done and let me know how it went."

Jim walked through the downstairs and out the patio door. He sat in one of the more comfortable lounge chairs and pulled out his phone. For all this buildup and drama, it dawned on him he'd probably just get Doug's voice mail. That's what happened most of the time. He listened as the phone rang several times. Sure enough, Doug's voice mail. "Hey, Doug, it's Dad. It's early Sunday evening. Give me a call when you get a chance."

He set the phone down and was just about to get up when the phone rang. It was Doug. He picked it up. "Hey, Doug."

"Hey, Dad. Sorry I missed your call. I was in the other room."

"Are you home? I mean, in your apartment. Figured you might be out with . . . your friends." He was going to say *Courtney* but couldn't quite do it.

"I will be shortly. I was out all afternoon, just came in to get cleaned up. What's up?"

"Nothing's really up, I guess. Just thought I'd follow up our conversation from Thursday. We kind of left things hanging there at the end."

"We did? Guess I didn't realize that."

What did that mean? "Don't you remember me suggesting that . . . well, you've kinda been living two lives. One with us and a different one at school. And that maybe this awkward incident between you and your mom flushed that out in the open. Just before we hung up, I suggested maybe you needed a little time to think this through some more. Figure out what you really want to do. Remember?"

"Yeah, I do remember you saying that now."

There was a pause. Jim thought Doug had more to say, but he didn't speak. "So . . . it's been three days. I'm wondering if you've had time to think about this, if you're any clearer now than you were then?"

"To be honest, Dad, I really haven't given it much thought. Things got pretty busy for me over the weekend."

Jim couldn't believe it. Hadn't given it much thought? It was pretty much all Jim and Marilyn had thought about since that last talk with Doug. Did they matter so little to him? "I'm sorry, Doug. I find that hard to believe."

"Find what hard to believe?"

"That you were too busy to think about something so important. This may not be a big deal to you, but it's a huge deal to us."

"I know it's a big deal," Doug said.

"Really? I'm sorry, but I don't think you do. I think you agreeing with me now is just like you always do when I play something back to you that you said. Something that sounds bad when you hear it repeated out loud."

"What are you talking about?"

"That you can't say now, yeah, you know it's a big deal when you just got done telling me you haven't even thought about it for three days. If you asked me to think about something that was really important to you, and I just put it out of my mind for the next three days, wouldn't you say, at the very least, it wasn't that important to me? That whatever else I paid attention to mattered a lot more?"

Doug didn't answer. Several seconds went by. "Dad, I think we should end this conversation. You're getting upset. I don't want to have to defend myself or explain what I've been doing the last three days, to see if it meets with your approval. I'm sorry you —"

"Doug, who do you think you're talking to right now? Las I checked, I'm still your dad, and you're still my son. Technically, you've left home, but I'm still responsible for you in every way that counts. Did you get a job I didn't know about?"

"No."

"Who's paying for the food you ate today? The gas you put in your car? For that matter, where's the money coming from for you to even be attending that school?"

A pause. "From you."

"See, if you were paying for all this yourself, then you could say you don't need to explain yourself to me or worry about meeting my approval. Ever heard of the term 'dependent'?"

"Yes."

"That's your official status right now, Doug. That's what I put on the IRS form after your name. When you graduate and get a job and start paying your own way, that's when you're no longer accountable to me. You can ask Tom and Jean if you want. Once they got to that point, I happily let them go with my blessing. They're not accountable to me anymore. But really, you still are. I know I'm pulling rank here, and you probably hate to hear me say all this, but I just don't think it's right, the way you treat your mom and me."

Jim waited to see if Doug had any reply, and to try to downshift his own emotions to a lower gear. He wasn't yelling, but he definitely had an edge to his voice.

A few more moments of silence. "Doug, I really need you to say something. I'm not going to hang up and leave things undefined like Thursday. If you need a little more time because you didn't take the time to think about things like I asked you to, I can call you back on, say, Tuesday. That'll give you forty-eight hours more."

He heard Doug breathing but still no reply. Finally, he said, "I don't need forty-eight hours more, Dad. I already know my answer. You can keep your money. You've prepaid my schooling and expenses to the end of the semester, which is just a couple of weeks away. I've got a plan to take care of things after that. I'll pay my own way. Thanks for getting me this far. Good-bye."

"Wait, Doug, don't do —"

He hung up. Just like that, he hung up.

41

Marilyn came to a stopping point in her book. She thought about Jim. He'd left the living room over twenty minutes ago to call Doug. They rarely talked on the phone together, and when they did, it was usually only for a few minutes. Was this a good or bad thing for them to be talking so long? She decided to get up and check. She would just open the patio door a crack. If they were still talking, she'd close it.

When she got to the door, it was already dark enough outside that she mostly saw her reflection in the glass. She turned the knob and pushed the door open a few inches. Silence. Total silence. Had Jim left the veranda? Sometimes he liked to pace when he was on the phone. Was he out by the pool?

"I'm here, Marilyn."

The tone of his voice made her tense up. He wasn't talking on the phone anymore.

Obviously, things had not gone well. She opened the door and stepped out. The light from the dining area revealed Jim sitting on one of the padded lounge chairs, staring up at the sky. Slowly, she walked toward him. "Are you okay?"

"No." Still looking up at the sky.

"How long have you been sitting there?"

"The phone call was less than five minutes."

"Not good, huh?"

"He hung up on me."

She sighed, then walked to the chair beside him. "Want to tell me about it?" She sat on the edge of the cushion. For the first time, he looked at her. Her eyes had adjusted enough to the darkness to see he had been crying.

"I blew it. I totally blew it."

She waited a few moments to see if he had anything to add. "Did you get angry?" He nodded. "How bad?"

"I didn't yell. I don't even think I raised my voice. But I knew as soon as he hung up I had pushed too hard."

She reached over and gently squeezed his foot. "I'm sorry. I was afraid that might happen."

"I really thought I could keep it together, no matter what he said. Thought I was past

308

behaving this way."

"I warned you because —"

"I know you did, it's just —"

"Let me finish," she said gently. "I warned you because of how angry I got at him Thursday morning. If I hadn't walked away when I did, I'm sure I'd have said a lot of things I'd regret."

He sat up and reached for her hand. "That's just the thing, I'm not sure I regret what I said. I regret the way I said it. Definitely fell into lecture mode. But he just got so smug with me, telling me he didn't need to explain himself to me or defend his actions."

"Were you talking about him sleeping with his girlfriend?"

"No, we didn't get into that at all. I kept the conversation to what you and I talked about . . . asking him if he'd reached any conclusions about what direction he wanted to go. That's how we had ended our conversation on Thursday night. He was supposed to think about what he really wanted to do and get back to me. Well, he hadn't made any progress on the subject. Turns out, he hadn't even thought about it since we talked."

"Really?"

"That's what he said. When I told him

that was kind of disappointing, because it was a pretty big deal to us, he said he knew it was a big deal. Clearly, it wasn't, and I told him so. That's when I slipped into full-on lecture mode, pointing out that until he was no longer dependent on us and was paying his own way, technically, he hadn't left home. And he needed to see himself as still accountable to us."

Marilyn shook her head. She knew how Doug would react to that, especially if Jim had shared it in the tone he was using now with her in this playback.

He sat back on the cushion. "Well, all of that is true, isn't it?"

"Technically, you're right. Doug is still dependent on us. And he should be accountable to us. I'm just not sure that's the right tone to use right now."

Jim looked back toward the sky. "I know. I know you're right. You just said the same thing I'm hearing inside. I've been out here wrestling with this, going over it and over it. Guess I've been wrestling with God."

"Well, don't beat yourself up. Remember that thing we learned in our small group last year? At the beginning of a big trial, don't be shocked if you experience anger or fear or any other negative emotion. Big things tend to shock our emotions. I think

310

that's what's happening here. I'm feeling it too. The more important thing is where our hearts go from here. If we let those negative emotions take over, we're sunk."

"I remember," he said. "And I know I have to start pushing myself to forgive him. But it's so frustrating."

"Yes, it is. But we've got to remember . . . Doug isn't seeing clearly right now. He's blinded by selfishness and immaturity. It's just sin. We can't take it personally, or we'll make it worse. For him and for us."

"I know."

"Remember what we're shooting for, what Uncle Henry said?"

"The Prodigal Son story. To respond like the father did."

"Do you feel like you have your answer at least? About which direction Doug wants to go?"

"Loud and clear," he said.

"You said he hung up. Before that, did you talk at all about what comes next?"

"That part was kind of bizarre. I have no idea what he was talking about."

"What do you mean?"

"He was talking like he didn't need our money anymore. That he could make it on his own. He said after this semester ends, which is in just a few weeks, he'd be taking care of himself. He meant financially. I have no idea what he's thinking or how he plans to pull that off."

Marilyn was confused too. Just then, the door opened to the garage apartment. They both turned to see Christina coming out, heading toward the main house. "We're over here, Christina," Marilyn yelled.

Christina turned toward her voice. "Oh, I was just coming over to talk to you guys about something. But it can wait."

"No, that's okay," Jim said. "We were just finishing up a conversation." He looked at Marilyn and whispered, "Maybe Christina could make some sense of this."

Marilyn didn't know if that was such a good idea, talking to Christina about all this. At least not while their emotions were so fresh.

She walked up and sat at the wrought-iron table in the chair nearest them. "Just wanted to let you know. After this new development with Doug, I'm kind of thinking I don't really want to check out that school in St. Augustine anymore. So if it's okay, I'll probably look into going to one of the schools within driving distance of River Oaks."

"That's great," Marilyn said. "I was hoping you wouldn't have to move out."

"Speaking of Doug," Jim said, "that's who we were talking about just now."

"Oh?"

"Yeah, the situation isn't good. I know you know that. But it's just gotten a little worse."

Christina's face fell. "How?"

"Last Thursday I had called him, asking him to think about the direction he wanted to go in. We kind of knew the answer, but I wanted to clarify things, so I talked to him tonight. It was a difficult conversation, and at least for now, it looks like he's pulling farther away."

"That's sad to hear," she said, "but not totally unexpected. For me, anyway."

"We're not really shocked, either," Marilyn said.

Jim sat up in his chair. "Doug said something at the end of our conversation that was very puzzling."

"What did he say?"

"He said at the end of this semester, he wouldn't need our help anymore. He was talking about money. He said he had something going on that would allow him to take care of himself from now on. Do you have any idea what he was talking about?"

Christina looked confused. "Do you mean things like food and gas money?"

"No," Jim said, "he was talking about everything, including school."

Christina shook her head. "That sounds crazy to me. Unless . . ."

"Unless what?" Marilyn said.

"There's only one thing I can think of, but it's hard to imagine he would talk about it like that. It's such an iffy thing."

"What is?" Jim said.

"You know that graphic novel contest he and Jason are entering? First prize is seventy-five-thousand dollars. Maybe he's thinking if they win that, he could handle his own expenses."

"Does that sound very realistic to you?" Marilyn said.

"Not really. I mean, Doug's a really talented artist. I have no idea how well Jason writes. But I'm guessing there's got to be hundreds of other people entered besides them."

They sat there a few moments in silence. Marilyn looked at Jim. "Do you think you should try to mend the fence a little with Doug?"

"I'll call him right now. Not that I think he'll answer."

"Try texting him," Christina said. "He still might not answer, but I can almost guarantee he'll read it."

42

A week had passed since the difficult conversation between Jim and Doug. No one had heard a word from Doug. He never responded to Jim's conciliatory text message sent that same night. Everyone had concluded the same thing from Doug's deafening silence. His heart had grown even harder, and he was moving even farther away from the family. Not just from them but from Christina as well. She was doing her best not to check his status on Facebook or Instagram, but she couldn't help noticing he'd made no efforts to contact her all week.

She was pretty sure that meant Doug had grouped her in with the family he had already decided to ignore. And she had given up any hopes of him "keeping her in the loop" with his graphic novel project. Both of those things made her sad, but she tried not to dwell on it.

Taking one last look at herself in the bathroom mirror, she made a few minor adjustments, then turned off the light. The rest of the Anderson family, minus Uncle Henry, Aunt Myra, and Doug, were already next door at the main house, getting ready for Sunday dinner. A first-time guest would make his appearance at the Anderson family dinner table today.

Ted.

Over the past week, they had met for dessert and coffee once and then again for another bike ride through River Oaks. Marilyn had suggested maybe it was time to invite Ted to a Sunday dinner. Christina could think of no serious reason to object.

She'd invited him yesterday afternoon by text, giving him a way out if this was too short a notice. He replied seconds later: *Are you kidding? Wild horses couldn't keep me away.*

Wild horses? Had he really said wild horses?

She walked slowly across the sidewalk toward the veranda, wishing she could be half as excited.

"Come on in," Christina said.

Ted stepped from the porch into the foyer, his eyes wide like a child's on Christmas morning. His head swiveled slowly, taking in the impressive sight of the home's architectural design and Marilyn's decorating expertise. Christina imagined his house must be almost as nice. She hadn't been inside yet, but the outside was just as big. His eyes finally rested on the dining room table on the far right. "Am I late?"

"You're right on time." He was referring to how many people were already sitting at the table. Marilyn and Michele were starting to serve the food. "Everyone else came right from church."

"Oh." He followed Christina toward the table.

Everyone turned when they saw them. "Is there anyone here you haven't met?" she asked.

"I don't think so. Hey, everybody." Everyone said hi. Ted walked around, shook hands with the men. He bent down and smiled at Ayana. "I don't think I've met you, though I've heard a lot about you." Ayana smiled. He held out his hand. She looked up at Michele, who had just walked into the room holding a basket of rolls.

"Shake his hand, Ayana. This is Ted. He's . . ."

Christina smiled. Michele didn't know what to call him.

"He's Christina's friend."

Ayana shook his hand.

Marilyn walked by and set a bowl of mashed potatoes down on the table. "Welcome, Ted. Glad you could join us."

"Thanks, Mrs. Anderson. For inviting me."

"We sit over here," Christina said, pointing to two empty chairs. She sat in hers. As Ted sat beside her, a picture of Doug sitting in the same seat two weeks ago flashed into her mind. She remembered feeling so happy, not just because he'd sat so close but because that was the day he seemed to be turning a corner, paying more attention to her. Out on the veranda and by the car when he left. It wasn't just her imagination. Michele, Marilyn, and even Jim had thought the same thing.

But apparently, she had it wrong. They all did.

"Christina?"

She looked up at Ted's face, then down at his hand reaching out to her, palm up. Was he thinking they were holding hands now?

"I guess we're going to say the blessing."

"Oh, right." She grasped his hand, reached for Jean with her other hand, and closed her eyes.

■ ■ ■ ■

By the time everyone had finished dinner, Christina was nearly exhausted. She didn't know why. Nothing had gone wrong. Ted seemed at ease the entire time, and everyone seemed to genuinely like him. And why wouldn't they? There wasn't anything not to like.

Then why didn't she like him? Well, she did like him, just not the way Ted liked her.

Not *that* way.

She looked up at him as he dabbed the edge of his mouth with the napkin. He smiled. She smiled back. Would that change in time, the way she felt about him? Is that all that was needed for something stronger to grow between them? More time?

She remembered a chat she and Marilyn had a few nights ago while watching a Jane Austen movie. *Emma,* the one with Gwyneth Paltrow. Marilyn and Michele loved Jane Austen movies, but Christina had never seen one before. Afterward, they'd gotten into a discussion. It centered around the obvious topic: whether one should marry for love or, as they put it in Jane Austen's time, to improve one's situation. Both Christina and Michele had said, of

319

course, one should only marry for love. Marilyn had agreed but said if you live long enough and see enough marriages that started out "for love" but ended terribly, it could make you wonder if there wasn't something to the idea of marrying for other considerations, like improving one's situation.

She'd gone on to say many couples who married back then for that reason, even some forced into arranged marriages by their parents, claimed that over time they came to deeply love their spouse and couldn't imagine their lives without them. She talked about a time just before Christina had met their family, when her own love for Jim had completely shriveled. She'd thought it had died for good. But now look. After Jim changed so thoroughly two years ago, he won back her heart, and now she loved him more than ever.

Maybe there was something to all this, Christina thought. Maybe, given enough time, she could develop feelings for Ted.

"What do you think, Christina?"

She looked up. Ted was smiling at her. "What?"

"Are you ready for dessert or do you want to wait a little while?"

"What do you want to do?" she asked.

"I'm fine either way."

She wanted to say, *Can't you just decide for once? Do you always have to defer to me? Don't you ever have any thoughts of your own? Aren't Christian men supposed to lead?* "I'm feeling a little full. Maybe we should wait awhile."

"Sounds like a good idea," he said. "Maybe we could take a little walk together."

Not a walk. We'd have to be alone if we took a walk.

Jane Austen was right. People should marry for love.

43

Doug didn't hear the door open, just the click of the latch when it closed. He was so focused on the drawing he'd been working on all afternoon, he didn't even turn around to see who it was. It could only be Jason or Courtney; they were his only friends who had a key.

"Hello?"

It was Courtney. They were officially a couple again, had been since the day after Doug's difficult phone call with his dad. She had asked him to choose which life he wanted, the one with her or the one without her. He'd told her he wanted the life that included her, Jason, and their friends.

"Hey, Courtney." He still didn't turn around.

"Thought I'd stop by. See if you're still alive."

"I am." He was so close to finishing this

panel. If she had only come ten minutes later.

"Is your phone turned off?" She came closer.

"Not off, just on vibrate." He swiveled around in his chair.

She picked up his phone off the couch. "You might hear it vibrate better if you put it on a hard surface, like the table."

"I'm sorry. Were you trying to reach me?"

"Uh . . . yeah. Three or four times. It's Sunday afternoon. We're boyfriend and girlfriend. It's a beautiful day out. Thought we might do something together." She said each of these things like a sarcastic question.

"I wish I could. I really do. But I've got to keep working."

She came over to see what was on his drawing board. He tensed up and swiveled his chair around to face it.

"This is what you're working on? A comic book? You've been ignoring me all afternoon because of a comic book? I thought maybe you were cramming for finals."

"It's not a comic book, Courtney. You know it's not." She was just saying that to be insulting.

"Okay, a graphic novel. Looks just like a comic book at this stage." She stepped back a few feet.

He glanced at the drawing. "Yeah, I guess it does. But I told you about that graphic novel contest Jason and I entered. This is for that."

"I know. Is that what you've been working on all week? I feel like we've hardly spent any time together."

"It is, and I'm sorry I've been shut up in here. But things are at a crucial stage right now. I've got to stay on this. It's super important."

She sat on the edge of the sofa. "I'm important too, Doug. You said I was. You said you wanted to make our relationship a priority. It felt like that for a few days, but . . . doesn't feel like that anymore."

"Courtney, I've only been working at this pace for a week. But I can't stop now. I don't really have a choice."

"What does that mean? Of course you have a choice. Nobody's forcing you to do this. You're doing it because you want to."

"That's not exactly true. I do enjoy drawing things like this, but I'm not doing this for fun. I have to finish it. I have to have it done in five days. And it has to be the best. We have to win this contest."

"Why? Why do you have to win? It's just a contest. The money would be great, but it's not like you need it."

Doug looked down, sighed.

"What? What's the matter?"

He looked up. "I do need the money, Courtney. It's not optional anymore."

"What do you mean it's not optional? What are you saying?"

He leaned forward. "I haven't told you everything that's going on with my parents. I'm not even sure I want to."

"That doesn't sound very nice. Don't you trust me?"

"It's not that. Not at all. It's something else."

"What? What is it?"

"I don't want you thinking bad things about my folks. Worse things than you already do. I told you the conversation didn't end well with my dad last week. It was a little worse than that. It's kind of complicated to explain."

"I'm not in a hurry."

He set down his drawing pencil. "Like you, I'm here at the school because of my folks. Well, my dad. He's paying for everything. I don't even have to have a part-time job. The deal's always been as long as I get As or Bs, he'll cover my expenses. But we're not rich. I don't have a blank check budget like Jason . . ."

"Neither do I," she said.

"My dad knows I'm not up here to goof off, so he's been willing to keep paying for it. But it's always been as long as I keep up my end, he'll keep funding my education."

"And now that's changed?"

"In a way? Yeah, it has. As of our last phone call."

"What, did he cut you off? Was it because of me?"

"In a way, he did. At least, he sounded like he was going in that direction. It wasn't really because of you, you were just part of the whole picture. We were discussing that whole which-life-do-you-want-to-live thing, the one I live at home or the one I live up here, when I'm not with them. Does that make sense?"

"Sort of," she said. "And you told him you were choosing the life you have when you're here, right?"

"I didn't say it flat out, but that's where I was heading. Actually, I was just trying to get him to stop treating me like a kid, like someone he could order around. I wanted him to treat me like an adult and let me live my life the way I choose to."

She got a look on her face.

"What?"

"So he pulled rank on you. Reminded you

who's paying the bills?"

"Pretty much."

"And you got angry."

"Pretty much. But in a way, I realized he's right. He's been paying my way, and I've been totally dependent on him. As long as that's the case, I don't really have a right to do as I please. I *am* answerable to him. He's just never yanked my leash before."

"And now he has?"

"Sure felt like it."

"So what did you do?"

"Guess I cut the leash."

She looked confused. "What does that mean?"

"I told him I didn't need his money. I could finish school without it."

She looked even more confused. Like he'd just started speaking a different language. She waited a moment, then said, "And how do you plan to do that?"

Doug sat back in his chair, pointed to the drawing on his drawing table. "Now you understand why I have to win this graphic novel contest. Why I've been working like a maniac all week. Why we can't go out this afternoon, and why I've gotta keep at this until I finish. Until I make this perfect. The deadline is five days away."

"Doug, you're not serious."

"I'm dead serious, Courtney. First prize is seventy-five-thousand dollars. I've only got the summer semester and one more year left to graduate. I figured it out. If Jason and I win this contest, I *can* pay the rest of my expenses without my dad's money. And that's exactly what I intend to do."

"Doug, your whole future, whether or not you can even stay in school, is dependent on you and Jason winning this contest? How many people have entered this thing, do you think?"

"I don't know, a few hundred?"

"What if it's a few thousand? Even if it is a few hundred, you're banking everything on you guys winning? All or nothing?"

"Jason thinks we can win. I think we can win too. You weren't there at the Comic-Con, Courtney. There was this whole row of amateurs with their drawings on display. Jason thought mine were in a different league than theirs. And if I'm being honest, I think he's right."

"Doug, you're really talented. You know I'm not a fan of comic books, but I've got eyes. Your stuff looks pretty professional. And maybe you might win, but it's gonna take more than just your artwork. You've got to have the best story too. I've read some of the things Jason has written. It didn't strike me as all that special. And while you've been shut up in here all week working like a maniac, as you say, and not spending time with me, seems like Jason's just being Jason. He's out goofing off right now. I've seen him at two parties this week, totally wasted both times."

"I know." She hit on something that was really starting to bug him.

"You know? Does he know there are only five days left till you have to turn this in? How can you even finish your drawings if he hasn't finished writing the story?"

"You're right. I'm gonna talk to him."

"And what about finals? They start up next week."

Doug hadn't given a thought to studying for finals. "I'll have to fit that in somehow."

She got up and walked toward the door, stopped with her hand on the knob. "Well, there's one thing I can see you won't have any time for this week."

"What's that?"

"Me," she said. "I know you said you were going to start making our relationship a priority. But I'm not feeling it, Doug." She opened the door. "Something else to think about. The week after finals we're off a week before the summer term begins. I've decided to go home that week and see my folks."

She opened the door. "I haven't seen you this past week, I'm not going to see you the week coming up, then I'm gone another week. That's three weeks. I like you, Doug. I really do. But that's not going to cut it for me. Between now and when I get back from visiting home, I want you to think about whether I really am going to be a priority in your life."

She turned and walked out the door.

44

About an hour after Courtney left, Doug finished the panel he'd been drawing. He spent some time taking stock of how many panels he needed to complete over the next five days and the deadline for submitting final entries to the contest. The rules called for ten completed pages, which meant everything on those pages had to look exactly the way you wanted them to appear in the final version. In addition, the judges wanted to see a complete script for the rest of the novel.

If they were going to win, the artwork had to be perfect. But Courtney was right: so did the writing. What Jason had given him so far wasn't bad, but it wasn't great. Already, Doug had to make several changes to tighten up the dialogue and increase the dramatic tension.

Besides that, Doug had just caught up to everything Jason had written so far. He couldn't even finish the artwork for the next page unless Jason gave him some more. At this pace, there was no way Jason would have the rest of the manuscript written in five days. "That's it," he said aloud. He set his pencil down on the drawing board and stood up.

He had to find Jason, tonight.

Doug had left several texts and voice mails on Jason's phone and spent the last hour searching all of Jason's regular haunts. But no luck. Doug finally drove to a location Jason sometimes went to, an abandoned dock on the river just north of town. You had to drive several hundred yards down a dirt road with thick brush on either side, pull off into a clearing to avoid getting stuck in the soft sand, then walk the rest of the way on foot.

Jason's truck was there, so he knew his search had paid off. By now, it was dark, but there was a big enough moon to get by. The wind was blowing east off the river, allowing Doug to smell the pot Jason was smoking well before he saw him.

When he reached the dock, he saw Drew there with him. Both were sitting on the edge, their feet dangling over the water. A joint passed between them. Doug figured they were already pretty stoned; neither one heard him approach, though several boards creaked as he walked. He wanted to be mad at Jason, when he thought about how hard he'd been working all week at the drawing board, but standing there listening to him educate Drew about the several reasons fish leap out of the water when they do, and watching Drew's head nod up and down like it mattered . . . Doug had to smile.

Jason had it all figured out. And Drew was easy to impress.

"You forgot the one about fish seeing insects flying just above the water, and how they leap out to catch them."

Jason turned around, the joint still in his mouth. "Left that one out on purpose, Doug. Seeing it's too dark out here for fish to see insects flying above the water."

"Can't they see at night?" Drew asked.

"What are you doing here?" Jason said.

"I've been trying to reach you for over an hour."

"Phone died. Left it in the car. Figured we'd just sit out here, take in the peace and quiet. What's on your mind? Some kind of emergency?"

"Important but not an emergency." Doug looked at Drew. "But it's also kind of private. Could we talk alone for a couple of minutes?"

Jason took a deep pull on the joint then handed it to Drew. After holding his breath a bit, he exhaled and said, "Drew, why don't you finish this off on your way back to the car? I'm getting kind of thirsty. Grab three beers out of the cooler in the trunk."

"None for me," Doug said.

"Oops, sorry. If I knew you were coming, I'd have packed a few Cokes."

"No problem. I can't stay long anyway. Got a lot of work ahead of me tonight."

Drew stood, nodded at Doug as he inhaled, and started walking toward the car.

"Work?" Jason said. "On a Sunday night? You get some kind of job I don't know about?"

"In a manner of speaking. And so did you."

"Not following you."

"The contest? The seventy-five-thousand dollars? The graphic novel we're supposed to be working on together?" Jason looked like he was trying to process what Doug had just said. Doug continued. "We need to send it in, finished and polished up, in five days."

"Five days? Okay . . . so why you stressing about that now?"

"Jason, the question is . . . why aren't *you*

stressing about it? Or better yet, why aren't you working on it now?"

"See, Doug, that's why you need to smoke pot. You're wound way too tight. You need to adopt my perspective. You'd enjoy life more."

No, I wouldn't get anything done, he thought.

"We got all kinds of time."

"No, we don't."

"I can finish what I got to write in two-three days tops. You got the hard part, doing all those drawings."

"Jason, I can't finish the drawings unless you write some more. I'm all caught up with you. We need ten pages. I've got two more left to do."

"See? The more you talk about this, the more tense you get."

"Jason, you're not taking this thing seriously."

"Serious as a heart attack," Jason said. "Which is what you're going to have if you don't lighten up."

Doug wasn't getting through to him. He walked a few steps closer. "Jason, have you even started studying for your finals? They start this week too. You've gotta finish our manuscript and you've gotta study, but instead all you're doing is sitting out here with Drew getting high."

"You are observant. I'll give you that. You're all tied up in knots, but you are observant." He shot Doug a big smile.

"Jason, there are still several hours left to this night. Hours I could spend working on the next page. If you had done your part. If you were keeping up."

"But you know what's coming next, right? We've talked about what should go on the first ten pages. Can't you improvise?"

Doug sighed. He was just about to let Jason have it. "I suppose I can. Suppose I'll have to. But you said it yourself, I'm doing the hard part, the part that takes ten times longer. Which kind of proves my point, don't you think, about you not holding up your end? It's like we're the tortoise and the hare, and the tortoise is buzzing right by the hare. You should be way ahead of me by now. Instead I'm waiting on you."

They stared at each other a few moments. The look on Jason's face said he was at least trying to comprehend.

"I don't know what to tell you, bro."

"Jason, you know what this means to me. I told you a few days ago about that conversation with my dad. I *have* to win this thing, or I won't be able to stay in school. Everything's riding on this."

"Gosh, Doug. That's so much pressure. This thing was supposed to be fun. You know? Like extra credit. I'm not sure I would've signed up for it if I thought our lives depended on it."

"I know. It wasn't all that serious at Comic-Con. But things have changed since then. Maybe not for you, but for me."

"The thing is, I don't do my best writing when I'm under pressure."

Doug wondered, was that what Jason had given him so far? His best writing? He thought of another solution. He didn't know why he hadn't thought of it before now. "I've got an idea, if you're okay with it."

"Sure, let's hear it."

"How about I just finish it myself? Your part and my part?"

"Can you do that? That even doable?"

"I think so. We've talked through the story a dozen times. I'm pretty sure I can take it from here."

"We do this, are you going to be mad at me? You know, for dropping the ball."

"I might be for a few minutes, but I'll get over it pretty quick. Like you said, when you agreed to it, there wasn't all this pressure. But you know, if I do the rest of it, and I win, we won't be splitting the money fifty-fifty."

"I'm cool with that. It's only fair. You win, the money's yours. All of it."

"All right then," Doug said. "Guess that's it."

They heard Drew whistling as he got closer. "We good?" Jason said.

"We're good. But look, I gotta go. I've gotta keep working on this thing."

"All right, good buddy. You do that. Drew and I will drink some beers, keep guarding this dock."

Doug smiled as Drew walked by. "You do that." He turned and headed back to his car.

45

For the next five days, Doug hardly came up for air. He worked day and night on his graphic novel. Mingled in, he crammed for final exams, stopping just long enough to take each test. But he applied only minimal effort to this "distraction," since he no longer had to satisfy his father's requirements to make As or Bs. Even with this reduced emphasis, he felt certain he hadn't slipped very far and wouldn't be surprised if he got a C or better in every class.

Late yesterday afternoon, he took his last final then worked late into the night putting the finishing touches on the manuscript for his novel. He'd already completed the artwork three days ago. It was the finest work he'd ever done. He'd never tell Jason this, but ending their creative partnership was the best thing that could have happened. It had completely escaped his notice before but became apparent as soon as Jason was off the project.

Jason was holding him back.

Here Doug was on Friday morning, holding the completed project in his hands. Today was the final day to turn it in. Had Jason stayed involved, Doug was certain he'd never have finished on time. Just as importantly, Jason's lackluster writing would have sunk any chance they had of winning. The rules stated that the judges' scores would include a breakdown between the artwork and writing, so Jason would have known he was to blame. He'd have been crushed; it could have ruined their friendship.

None of that mattered, though, because Jason had bowed out cheerfully, and now all the writing matched the skill of Doug's drawings. A win-win situation for sure. Besides all this, it was probably better for Doug's future career as a graphic novelist that he and Jason stopped collaborating. For one thing, they didn't share the same priorities. Jason was only marginally committed to his writing. Doug was dead serious about both his writing and his art.

Doug picked up his keys and headed toward the front door. The contest instructions stated the submission had to be postmarked no later than today and sent first class. As he walked through the door, his phone rang. It was Courtney. He'd hardly seen her all week. They had talked about this, and she said she understood.

"Hey, Courtney."

"Hi, Doug. Well, did you finish it?"

"I did. I'm on my way to the post office right now."

"You're not even going to let me see it before you send it in?"

"I . . . I didn't think you'd want to."

"Well, I do. I'm at the dining hall. But I'm only going to be here another hour, then I'm heading home."

"Home?"

"Yeah, don't you remember? I told you, after finals were over I was going home for a week to see my folks."

"You're leaving today?"

"Yeah, I guess you haven't looked at your phone the last couple days. I texted you and left voice mails about this. Well, look, just get over here so I can at least see you a little bit before I have to leave."

Doug easily found Courtney in the dining hall. She always sat in the same spot. He called to her. She turned and waved him over. Doug was glad her two friends got up and left as he turned down the aisle leading to her table. He knew that, like Courtney, they weren't big fans of comic book art, and he didn't care to hear their sarcastic remarks.

She got up as he reached her, gave him a quick kiss. Her cheerful disposition surprised him. He had pretty much ignored her all week. She was probably just excited to be going home, he thought. They hadn't talked too much about her family life when they were together, but she had said she got along with her parents pretty well. It didn't sound like they had too many rules, much like Jason's parents.

"Is that it?" she said, pointing to the big envelope he carried.

"That's it." He sat and carefully pulled out the drawings, leaving the manuscript pages inside. He set them in front of her. "Could you just grab the edges as you flip through them?"

"I think I know how to handle artwork," she said, looking down at the first page.

"Sorry." There was just so much at stake here.

She looked at several more, taking time with each one. Not enough to read the story but enough to express more than a casual interest. "You know I'm not a big fan of comic books —"

"Graphic novels," Doug said.

"I'm just playing with you," she continued. "But these are very good, Doug. I wouldn't be able to tell the difference between these drawings and ones done by professionals."

"Thanks." That meant a lot, coming from her. "Hope the judges feel the same way."

About halfway through, she stopped and looked up at the dining hall ceiling, then all around the room, then back down at the drawing. "The throne room in this panel looks very familiar," she said with a smile.

"Probably because we're in it right now," he said. "I modeled it after this hall." The dining hall at Flagler was, like so many other buildings on campus, an architectural masterpiece. Multiple arches rested on ornate, hand-carved wooden pillars. Beautiful frescoes adorned every flat surface in the ceiling.

Doug saw Jason approaching their table. "Hey, Doug." He stood over Courtney's shoulder. "What have we got here? Is this it? Did you finish?"

"That's it. *The Prodigal,* ready for prime time."

"Cutting it close, aren't you? Isn't today the deadline?"

Doug nodded. "I'm bringing it over to the post office as soon as I leave here."

343

"Let me see the cover." Jason slid it out from under the stack. "Whoa, dude. You hit it out of the park. This is way better than the one we started with."

"I just finished this one last night. After writing the ending, it gave me some new ideas."

Jason carefully set the cover back in place. "Are we still good about this? About me bailing out?"

"Yeah, don't worry about it. We're fine."

Courtney finished looking at the drawings; Jason picked up where she left off. She looked up. "When do you find out if you win?"

"In ten days. Think I have a good chance?"

"Definitely," she said.

"Bro," Jason said, "there's no way this doesn't win. I'd buy this in a heartbeat. The cover alone is as good as anything out there."

Doug smiled. He knew it was good, the best he'd ever done. Hearing them say it was reassuring.

Courtney pushed her chair back and stood. "Well, I've got to go. Got a long drive to get back home, and I wanna get there before dark. Walk me out, Doug?"

Doug stood. "Sure." He looked at Jason. "Guess I need to go too." Jason handed the drawings to him. Doug sealed up the package.

As she walked toward the front door, she reached for Doug's hand. He grabbed it and followed her. They walked down the steps, through the lobby, and out into the sunlight. She walked them over to a shady tree. "This kind of stinks, you finish your graphic novel and I have to leave for a week."

"I know," Doug said. "Lousy timing, right?"

"What are you going to do while I'm gone?"

"I don't know. Guess I'll just hang out with Jason and the guys."

"You going to miss me?"

"What? Yeah, sure I am. But we can stay connected."

She put her arms around his neck, looked into his eyes with a more serious face. "I meant what I said before. I want you to make up your mind while I'm gone that things are going to be different between us. I don't want to be second fiddle anymore. Not to any art projects, not to Jason and your friends, or anything else."

"I know. I will."

"You will what?"

"I'll think about it."

"You're not supposed to think about it.

That's just an expression. You're supposed to just do it. Just make up your mind and do it."

He had no idea what she was saying. "Okay," he said.

She pulled him toward her, and they kissed. She kissed him again with more passion. He pretended to feel the same, but it just wasn't there. She pulled him closer for a good-bye hug. Then they parted and she started to walk away.

"Miss me," she said, smiling.

"I will." He watched as she strolled out of sight. But as he walked toward his car, he felt no sorrow that Courtney was gone. If anything, he felt . . . relief.

46

It was late in the afternoon on Friday, one hour before quitting time for Christina. She and Marilyn were minding the store; Harriet, the owner, had left for a quick trip to the bank. At the moment, there were no customers, so they used the time to do some blocking, a retail term where you straightened out the shelves and pulled everything toward the front. Marilyn was one aisle over. Christina could see her through the glass shelves.

"So, where's Ted taking you for dinner tonight?"

Marilyn's voice sounded way more excited than Christina's reply would be. She still wasn't sure she'd made the right decision saying yes to Ted. "We're going to Giovanni's."

"My favorite Italian place," Marilyn said.

"Mine too. It's the first place I ever ate in River Oaks, when you invited me there shortly after we met."

"I remember."

"That was the first time I ever ate at a restaurant with linen napkins," Christina said.

"It is very elegant. And the portions are so big, you always get to bring home leftovers for lunch." Marilyn moved one rack closer toward Christina. "I think Italian food is even better the second day."

"Me too."

"Are you excited about it?"

Christina paused. Over the last few weeks, she and Ted had been out several more times: at the coffee shop, on more bike rides, even to a movie once. They sat together at church and at a Bible study. Christina was sure everyone was starting to view them as a couple. "I wish I was."

"The sparks still aren't flying yet?"

"Not yet. I mean, he's still nice, and I still like him."

"Is tonight your first dinner out?"

Christina straightened up some candle holders. "Yes. It will also be the first time I've let him pay my way. He insisted when he asked me."

"Does that matter to you? I just assumed he was paying all along, like when you guys went out for coffee. Jim always did when we dated."

"Oh, Ted wanted to. I just never let him."

"How did you handle that?"

"It wasn't hard. I'd usually just get there first and pay for mine. It's not a big deal. Maybe I'm making too big a deal out of it. I guess, as long as I was paying, we weren't officially dating."

"Is that what's making you nervous about tonight? That this will make you guys . . . official?"

She realized . . . that was exactly what was bothering her. That Ted would see tonight as a step forward in their relationship. "Yes."

"It doesn't have to be," Marilyn said. "You're just going out to dinner, right? To a very nice place, but still, it's just a dinner. Do you feel like Ted is pressuring you in any way?"

"Not exactly. He's been a perfect gentleman. But I can tell, he wants this way more than I do."

"Well, you just take it as slow as you need to." Marilyn knocked something over. "Uhoh. Glad it was just plastic. I better pay more attention."

"But what if he tries to hold my hand tonight, or expects a good night kiss when we say good-bye? I can tell he wants the relationship to move beyond where it's been."

"You haven't been doing anything like that so far?" Marilyn said.

"So far I've been able to dodge that bullet." Gosh, did she just say that? Was that how she viewed any physical affection coming from Ted?

"If you're not ready for that step, you just tell him the truth. Like you said, Ted's a gentleman. I'm sure he'll respect that."

They worked in silence a few moments. Christina said, "Have you guys heard anything more from Doug?"

"Not a sound. It's so hard, wondering how he's doing, especially at night. All we can do is pray. We're doing a lot of that."

"I am too," Christina said. She thought about something, wondered if she should say it. "I did a little snooping online last night."

"You did? About Doug? What did you find out?"

"Not a whole lot. Apparently, Doug's been locked up in his apartment working on his graphic novel."

"For that contest, right?"

"Yep, that's the one."

"Well, at least it'll keep him from getting into trouble with Jason."

Christina had thought the same thing. Not just about Jason but about Courtney too. She didn't see any interaction between them on Facebook. Of course, that didn't mean a whole lot. They lived in the same town, went to the same school; they could still be seeing each other in person.

The only thing Christina knew for sure was . . . she and Doug hadn't interacted on any level since he'd pulled away from the family. And she'd been right about the graphic arts novel. Today was the last day for contestants to enter. If Doug had completed the project, he did so without running anything by her. She was most definitely not in the loop.

Did he even think about her anymore?

47

The following morning, Christina sat in a booth, drinking coffee. When she'd gotten home last night from her dinner date with Ted, she'd been so conflicted she had to talk to someone. It was only a little after nine, so she took a chance and called Michele. Michele and Allan were in the middle of a movie, but Michele could instantly tell Christina needed help and agreed to call her back after. By then, it was pretty late, so Michele suggested they meet for breakfast. Allan had the morning off and said he would be happy to watch Ayana.

Christina saw Michele coming through the front door and waved. A moment later, Michele slid in across from her. "Good morning," Christina said. "I'm so glad you could come."

"Me too," Michele said. "I've been wanting to try this place ever since it opened."

"The coffee's good." Christina took

another sip.

"I'm glad. I've been to so many breakfast places that have great food but lousy coffee."

"Can't vouch for the food yet. It's my first time here too."

"Did you order yet?"

"Just got here myself a few minutes before you did." Christina picked up the menu.

They read the menu over and chatted awhile. The waitress brought Michele her coffee. Christina asked her how things were going with Ayana, and Michele filled her in. Sounded like Ayana was adjusting nicely, learning a bunch of new English words like fried chicken, milkshake, and cartoons. Michele said Ayana especially loved discovering they made TV shows just for kids.

Michele told Christina about a small group she had just begun attending, made up of moms with children Ayana's age. Between that and the help she was getting from Jean, Michele felt confident she wouldn't stray too far off track. About that time, the waitress came and took their breakfast order.

"So, enough about me," Michele said. "Fill me in on how things are going with Ted. Last night you ate at Giovanni's?"

Christina nodded. "Our first dinner out. And the first time I let him pay."

"From what you said last night and by the look on your face, I'm guessing it didn't go so well."

"It went fine. Nothing went wrong. Ted was as nice as ever. The food was fantastic. Of course, I knew it would be. It's Giovanni's. We didn't fight. I don't think we've even had what you could call a conflict."

"But you're just not feeling it," Michele said.

Christina made a face that said no.

"How long has it been? I mean, how long have you guys been something of a couple?"

"I know he's been interested in me for about six weeks. We went out for coffee for the first time I guess about a month ago. Do you think I just need to give it more time?"

Michele set down her coffee cup. "I don't know. It's hard for me to say. I think I loved Allan by the end of our first date. I'm sure I did by the end of our second."

"It would be so much easier if Ted had some glaring faults. Then my lack of feelings for him would make a lot more sense."

"Have you ever gone out with someone like Ted before?" Michele said.

Christina laughed. "Not even close. See, even that doesn't make sense. By all accounts, Ted should be out of my league. He should be the one who's uncertain, not me."

"But he's not," Michele said. "To be honest, I'd say he's in love with you."

Christina sighed. "Did you have to say that?"

"You don't think he is?"

"No, I get that feeling too. I try to ignore it when we're together. But I think you're right."

Michele sat back. "Was there any new . . . evidence last night?"

"Nothing he said. But he kept looking at me that way, right into my eyes. Every time he did, I looked away or thought of something to say to break the tension. You know, like, 'How's your lasagna?' or 'Want another breadstick?' "

Michele laughed. "Have you guys started holding hands? Has he kissed you yet?"

"No, but last night he tried, several times."

"Which one, holding hands or kissing?"

"Both."

"At the same time?"

"No. Different times. During dinner, he reached for my hand across the table twice."

"What did you do?"

"The first time, I wasn't expecting it. I

yanked my hand back like a bug just crawled on me. I apologized but then grabbed a breadstick, so he wouldn't reach for it again. The other time I was looking out for it. When he touched me, I didn't freak out. But I moved my hand away pretty quick."

"What about him trying to kiss you?"

"That happened when we were saying good night at the door. He didn't actually try to kiss me. There was just that terrible, awkward moment when I could tell he wanted to, and he was giving me that look as though asking if I wanted to kiss him too."

"How did you handle that?"

Christina looked down. She felt awful saying it. "I pretended I didn't catch the signal he was sending and said a quick, 'Well, guess I better go. Good night.' "

The waitress came up with their food order. Christina got two eggs over medium, applewood bacon, and rye toast. Michele was in the mood for a Belgian waffle with pecans. She prayed a quick blessing over the food and said, "I know we're going to talk about this some more, but Christina, I think you know what this means, don't you? It means you need to break things off with Ted."

Christina cut off a piece of egg with her

fork. "That's what I've been thinking too. But I wasn't sure if I should give it more time."

Michele looked up at her. "Do you really think more time is going to change anything?"

"No, I don't. I keep waiting for something to happen when we're together, but it never does."

"And there's nothing wrong with that. Love isn't something we can just turn on or off."

"But I don't want to hurt Ted."

"Which is precisely why you need to do this very soon. The longer you wait, the greater the chance you will hurt him. Do you think he has any idea you don't feel the same way?"

"I'm thinking he'd have to by now, don't you think? Especially after last night."

Michele finished chewing. "Not necessarily. He might just think you're taking it slow. And if he is in love with you, and he's a gentleman — and I think both of those things are true — he might just think he needs to be patient. In a little while, you'll come around."

They stopped talking a few minutes and ate some food.

"Do you think it's going to be a problem,"

Christina said, "you know, at church, after I break it off? When I used to break up with a guy before I was a Christian, we usually avoided each other."

"I don't think so. Especially if you guys haven't been physical yet. He might feel a little hurt, but not because you've done anything wrong. It'll just be the usual disappointment that always happens when we don't get something we were hoping for."

They both took a few more bites.

"I really don't want to hurt him," Christina said. "He is a nice guy."

"He is. And he'll make somebody very happy someday," Michele said.

"I like that," Christina said. "I'm going to use that when I talk to him."

They ate a little bit more.

Finally, Michele said, "So, are we going to talk about it?"

"Talk about what?"

"The real reason you don't have room in your heart for Ted. We both know what it is. Or should I say, *who* it is."

48

Doug did something that morning he hadn't done for months. With his finals out of the way, his graphic novel project sent in, and Courtney safely out of town, he had absolutely nothing to do, no place to be. So he grabbed his skateboard out of the closet and rode it all over the college campus and historic downtown area. At least, everywhere skateboards were allowed.

He felt a little rusty sailing through the streets and sidewalks, but for the most part, he held his own. He only tripped twice, flying off two different curbs, but regained his balance both times before hitting the street. Afterward, he took a cool shower, letting the water run about twice as long as usual.

As he skateboarded through town, he found himself thinking mostly about Christina. How she was doing, what she was doing these days. He'd actually started thinking about her yesterday when he dropped the big envelope containing his graphic novel in the mail. At that moment, a conversation with Christina had flashed into his head, bringing with it a fresh feeling of guilt. They were talking in front of his house in River Oaks the last Sunday he'd visited. Doug was in his car talking to her through the window, asking her if she'd be willing to look at his drawings and give him some honest feedback as he worked on the project.

That never happened. He'd never given her the chance. It didn't seem like an appropriate thing to do anymore after that fiasco at his apartment when his mom caught him with Courtney a few weeks back. Felt like months had passed since then. Doug remembered that look on Christina's face when their eyes locked for that brief moment before he closed the door. It wasn't anger. More a combination of hurt, confusion, and disappointment.

Whatever it was, he felt horrible every time he thought of it.

The saddest part of it was, he had really enjoyed spending time with her that Sunday at the house. He remembered thinking on the drive home that it was the single most enjoyable conversation he'd ever had with a girl. It got him thinking about all the other conversations he'd had with Christina and how much he'd liked them. He'd really been looking forward to the two of them reconnecting again. And she'd seemed to like the idea too.

Later that Sunday, he'd thought about Christina some more. This time it happened after spending a few hours with Courtney. Which, by contrast, felt boring and flat. They had almost nothing in common, and other than her looks, he felt no attraction to her. By the end of the night, he had decided he wanted to start winding down this relationship altogether.

If only he had acted on those thoughts right away. Instead, he'd let things continue to drift until that awful exchange by the front door. Things between him and Courtney were still adrift.

He was dressed now and planning to head over to the dining hall to grab some lunch. Jason had texted him a few minutes ago, saying he and Drew were on their way there. But Doug thought he'd first spend a few moments getting caught up on Facebook.

So he grabbed his iPad, plopped down in his favorite chair, and clicked on the Facebook app. He and Christina were still friends on Facebook, but, due to inactivity, she no longer showed up in his newsfeed.

But there was Courtney, front and center. She had already uploaded four different times today, including a number of pics. Looked like she had already reconnected with a number of her high school friends back home. And she had sent him a message.

He was about to click on it and knew that he should, when it dawned on him . . . he really didn't want to. One of the distinct sensations he'd felt that morning as he skateboarded around town was the freedom in knowing he wouldn't have to see Courtney today. Or tomorrow. Or for an entire week. According to Jason, Doug's stock would plummet if he broke it off with Courtney, and so would theirs.

He didn't care. He decided right then that he had to end the relationship. Not now, not on Facebook, or with a text, or by phone. But as soon as she returned, he'd tell her in person.

He quickly found Christina's Facebook page and began scrolling through the posts she'd made since the last time they were together. As he did, his heart sank. It quickly became obvious that thing with Ted had escalated. Doug had thought, from what Christina had said that Sunday out by the car, that she wasn't interested in him. But clearly, something had changed. Doug was looking at pictures of the two of them together, taken from a number of different places over several different occasions.

They were dating. And she looked happy. Clicking on Ted's Facebook page only made it worse. More pictures of them together. A lot more. He read all the captions, comments, and replies. Nothing overtly romantic, but it was clear they were in a relationship, and it was growing.

Doug set the iPad down on his lap. Why should this be a surprise?

Christina's face flashed into his mind, of that moment when he stood there in the doorway of his apartment. She was standing behind his mom, Courtney behind him.

He was sure Christina wanted nothing more to do with him now. When he closed the door on her that day, he'd closed the door on any chance he'd ever have with her.

49

Christina was nervous, with good reason.

It was Saturday evening, shortly after dinner. She was sitting at an outdoor table in the Starbucks in downtown River Oaks, watching Ted get out of his car. He had parked along the curb a few car lengths down. She glanced over at a familiar table on the other side of the courtyard. Over the last six weeks it had become "their table." The table where they'd first had coffee together, and the table they sat at every trip to Starbucks since.

It was empty.

She sat at *this* table on purpose.

Ted smiled as he walked up, then noticed their table was available. His puzzled look disappeared after looking in her eyes. He seemed to understand something was up.

"Hey, Christina." He pulled the iron chair out and sat.

"Hi, Ted." She had rehearsed how she'd

start things off, but now that he was here, she'd forgotten what she planned to say.

"What's up? Is anything wrong?"

She took too long a breath, let it out slowly. "I guess you could say that."

"Did I do something wrong?"

"No, Ted. It's not that kind of wrong." His puzzled look returned. "And you certainly haven't done anything wrong. Since that first time we came here, you've been . . ." What should she say? "Very nice."

"But something's bothering you. I can tell."

"You're right. Something is bothering me. And it's been bothering me for a while now."

"Whatever it is, if I can help, I will."

Don't do that now. Don't be nice. That's only gonna make this harder. "You can't really help with this kind of thing, Ted. I'm not sure how to say this. Especially because you've been so nice. This is really me, something with me. It's just . . ." She had to stop looking at his face. Now she understood why people chickened out when they broke up, left a voice mail message or a note on a table.

"You want to stop seeing each other? Is that it?"

Still looking down at the table, she nodded her head. "Yes, Ted." She looked up.

"That's what I'm trying to say."

"I had a feeling that was it. I could kind of tell this was mostly one-sided. In the beginning, I thought it was just because you didn't know me. But I don't think that's the reason anymore." He seemed a little sad but not crushed.

"I've really tried to like you, Ted. Of course, I like you. I mean *that* way. But the things that are supposed to happen aren't happening for me. Every time I see you, I see you as a friend. Do you understand?"

"I think so. I was hoping it would become more." He paused, then said, "Are you sure it can't happen if we give it more time?"

"I don't think so. That's why I've waited this long to talk about it." She looked into his eyes, trying to measure his mood. "But I'm hoping we can at least still be friends."

He returned her gaze without saying anything for a moment. "Sure. We're still friends." He looked away, then looked back and said, "Can I ask you something? If you don't want to answer, you don't have to."

"Sure. What is it?"

"Is there anyone else? Is that what's holding you back?"

Two things instantly came to mind, one right after the other. First, an image of Doug's face. Not the last time they saw each other at his apartment, but the look on his face the last time he came home, when he was sitting in his car at the house. The second thing was a quote from one of her favorite movies, *You've Got Mail.* After they had just broken up, Greg Kinnear's character asked Meg Ryan's character if there was anyone else. Meg Ryan replied, "No, but there's the dream of someone else."

Of course, Christina couldn't say that.

"No, not really," she said.

Just before dark, Jim and Marilyn were coming back from a walk around the neighborhood. They had been taking walks more often, ever since Doug had pretty much cut all ties with the family. Some days Jim's anxiety level about Doug would get the better of him, and he'd struggle with feelings of depression. Walks like this really helped.

He didn't know why, but today had been particularly hard. Maybe it was because it was Saturday, and he'd had the day off. Too much downtime. Too much time to think. The fresh air did great things to clear his head and Marilyn's comforting counsel, like a lighthouse, always helped point his heart toward the shore.

They were still talking as they walked through the front porch into the house. "Why don't we finish chatting out on the veranda?" Marilyn said. "I'll grab two bottles of water from the fridge."

"Great idea," Jim said. "I'll meet you out there." He sat in the padded lounge chair he usually used and looked up at the sky. To his left, the sun had disappeared. The blue sky was following right behind it. The brightest stars were already making their presence known. "God," he prayed quietly, "here I am, again, needing to surrender Doug to you. Help me to trust you with his life. I know what Marilyn said is true. You care about him more than we do. But I don't own it. If I did, I wouldn't keep worrying so much. You're the only one who can change his heart. Help me to settle that in my heart as we wait for you to turn things around." He turned when he heard Marilyn open the patio door.

"Here you go." She set the water bottle beside him and sat in her usual spot. "Are you doing any better?"

"I am. I just wish I'd get to the place where I could set my heart on trusting God and it would just stay there. Like flipping a switch. In my head I know everything you and Uncle Henry have said is true. But you both seem to do a much better job of staying on track than me."

Marilyn opened her bottle of water. "I think I know one reason it might be harder for you. Do you want me to tell you what I think?"

"Of course I do. Why wouldn't I?"

"It might sting a little."

"I still want to hear it."

"Remember that whole dance metaphor Audrey Windsor taught us? The fear dance?"

Jim nodded. "About identifying our core fears?"

"Remember one of yours? About feeling helpless or losing control?"

Jim remembered. "You're right. That's exactly what's going on here. I'm still not used to resting in God when things are out of my control." He reached over, squeezed her hand, and grabbed the water bottle.

"And this situation with Doug is totally out of our control, from beginning to end. I'm kind of used to living with things out of my control. For most of our marriage, I hardly had any. You were in control. It's different now, but it was like that for so long, I think letting go and trusting God just comes easier to me."

That made sense to Jim. "I hope it doesn't take me twenty-seven years to catch up."

The garage door opened.

"Must be Christina coming home from her meeting with Ted," Marilyn said.

"Meeting? Don't you mean date?"

"No, I mean meeting. We talked about it this afternoon. She's breaking things off with him." Marilyn looked toward the door that led into the garage apartment. "I hope things went well."

"Can't say I'm really surprised," Jim said. "They didn't seem like a good fit to me." Jim remembered what Marilyn had said about Christina's feelings for Doug. He really liked Christina and wished Doug was in a better place, but considering where he was at now, Jim didn't see how anything could ever happen between them.

50

Today was the big day. The day that would change everything.

Ten days had passed since Doug had mailed in his graphic novel. The contest organizers had announced they would name the winner of the $75,000 first prize on their website this morning at 10:00 a.m., a few minutes from now. Doug wasn't sure why they'd picked a Monday. Seemed like a Friday night made more sense for something like that.

He'd managed to keep himself preoccupied with other things most of the week, but all weekend long he could barely think of anything else. He'd hardly slept at all last night. He brought his coffee mug to the couch, set it on the coffee table, and picked up his iPad. Jason had just sent a text saying he'd be over any minute. He wanted to be there when they announced the winner and help him celebrate.

Doug checked the contest website first, but there was still nothing there. He noticed a red number one on his Facebook icon, indicating someone had contacted him. He clicked on it, a message. He clicked on that, saw it was from Courtney.

Courtney, that's right. She was supposed to be back at school today. Probably letting him know when she'd be there and setting up a time for them to meet. Students were already signing up for summer classes. In fact, Doug was getting a little nervous; there were only two days left. He hoped the contest organizers planned to pay out the prize money right away. He'd need it for tuition and books.

He scrolled down and read the following message from Courtney.

Doug,

You were probably expecting a call from me or maybe a text, saying I've arrived back at school. Well, my plans have changed. I hope you can be happy for me and that what I'm about to tell you doesn't make you too sad. The thing is, I'm not coming back to school. Not to Flagler anyway. Something kind of wonderful has happened, something totally unexpected.

I don't know if I ever mentioned to you my old high school boyfriend, Rick. We went out all through high school. I thought we were in love and would always be together, but he wound up breaking up with me a few months after I left for Flagler. I was crushed, at least for a little while.

It's a long story, but the thing is, we started seeing each other again since I came home, and it's like we were never apart. All the love we felt for each other, it's like it's all back good as new. He wants me to stay here, go to a college closer to my house. I talked to my parents about it, and they're fine with it. So . . . I guess this is good-bye. We had some fun times together, but I think you'll agree we never let it get too serious. You're a great guy. I know you'll meet someone special (I know a couple of girls up there who were pretty jealous that we were going out).

Hope you have a great summer! Hope you win your comic book thing!

Love, Courtney

Comic book thing? How many times had he told her, graphic novels are totally different than comic books. And this was how she was breaking up with him? On Facebook? There was a knock on the door. "It's unlocked, Jason."

Jason walked in. "Did I miss it? Did they announce who won yet?"

Doug looked at the time. "Still three minutes." Jason came up behind him.

"Whatcha doing?"

"You believe this?" Doug said. "It's Courtney. She just broke up with me on Facebook."

Jason walked around the couch and sat beside him. "You're kidding."

"Why would I kid about that? She and her old boyfriend from high school started up again. She says they're in love. She's not even coming back to Flagler."

"Really? Man, that stinks. Sorry, bro."

Doug closed the Facebook app.

"Aren't you going to say anything back to her?"

"Maybe, but not now."

"Are you okay with it? You don't seem too upset."

"I guess I am. No one ever broke up with me before."

"Somehow I think you'll survive the blow.

It's not like you two were in love or anything, right?"

"No. Whatever we had, it wasn't love."

Jason laughed. "I will miss having her around. Not gonna lie. She was fun to look at."

Doug didn't answer. He clicked on the contest website.

Jason leaned over and looked at the screen. "Man, only one more minute. You excited?"

Excited wasn't the word. His stomach was in knots. He had to win. Everything was riding on this. He stared at the clock in the corner.

"How are they going to announce the winner?" Jason said. "Just flash the name up on the screen?"

"The name and the cover."

"What do the second- and third-prize winners get? I forget."

Doug didn't want to think about that. "Second prize is $5,000. Third prize gets some fancy mountain bike, I think." He kept his eyes on the clock. Thirty seconds.

"You're going to win, Doug. No way you're not."

They both stared at the screen as the seconds ticked down. The clock turned over. It was now 10:00 a.m. But nothing happened. They kept staring. Several more seconds went by. Still, nothing.

"What's going on?" Doug said.

"You sure it's 10:00 a.m., Eastern time?" Jason said. "Maybe they live in a different time zone. Maybe it's 10:00 a.m. a few hours from now."

"No, I checked. I'm sure it's our 10:00 a.m." He scrolled and scanned around the home page, found a link for the contest instructions. He clicked on it and glanced down at the bottom. "See, right there. It says today's date, 10:00 a.m., EST. That means Eastern Standard Time." He hit the back button. Still, no change on the screen.

"Maybe they're just running late," Jason said. "Maybe they're having some problems uploading the cover."

Doug didn't answer. He just kept staring at the spot on the screen where the winner was supposed to be announced. He looked up at the clock. Two minutes had gone by.

"You thought about what you're gonna do with the prize money?"

Jason was just trying to ease the tension. "I already told you," Doug said. "I need to use it for school."

"All of it?"

"Most of it. I haven't figured it all out yet. You ever looked into the costs to go here?"

"No. I know it's a shame you gotta spend

that money on something like school."

"Wait, something's happening," Doug said. "The page is reloading." Jason leaned in. Doug read aloud the words that had just appeared: "And the Winner Is . . ."

A name flashed onscreen, then the cover. Doug read them, but not aloud.

It wasn't him.

"What?" Jason yelled. "Takumi Matsui and *Mako Man*? What kind of crap is that? Look at the cover. A man who turns into a shark? Are you kidding me? That cover's ridiculous. What were they thinking? They picked him over you?"

Doug barely heard Jason's rant. His eyes locked onto the screen. He hadn't even considered another name or another cover appearing in the winner's box. How could this happen? His mind finally comprehended the information he had just read. Someone else was getting his $75,000. He focused on the cover. *Mako Man.* It wasn't bad. Certainly better than average. But Jason was right, it wasn't even close to the quality of what he'd sent in.

"Does it say who got second and third?" Jason said. "Scroll down."

Doug did.

"No way. No stinking way. You didn't even get second or third. What a rip-off. This thing was rigged. Look at those other covers. I wouldn't even pick those up for a second look if I saw them on the shelf. Doug, I'm so sorry. You got ripped off, bro. Totally ripped off."

Not even second or third. All that work, all those late hours. All for nothing. He let the iPad fall to his lap. What was he supposed to do now? He needed several thousand dollars for tuition and books in the next two days.

He barely had enough food and gas money to last through the week.

51

Jim sat at his desk in his home office, his computer open to QuickBooks. It was bill-paying time. He didn't love or hate the task; it was just something that had to be done. He tried to remain thankful that at least they had sufficient funds to cover their expenses. Like every year, Jim had set up a budget and a bill schedule in January, so that bill-paying time wouldn't be such a headache. But he felt that headache starting to form as he stared at one troubling item on the screen.

Doug's college tuition.

His bill schedule suggested that right about now he should be transferring funds and sending a major payment to Flagler College to cover Doug's tuition for the summer semester. They hadn't heard from Doug in weeks, ever since the night he'd hung up on Jim, saying he could take care of his own expenses from now on. Jim seriously doubted that was true, but what should he do with this?

Marilyn walked by, heading from their bedroom to the kitchen.

"Hon, can you come here a minute? I could use your help with a debate I'm having."

"With who?"

"Myself."

"Sure." She stepped past the open French doors, looked at his screen. "Guess it has something to do with the bills?"

"Just one bill. A big one. You haven't heard anything new from Doug in the last few days, have you?"

A pained expression came over her face as she sat on the edge of an upholstered chair. "Not a word. I send him a text every few days, but he hasn't responded. The silence is killing me."

That made him angry. He could understand Doug being a little miffed at him. But there was no way Marilyn deserved to be treated that way. He looked at the screen. "Maybe that's my answer then. He doesn't want to hear from us, maybe I should just leave it that way."

"Why? What's going on?"

"It's about his college money. I built into the budget little reminders that tell me when I should move money from the college fund to the checkbook. I got one of them today. Which means I should be paying a pretty big chunk of money to Flagler College right now to cover Doug's summer semester. But the last thing he said when he *was* talking to us was he didn't need our money anymore, remember? He'd figured out a way to make it on his own from now on."

Marilyn nodded. "You mean that contest he entered. Do we even know if he won?"

"I don't know. I never thought of it as a solid plan. Like banking on a poker game. But if by some slim chance he did win, then I don't need to pay this bill. If he didn't win — which seems more likely — and I don't pay it, he can't stay at school. I checked the school's website, and the last day to sign up for summer classes is Wednesday."

Marilyn thought a moment. "I know Christina's home. I just saw her doing her laundry."

"Has Doug been staying in touch with her?"

"I don't think so. But she might know a little more about this contest he entered. Or maybe where to find out about it on the internet. If you find out he didn't win, are you thinking of not paying his tuition?"

"I don't know. Part of me is thinking that. If he wants to be on his own so bad, maybe we should let him find out what it's really like. But I don't think that's what God wants. I keep trying to remind myself of that Prodigal Son story, and what Uncle Henry said my goal should be."

"You mean to be like the father in the story?"

Jim nodded. "My instincts run just about the opposite. The father in the story gave his son his inheritance early, knowing what he'd probably do with it. I'd have said no way. I'm not going to help you screw up your entire life and fund your rebellion. But he didn't do that. He gave him the money."

She reached over and squeezed his hand.

"I'll give Christina a call," he said. "See if she knows anything more about that contest." Jim picked up his phone and dialed Christina's number.

Christina was sitting on her sofa folding some towels when her phone rang. She picked it up, saw who it was. This was different. "Hi, Jim," she said. "What's up?"

"Marilyn and I are over here in my home office. We've been talking about Doug's situation, and we're wondering if you could help us solve a little problem. Do you remember that graphic novel contest Doug entered a few weeks ago? The one you thought was his great plan for paying his own way at school?"

"I do. But I don't really know anything about it. Doug and I aren't connecting anymore."

"Do you happen to know who was running the contest? Or have any way of checking out their website?"

"Not off the top of my head," she said. "But I can look it up on Facebook. I remember he posted something about them a few days ago."

"Can you find out the date they'll pick the winner? I know Doug's banking on winning that prize money to pay for his school expenses. The tuition's due this Wednesday."

"I'm sure I can find that out. Let me go check, and I'll call you right back."

She hung up and picked up her iPad from the dinette table. In a few minutes she found Doug's post about the contest. She clicked on the link and saw what they needed to know, right there on the home page. The winners had been announced today, and Doug's name wasn't on the list. Not even in second or third place. Poor Doug, she thought. He must be feeling horrible about now.

She picked up her phone to call Jim back with the news.

Doug sat alone in his apartment, his eyes incrementally adjusting to the darkness overtaking the room. He'd pretty much sat in the same spot all afternoon. After getting the heartbreaking news about the contest, Jason had done his best to cheer him up. He'd offered to take Doug out to his favorite restaurant, then he tried a few movie possibilities, then suggested a video game marathon. Nothing worked.

Jason didn't understand. How could he? He had all the money he could ever want and parents who didn't care what he did or didn't do.

Doug still couldn't believe he had lost the contest. He hadn't even placed. How could he call his dad back now and tell him that? Would his father even help out, after the things Doug had said? And if he did, what kind of things would Doug have to agree to?

His stomach was growling. It had been for the last hour. He needed to get up and get something to eat. But he wasn't hungry. Willing himself out of the chair, he stood and walked toward the kitchen. His phone rang. He'd gotten a call a couple hours ago, but he didn't answer it. He figured it was just Jason again, and he wasn't in the mood to talk.

This time he picked it up. It was Jason. Might as well answer it. "Hey."

"You doing any better?"

"Not really."

"Well, Drew and I are on our way over. We'll be there in ten minutes."

"Jason, I'm really not —"

"I won't take no for an answer. We're going out. Trust me, what we have in mind is exactly what you need."

"I don't know."

"That's right, you don't. But I do. You can't just sit around there moping by yourself. Let's go blow off some steam."

"I haven't even eaten yet."

"We'll get something at a drive-through."

"Is this what you called about earlier?"

"I didn't call you earlier. Just be ready in ten minutes."

Doug hung up. After checking his phone, he saw the earlier call was from his dad, and that he'd left a voice mail. He wanted to ignore it, but curiosity got the better of him, so he clicked a few buttons and listened to the message.

"Doug, this is Dad. I know you're not talking to us right now. Mom said you haven't even

returned any of her text messages since we last talked. But don't ignore this call. We know you didn't win that contest. I'm guessing that was your big plan when you said you could take care of your own expenses from now on. I don't know what you're thinking now, but we really need to talk. Please call me back."

Doug deleted the message. He would have to get back with his dad sometime, but not now.

52

"You gotta admit, this is just what the doctor ordered." From the front seat, Jason turned all the way around, yelling over the music. Doug was in the backseat of Jason's four-door Nissan pickup. Drew sat in the passenger seat.

"Yeah, this is great," Doug said. "Turn around and look at the road."

"Relax, bro. I got this." Jason did as he asked.

Doug hated riding with Jason, even when he wasn't stoned, because of this very thing. If Jason was talking, he had to be looking at you. Judging by the glassy look in his eyes, the dumb look on Drew's face, and the lingering aroma in the truck cab, Doug knew the two of them had already smoked a joint before they picked Doug up. "Where are we going anyway?" Jason started to turn around again. "Don't look at me, just drive."

"Chill, Doug," Drew said. "This is supposed to be a fun time."

Jason glanced at Doug through the rearview mirror. "I told you, where we're going is a secret. But I saw you eyeing that pile of wood when you got in, and those lounge chairs in the back of my truck. Those are clues. If you reach behind your seat, there's another clue. That cooler's holding an ice-cold six-pack of Buds."

"Campfire on the beach," Drew said. "Looking at the stars, drinking some brews."

Jason couldn't help himself; he turned around again. "Now, before you object, that's only two beers apiece. No way you can get drunk on that. I asked you once, if you ever did drink beer, what would you drink? You said Budweiser. So there you go."

Drew said, "Jason told me what happened. After the day you had, you could use some liquid refreshment."

Maybe they were right. It was just two beers. He looked at Jason. "All right, but could you stop looking back here every time you talk?"

Jason smiled through the rearview mirror then turned to Drew. "See? I told you Doug could be reasonable."

"When did you tell me that?"

Jason shook his head. Drew could be so dull.

"So Doug," Drew said, "since you lost that contest, you still going to finish the comic book?"

"Not you too," Doug said.

"What? What did I say?"

"Comic book?" Jason said. "Really?"

"Okay, I meant graphic novel. I know the difference. Anyway, you going to finish it?"

"I haven't decided." He looked out the window. After leaving the college, they'd crossed the Bridge of Lions separating the historic area from Anastasia Island. They'd grabbed some burgers and fries, which they'd already eaten. They had driven south down A1A, through St. Augustine Beach and Crescent Beach. No more signs of city life now, just palms scrubs and ocean shrubs, broken up by the occasional driveway leading to a beach house. "How far we going?"

"Past Marineland," Jason said. "Far enough south till we get past all these houses. Don't want anyone calling the cops on us because of the fire. I've got the place marked on my GPS. Went to a keg party there a few weeks ago."

"It's so cool," added Drew. "There's a little cutaway in the bushes. You just follow the path about a hundred feet, and it dumps out right on the beach. No one on either side as far as you can see."

"Trust me, Doug. You're going to love it," Jason said.

It did sound kind of appealing.

"And of course," Drew said, "to sweeten the experience, at least for Jason and I . . ."

Doug heard him wrestling something out of his pocket. A moment later, the familiar click of a lighter. A red glow in the front seat, followed by a deep inhale. The fragrant telltale aroma of pot drifted into the backseat. "Can't you guys wait till we're out of the car?"

"Why put off a good thing?" Jason said, reaching for the joint.

"Why? Because you're driving."

"There you go, being paranoid again."

"I'm not paranoid."

"Beg to differ, bro," Drew said. "Pot's not like booze. It's perfectly safe to drive when you're stoned." He reached for the joint.

"That's not true, Drew." Only an idiot would say something like that.

Jason exhaled a long puff of smoke. "See how uptight you are? It's a shame you don't like this. All that tension you feel inside? It would be gone just like that." He snapped his fingers.

Doug rolled his window down. Jason was right. He didn't like the feeling of being high, but he did like the smell. But in a confined space like this, he couldn't help but breathe it in.

"You're wasting all this fine secondhand smoke," Drew said.

Doug didn't answer. He just looked out the window again, tried to get lost in the music. They drove through an uninhabited section. Doug could see a thin strip of ocean over the tops of the bushes, partially lit by a three-quarter moon. Way out on the horizon, the lights of a lone shrimp boat flickered like a low-hanging star. In the front seat, Jason and Drew worked feverishly on the joint, quickly reducing it to a nub.

A minute later, Jason flicked the rest of the joint out the window. The song on his playlist changed to one with a driving beat. Doug had heard it many times before but couldn't remember the name. He and Jason didn't exactly share the same musical tastes. Jason and Drew's heads instantly rocked up and down in sync with the bass and drums. Drew started playing the dashboard like bongos. Doug knew what came next. Both of them started butchering the chorus. He had to laugh. It was like a scene from a bad college movie.

Doug noticed bodies of water out both windows now. They must be coming up on the Matanzas Inlet. But it seemed like Jason and Drew were somewhere else, maybe the front row of a live concert. There was a slight curve in the road. Jason seemed to miss it. "Jason!" Doug shouted.

Jason reacted and corrected his drift but stayed locked into the song. Doug looked up ahead, saw headlights coming the opposite direction, from the bridge that crossed over the inlet.

The chorus of the song began again as they crossed the threshold of the bridge. Jason and Drew were singing their hearts out, their heads still banging back and forth to the music. Doug felt a tinge of fear and made sure his seatbelt was clicked tight. Then Jason did something insane. As the chorus repeated, he started pushing the truck headlights off and on in time with the beat.

"Jason, what are you doing? Stop!"

But he didn't stop.

"Stop messing with the lights!" Jason ignored him. The next few seconds seemed to move in slow motion. Doug looked through the front windshield, saw their headlights and dashboard lights flicking on and off. The approaching car's headlights flashed brightly in Doug's eyes. Something seemed wrong. The angle was off. "Jason, stop!" They were too close. The pickup had crossed the centerline. Doug reached toward the steering wheel, but the seatbelt caught his shoulder. "Jason look out!"

Jason looked up, saw what he'd done, and yanked the steering wheel to the right. But he was too late. The other car rushed past them, horn blaring, sideswiping both doors. A loud crunch. Screeching metal. The pickup bounced far to the right. Drew screamed. They jumped the curb and slammed into the cement guardrail. Jason and Drew's heads hit the ceiling. The truck careened toward the other side of the bridge. Through the windshield, Doug saw nothing but the other guardrail and lots of ocean.

The truck hit the opposite curb and went airborne. It felt like the tires bounced off the guardrail. Everyone screamed as the truck began to dive and spin sideways. Doug was upside down now, hanging by the seatbelt. More screams. He closed his eyes. Falling, spinning. A loud boom as they landed.

What? No splash?

He blacked out.

53

"Oh my gosh, what a mess. Hardly even looks like a truck."

"You see the way it went over that guardrail? Must've flipped three or four times 'fore it hit the ground."

"You call 911?"

"Already on their way."

"I don't see anybody moving in there."

"How many people do you see?"

"Looks like three."

"Reach in there, see if any of 'em have a pulse."

"I ain't gonna touch 'em."

"Geez, what a wimp. Move out of the way."

Doug heard voices but didn't recognize them. He'd woken up a few moments ago, didn't know where he was. Everything was black. He hurt all over but especially his head, his right hip, and leg. He tried to move but couldn't. Why couldn't he? Where was he? He heard waves breaking on the beach. Sounded far away. Why was that?

"No pulse on this one."

"That the driver?"

"Think so. Hard to tell, the way they're all twisted up together. Can you reach through the passenger window, see if you can reach the other guy's wrist?"

"The opening's too small."

"I can see light coming through from over here."

"Why don't we just wait for the paramedics? They'll be here any minute. It's not like we can do anything. If he is alive, they're going to have to cut him out."

"Just try, see if there's a pulse."

Doug felt movement, heard something in front of him. Little specks of light here and there. Still couldn't move.

"I think I feel one. Yeah, pretty sure this one's got a pulse. Real weak, though."

"There's one in the backseat. I think I can reach him."

Doug felt something touch him, then a sharp pain. "Ow!" he screamed.

"Sorry, man. Guess we know you're alive. Are you okay? Can you hear me?"

"I can hear you," Doug said. "What happened?"

"You've been in an accident. A pretty bad

one. My friend and I were fishing down the beach a ways, saw the whole thing. Your pickup truck smacked into a car up on the bridge. You guys went flying over the guardrail. Ambulance is on its way. They'll get you out of there."

"Where are we?"

"Matanzas Inlet. You guys are lucky in a way. Well, two of you are. If that accident happened fifty yards sooner, your truck would've landed upside down in the water. You'd have all drowned."

Doug felt like he was clinging to a dream that was slipping away. Jason and Drew, the loud music, banging into that oncoming car. That was what happened. A car accident. What did he mean, two of them were lucky? He looked toward the front seat but couldn't make it out. Nothing looked right. "Are my friends okay? Jason? Drew? Can you hear me?"

No answer.

"I don't think they can hear you. One of them can't, for sure. I think the other one's unconscious."

"What do you mean?"

"Sorry to have to tell you this, but I can't find a pulse. I think one of your friends is dead."

"Dead? Which one?"

"Looks like the driver. But the other guy's not doing so hot, either. But he's still alive."

Jason is . . . dead?

"How are you doing? You hurt bad?"

"Not sure. I can't move. My hip and right leg are killing me."

"But you can feel them, right?"

"Yes."

"How about the other leg? Can you feel that one?"

Doug tried to wiggle his toes. They moved fine. That leg only hurt a little. "It seems fine."

He couldn't believe it. Jason was dead.

"I hear the sirens," the other man said.

"I hear them too. They should be here any minute. They'll take good care of you. You'll be all right."

All right? How could he be all right? His best friend was dead. Just like that. The three of them were laughing and goofing off, on their way to a fun night at the beach. He heard Drew's voice in his head. *Campfire on the beach. Looking at the stars, drinking some brews.* But that didn't happen. It would never happen. The three of them would never laugh or goof off ever again. Drew was unconscious and Jason was dead.

It all happened so fast. Doug realized . . . he could have died just as easily a few moments ago. But he hadn't.

Had God spared him?

Jim's phone rang a little after 9:00 p.m. He and Marilyn were sitting together on the sofa watching a show on Netflix.

Marilyn picked up the phone. "It's Doug."

"Maybe he's finally returning my call."

Handing him the phone, she said, "Remember the father in the Prodigal Son story."

"I'll be nice." He clicked on the answer button. "Hey, Doug. Thanks for returning my call."

"I'm sorry. This isn't Doug." It was a much deeper voice. "Can I assume this is Doug Anderson's father?"

"Uh, yes. And who is this?"

"Hello, Mr. Anderson. This is Deputy Sheriff Ben Berlin with the St. John's Sheriff's Department. I'm calling on behalf of your son."

"My son? Is he in some kind of trouble?"

"He's been in a car accident, sir. Just about an hour ago. A pretty serious one. He's alive, but he's been hurt pretty bad. They brought him to Flagler Hospital emergency room in St. Augustine. I'm sorry for calling you this way, but I thought it would be the quickest way to reach you. I just hit the Dad button on his contact list."

"Excuse me, Sheriff." Jim put his hand over the phone and explained what he'd just been told to Marilyn. She already knew something was very wrong. "If you don't mind, I'm going to put you on speakerphone so my wife can hear everything we say."

"That's fine. I don't have a lot of details yet. Other officers are still investigating the scene. But I'm sure I can answer a few of your questions."

"Do you know how badly Doug was hurt?" Jim said.

"He's still in with the doctors as we speak. But I asked one of them for a brief update before calling you. They're listing his condition as serious but not critical. One of the other passengers in the car is also here. He's in critical condition. In surgery right now."

"You said other passengers," Jim said. "Does that mean Doug wasn't driving?"

"No, it looks like he was in the backseat of the vehicle, a pickup truck."

"Jason owns a pickup," Marilyn said.

"I believe that is the driver's name," the deputy said. "Yes, I just confirmed on my notes. His first name is Jason. We've already contacted his family, so I guess I can tell you. He is deceased. I'm sorry, but Jason didn't make it."

"What?" Jim said. "Jason is dead?"

"I'm afraid so, sir."

"Oh no," Marilyn said. "This is terrible." She began to cry. "But Doug is okay? You're sure he's okay?"

"He's been badly injured, ma'am. But I am told his injuries are not considered life-threatening."

"Can you tell us anything more about the accident?" Jim asked. "Were there any other cars involved? Was anyone else hurt?"

"There was another car on the bridge, but it wasn't badly damaged. Neither of the occupants were hurt. From what we were told by some fishermen on the bridge and the evidence at the scene, it appears the pickup truck crossed the centerline briefly, sideswiped a car going the other direction, then the driver of the pickup overcorrected. He hit one guardrail then went flying across to the other side of the bridge. At that point, the truck went airborne and then over the side."

"Oh, Lord," Jim said. "And it fell in the water?"

"Fortunately, no. The truck landed in some hard-packed sand near the water's edge. That section of the bridge is not very high off the ground, so they didn't fall very far. Maybe twenty feet."

"Can we come up there and see him?" Marilyn asked.

"I'm sure that would be fine. You can ask the nurses at the front desk about him. I do need to mention something else to you . . . in the wreckage we found a smashed-up cooler filled with broken beer bottles. And the truck cab smelled heavily of marijuana. We're not sure if Doug was involved in this activity, but we have ordered a blood test. It's clear he wasn't the driver. But we still need to check."

"We understand, Sheriff."

"I'm just a deputy."

"Right. Well, thank you for the call. We'll be heading your way any minute."

Jim hung up the phone, held on to Marilyn. She had already started to cry. He joined her.

A few moments later, Jim said, "I think we should tell Christina, see if she wants to come with us."

54

Christina, Jim, and Marilyn had just pulled into the Flagler Hospital parking lot in St. Augustine. They were walking toward the Emergency Department door. On the way there, they'd prayed for Doug, for Drew, for Jason's family, and, lastly, for themselves. That God would give them peace and would somehow use the situation for his glory.

Christina loved it when Jim prayed. He always sounded so eloquent, and she always felt so calm after. When she prayed, she still sounded like a New Yorker. Anyway, God didn't care about things like that.

The peace and calm she felt all but vanished when they stepped through the doors of the emergency room. So many people sick and injured in the lobby and waiting room, so much fear and anxiety on their faces. She probably looked just the same to them. Jim and Marilyn walked right to the nurse's station, so she followed.

"Hello, my name is Jim Anderson. A sheriff's deputy called us about an hour and a half ago, saying our son had been involved in a car accident. He said the ambulance brought him here. His name is Doug, or Douglas Anderson."

"Let me check," the nurse said. She checked her computer screen, clicked a few keys. "Yes, there he is. He's out of surgery now but still in the recovery room."

"Surgery?" Marilyn said. "He needed surgery?" She grabbed hold of Jim's arm.

Christina tensed up.

"Yes. Why don't you all have a seat over there in the waiting room? I'll have one of the doctors come over and brief you. Shouldn't take but a few minutes."

"Okay, thanks," Jim said.

"When can we see him?" Marilyn said.

"I'm sure they'll let you see him as soon as they bring him into a room."

Jim led them over to an uncrowded section of the waiting room. Marilyn and Christina took a seat. Jim stood a moment longer. "Can I get you guys anything? There's a machine over there. I'm going to get a bottle of water."

"I'm fine," Christina said.

Marilyn looked through her purse. "I

brought one from home, guess I left it in the car. I'll just take a few sips of yours." After Jim left, she said to Christina, "I didn't know he needed surgery. I hope it's not anything serious." She looked around the waiting room. "Listen to me, I should just be thankful he's alive. Jason's poor parents. I can't believe he's gone."

"Did you know them very well?"

"Hardly at all," Marilyn said. "Doug and Jason have been friends for years. You'd think we'd be much closer. But we're kind of from two different worlds. For the most part, when the two of them get together, Jason and Doug, I mean, they mostly hang out over at Jason's house. He hardly ever comes to our place." Tears welled up in her eyes. "Here I am talking about him in the present tense, as if he's still alive. I can't believe he's gone."

Various pictures Christina had seen on Facebook of Jason and Doug together began to flash through her mind. In every one she could think of, Jason was smiling, and he always looked either drunk or stoned. On the car drive here, they had talked about what the deputy had said about the beer bottles in the pickup and smelling marijuana. Beyond the obvious anxiety about Doug's injuries, they were concerned about whether he might be arrested.

Christina had told them she didn't think he would be, since he wasn't the driver. She also said she was almost certain Doug didn't drink or smoke pot. He had told her that, and she didn't think he was lying. She hoped that still held true, that Doug hadn't given in this time to help him deal with his disappointment about losing the contest.

As Jim walked back with his water bottle, Christina noticed a man dressed in doctor gear coming through the doorway behind him. Jim turned and said something to him. The doctor nodded. Jim pointed to where Christina and Marilyn sat, and both men walked over.

"Hello, Mr. and Mrs. Anderson, I'm Dr. Rodriguez. I was one of the doctors caring for your son, Doug."

Jim introduced Christina, and everyone shook hands.

"What can you tell us about Doug?" Marilyn said. "What kind of surgery did he have? Is he okay now?"

"I'm an orthopedic surgeon," Dr. Rodriguez said. "Doug broke his right leg in two places during the accident. They were severe breaks, but I feel very good about the procedure we just performed. With some physical therapy and some time, he should experience a full recovery. He's also pretty banged up all along his right side, especially the hip area. I'm guessing that's where Doug's body made impact with the ground. But we saw no signs of internal bleeding. He did sustain a mild concussion. But other than that, and a few minor scrapes and cuts, I'd say he made out pretty well compared to the other two young men in the car."

"Jason and Drew," Jim said. "The deputy sheriff told us what happened."

"Speaking of the sheriff," Dr. Rodriguez said, "I haven't informed him yet, but we have the blood test results on Doug. We found no traces of alcohol or marijuana in his system. I thought you'd be happy to hear that."

"We are, Doctor. Thank you for telling us."

Christina was relieved, though not surprised.

"Do you have any idea how long he'll be in here?" Marilyn asked.

"I think at least a few days. His leg was seriously injured. I want to make sure it's healing up right before we release him."

"You know when we can see him?" Christina asked.

The doctor looked at his watch. "They should be moving him to a room any minute. I'll go check on that and have someone come get you as soon as possible. It shouldn't be very long at all."

"Thank you so much, Dr. Rodriguez," Jim said. "Thank you for taking such good care of Doug."

"You're very welcome. Doug had a very close call tonight, but I think he'll be just fine."

He shook their hands and left the waiting room. Instantly, Jim and Marilyn embraced. Marilyn cried gently on his shoulder. Jim wiped his eyes and patted her back. Christina excused herself, saying she needed to find the restroom.

She was glad to find it empty and closed herself inside the biggest stall. Then she started crying. The cries became sobs. She was so relieved. Doug was okay. The doctor said he would be just fine.

"Thank you, Lord. Thank you."

55

Doug heard a familiar voice softly call his name, felt a warm hand touching his left arm. When he opened his eyes, his mom and dad's faces came into view, one on either side of his bed.

"We're here, Doug," his mother said. "Christina's here too. She's just down the hall in the waiting room. How do you feel? Are you in any pain?"

Was he? He tried to move. He could move some, but his entire right side from the waist down felt heavy. Something was on his head. Was he wearing a hat? "I feel achy and stiff. But it doesn't hurt as much as it did before, when I was in the ambulance."

"Do you remember what happened?" his dad asked. "About the accident?"

"Some of it." An image of that slow-motion moment on the bridge came into view. Jason, flicking the headlights on and off. He and Drew, their heads bouncing up and down with the music. Doug screaming for Jason to stop. Headlights flashing in his eyes. The other car slamming into their left side. Jason jerking the steering wheel hard to the right. Then he remembered. "Jason . . . Jason is dead."

His father nodded. "We're so sorry, son."

"Drew. Did Drew make it?"

"He did, but he's in much worse shape than you are. We don't know any details, but he's in critical condition in the intensive care unit."

"I told him to wear his seatbelt. But he never would."

"Drew?"

"Jason. Both of them."

"Did we ever meet Drew?" his mom asked. "I don't remember him."

"I don't think so. We weren't that close. He was more Jason's friend than mine." But Jason, he and Jason were friends back in River Oaks for as long as he could remember. "I can't believe Jason's gone." No one said anything for a moment. "I'm so glad you're here."

"We came as soon as we got the call."

"Who called you?"

"A deputy sheriff. He used your cell phone."

Doug reached up to touch his head, using

his right arm, but it was so weak. His left arm felt stronger, but his mom was still stroking it gently. He didn't want her to stop. "Am I wearing a hat?"

"You suffered a concussion," his father said. "A mild one. Those are bandages you're feeling. You've also got quite a few cuts, some with stitches. You're probably not feeling them because of the pain meds."

"You see this?" his mother said. She held up a brown plastic cylinder with a button on top and a tube sticking out the bottom. "It's a morphine drip. The nurse said you can push it if the pain gets too bad. How are you feeling now?"

"I'm okay."

"Does your leg hurt very much?"

"A little. Kind of a dull ache. Feels very heavy."

"It's in a cast," his dad said. "From the bottom of your foot halfway up your thigh. It was broken in two places during the accident. The doctor said that's your worst injury."

"Did they say how long I would be in here?"

"He thought a few days."

"So are you guys going back home tonight?"

"No, we're staying right here," his father

said. "Booked two rooms in a nearby hotel."

"Two rooms?"

"Guess you were a little groggy when I said it before," his mother said. "Christina's here with us."

"Christina? Where is she?"

"She's right down the hall in the waiting room. She'd like to see you, if you're up to it."

Was he? He did want to see her. He couldn't believe she wanted to see him after the way he'd treated her. For that matter, he couldn't believe how nice his parents were being to him right now. He'd treated them so badly. "I'm feeling pretty tired, but if you think she's really okay about seeing me, I would like to see her."

"Then we'll say good night now," his father said. "You need your rest, and she's really hoping to see you tonight."

"She is?"

"She's been worried sick," his mother said. "We all have."

"Does the rest of the family know what happened?"

"I'm sure they do by now. We called Michele while we were waiting for the doctor to give us the okay to come in. She's calling everyone else to get them praying for you."

"Well," his father said, "we better go and get Christina."

"Good night, honey." His mother stepped closer, leaned forward, and kissed him on the forehead. "Hope that didn't hurt."

Not a bit, he thought.

They walked toward the door. His mother turned and said, "We love you."

"I love you too." He almost added the words, "More than ever."

His father said, "We're so glad you're okay, son. I don't know what I would've done if —" Tears filled his eyes, and he couldn't finish.

56

Christina stepped through the doorway into Doug's room. Jim and Marilyn had spoken to her briefly in the hall. They said Doug seemed a lot better than they had feared on the drive here. Of course, he was heavily sedated. No telling how much pain he'd be in otherwise. He was a bit groggy but definitely able to talk.

She saw his feet first; the left leg was under a blanket, the right leg in a cast. She peeked around the curtain. The bed was slightly elevated, his head wrapped in gauze bandages, his eyes closed. Should she wake him? Should she leave, just come back tomorrow? She looked toward the door, hoping a nurse might walk by.

"Christina?"

"I thought you might be asleep." She walked up to his bed.

"I was. Guess it's this morphine. Makes me pretty sleepy."

"And you probably still have some of the anesthesia meds in your system. But sleeping is good. That's probably what your body needs the most. I won't stay long."

"I'm glad you came."

She was glad too. "You gave us all a good scare."

"Scared me too." He inhaled deeply, sighed. "You hear what happened to Jason?"

She nodded. "I'm so sorry, Doug. I know you guys were great friends."

He looked toward the window. "We were. Though sometimes I don't know why."

"What do you mean?"

He looked back at her. "We were so different. You know? He always had his own way of doing things, his own way of seeing things. Although right now, I wish he was a little more like me."

Christina wasn't sure what Doug meant. After what he'd just been through, she wasn't sure she should ask.

"He was so reckless," he continued. "He always said I was too cautious, too stiff. He liked to be spontaneous, live in the moment. He always said I was wound too tight, that I'd be so much happier if I were more like him. But look what it got him. He's dead, Christina. I told him to stop. But he wouldn't listen. He and Drew, they were headbanging in the front seat, stoned out of their minds. There I was, stuck in the backseat. We're driving over a bridge, and you know what he does?" He was getting angry; tears rolled down both cheeks. "He starts flicking the headlights on and off. Can you believe that? Over and over again. I'm screaming for him to stop. But he won't stop. I can't even believe what I'm seeing. It was like a nightmare. Then this car is coming right at us. I'm saying, 'Jason watch out.' But it's too late. I knew right then, we were done for. Sure enough, the guy smacks into us. We go bouncing all over the bridge, then the truck starts flying in the air. Spinning and falling."

He closed his eyes and grimaced, as if reliving the impact. She put her hand on his forearm, careful not to touch the IV.

Doug opened his eyes. He looked down at his chest. "When I woke up, it was pitch black. I didn't even know where I was. I hear these guys talking outside the truck, the waves breaking in the background. I start to remember where I am. I listen to them talking some more, and I can tell by what they're saying, they think Jason is dead. I can't see him, him or Drew. But I start calling them. They don't answer. They can't answer. And you know why? Because

Drew is unconscious, and Jason *is* dead."

He looked up at her, more tears in his eyes. "He's dead, Christina. It didn't have to happen. None of it had to happen. If he would've just listened to me. Just this once." He closed his eyes again then brought his left hand up and rubbed his eyes.

She could tell he was trying to stop the tears. She rubbed his forearm gently. "It's okay to cry, Doug."

So he did. Quietly at first, then much louder. She put her hand on his shoulder and said softly, "It's okay." Then she said a silent prayer.

A minute or two later, she could tell he was done crying. She walked over to a little dresser in the corner and grabbed several tissues out of a box and handed them to Doug.

After wiping his eyes, he said, "Thanks." He looked up at her. "Even though he was such a jerk sometimes . . . I'm going to miss him so much." The tears came again.

She walked back to the dresser and grabbed the tissue box. This time, they weren't just for him.

A few minutes later, a thought popped into Christina's head. She was almost reluctant to share it but knew it was the right thing to do. "Has anyone called Courtney to let her know what's happened?"

"I doubt it," he said. "Although, I'm not sure how much she'll care."

This reaction made no sense to Christina.

"She didn't really like Jason or Drew," he said, "and now that we're no longer together —"

"You two broke up?"

Doug nodded. "It's been coming for some time. Truth is, we had no business being a couple. Last week she went back to visit her folks. I finally realized it when she was gone. I was going to break it off when she got back into town. It was supposed to happen this morning. But she sent me a Facebook message, saying she and her old high school boyfriend were back together again. She wasn't even coming back to Flagler anymore. I wasn't sad. All I felt was relief."

"She broke up with you on Facebook?"

Doug nodded. A nurse came in to check on him. She asked about his level of pain. He said it was a little worse than it was when he first woke up. She reminded him of the morphine drip, then politely suggested that maybe he'd had enough excitement for one night.

"I really should go," Christina said. "Let you get some sleep."

"I am feeling pretty tired. But I'm really

glad you came."

"I'm glad too. We'll be praying for you."

"Can you come back tomorrow?"

"I think so. Your dad said we're going to stay here until they're ready to send you home." Then she wondered, did that mean home as in back to his apartment, or home as in River Oaks?

57

Doug watched as Christina disappeared behind the curtain divider. It was so good to see her. She didn't seem even a little upset with him after the way he'd treated her. Of course, someone like her would hide the hurt at a time like this. Is that what she was doing? It didn't seem like it. Seemed like she genuinely cared about him.

But why would she, how could she? He had been such a lousy friend.

And his parents. He'd treated them even worse. Yet here they were, dropping everything they were doing and driving all the way up here. Didn't think twice about it. The last time he'd talked with his dad, he'd told him to keep his money. Doug could take care of himself from now on. He was such an idiot. Pinning all his hopes on winning that contest, and he didn't even get an honorable mention.

The last time he'd talked with his mom,

he had yelled at her and accused her of spying on him. When all she'd wanted was to take him out for a surprise breakfast. He pictured her arriving to his apartment, her heart filled with all kinds of love for him . . . just like always. He'd been so mean to her. Now he realized, it was just to cover up the shame and embarrassment he felt.

Just like always. The phrase repeated in his mind. Because it was true. That was how she always treated him. With love. All through his childhood, the teen years, and even tonight. After everything he'd done. Love was all he saw in her eyes. He hadn't even asked her or his dad to forgive him. But he could tell, they already had.

God, I'm so sorry for the way I've treated my parents. All I've ever done is use them, and all they've ever done is try to help me. I've treated my whole family so badly, for years. And I've treated you even worse.

He looked down at his IV, then the cast on his leg. For an instant, an image flashed into his mind. He was pinned in the truck as it lay smashed upside down under the bridge. He felt the same fear he felt then, the moment he realized where he was and what had happened.

And what had almost happened.

I could've died tonight. Just like that. You

*had every right to take me, but you didn't.
Thank you for not giving me what I deserved.
I don't want to be the way I've been anymore,
Lord. Running from you, hiding from them. I
want to know you the way they do, Jesus. The
way Christina does.*

He took a few breaths. His body was
almost crying out for sleep.

Jim quietly stepped into Doug's room
behind the curtain. He wanted to say a
quick prayer for Doug before heading over
to the hotel. Doug was probably asleep
already. He stepped around the curtain and
looked at him. It looked like he was crying.
He rushed to his side. "Doug, are you all
right? Where does it hurt? You want me to
get the nurse?"

Doug looked up at him. "Dad, I'm so
sorry. For everything. I've been such a lousy
son. I can't believe how I've treated you and
Mom."

Through the tears, Jim saw a totally different look in Doug's eyes. He put his hand
on his shoulder. "It's okay, Doug. Your mom
and I love you. That's never changed."

Doug reached for his father's hand. "No,
it's not okay."

Jim leaned forward now and hugged him
gently.

Doug rested his head on Jim's shoulder and cried. The cries became sobs. "It's not okay."

Jim began to cry too.

Doug looked up at him. "Can I come home?"

"Of course you can come home, son. Nothing would please me more." He hugged Doug again.

A few moments later, Jim looked at Doug and said, "I'm going to call the office tomorrow and rearrange my schedule. Your mom already got the next few days off. I don't know if Christina can stay that long. I'm sure she would if she could. But your mom and I are gonna be here every day until we can all go home together."

58

Two weeks after the accident, Doug was doing better convalescing at home. At least physically. To keep from having to go up and down the stairs, he slept on the sofa bed in his father's home office. During the day, they moved him out onto the living room couch. He was starting to get around a little better on crutches; the headaches from his concussion had subsided a great deal, and a few days ago the doctor had removed the last of his stitches.

Of course, the biggest hurdle to overcome had been attending Jason's funeral last Saturday. His mom had suggested he could stay home. No one would be offended, considering his injuries. But he needed to be there. Jason's family weren't churchgoers, so they'd held the memorial service at a funeral home. A number of people stood up and tearfully recalled their fondest memories. Doug had wanted to, but he knew he'd never make it through. Instead, his dad had read something Doug had written.

After the service, a brief reception was held at Jason's house. Doug didn't have the strength to go. He'd heard the funeral home had cremated Jason's body the day before. He didn't want to think about that, even less than he wanted to think about where Jason might be right now. The whole thing made him feel dark and confused. He had to stop thinking about it before he got sucked into full-blown depression.

He refocused his gaze on the laptop screen in front of him. For the last hour or so, he had been exploring degree programs for the Florida colleges within driving distance of River Oaks. For the most part, he'd enjoyed attending Flagler College but felt pretty sure God wanted him to finish his schooling closer to home.

There were too many bad memories for him at Flagler. He really needed a fresh start. It was also clear that Flagler hadn't been a healthy spiritual atmosphere for him, either. He had never attended church there. His whole family liked the church they were attending here in River Oaks. Doug had never given it a fair chance before and planned to do that as soon as he was able.

But one of the biggest reasons for going to school closer to home was Christina.

He wasn't sure they had a chance of becoming more than friends, but he wanted to find out. Since he'd been home, she had only treated him with kindness and care. It was certainly more than he deserved. But for the most part, it was the same way she had treated him before. It didn't necessarily mean anything; she was just a kind and thoughtful person.

But he couldn't stop thinking about her.

He wondered if she could ever get past the memories of that awful morning when she and his mom had caught him with Courtney. He regretted his entire relationship with Courtney, not just that moment. Christina wasn't stupid. She would know what kind of relationship they had, and what kind of guy Doug was. He was no different than all of the loser guys Christina had left behind last year before she'd started following Christ.

He was such a hypocrite. He remembered a conversation with his mom about Christina, back when she'd first moved into the garage apartment. She was still pregnant then, and his mom had hinted at the possibility of Doug being interested in her. He didn't remember his exact words, but his meaning was clear. He considered Christina damaged goods, and talked as if she wasn't good enough for him.

Now who was the damaged goods?

That knowledge made him tense up whenever she came around. It was like an invisible wall existed between them. He could barely look her in the eye. He prayed about it, every day. But it didn't seem like God was giving him any answers.

"I was going to head back to my apartment for a little while. Maybe put in a load of wash. Is there anything I can get you before I go?"

Doug looked up into Christina's smiling face. It was her turn to take care of him today. She and Doug's mother were taking turns. Harriet, their boss down at Odds-n-Ends, was kind enough to rearrange their work schedule for a few weeks. "Uh, no. Thanks. I'm okay. You go ahead and do what you need to do."

"You sure?"

Doug looked away, back to his computer screen. "Sure, I'm fine. Thanks for asking."

In his peripheral vision, he saw her walk away.

"Call me if you need anything."

"I will." He turned and watched her walk through the living room, the dining room, then out the patio door.

That evening, Christina had eaten alone at her dinette table in the garage apartment. Marilyn had called on her way home from work and invited Christina to eat with them in the main house. She was picking up Chinese takeout and wondered what she could order for Christina. Christina had thanked her but said she wasn't up to it tonight.

Marilyn could read her moods and had asked what was wrong. Christina said it wasn't something she wanted to talk about over the phone. Marilyn asked if it had something to do with Doug. Christina said yes, then did a good job of keeping her tears at bay. Marilyn said she'd be coming over as soon as she had cleaned up their dinner.

Christina got up from the table, picked up her half-eaten Lean Cuisine dinner, and dropped it into the trash can. A moment later, the door downstairs opened and closed, then footsteps came up the stairwell. When she heard them stop at the landing, she said, "It's not locked, Marilyn."

Marilyn walked in. They hugged briefly and both sat in their usual spots in the living area. "Okay, so what's this all about?"

"You already know it's about Doug."

"I know there seems to be a lot of awkwardness and tension between the two of you, ever since he came home. I can't say I know why. We've been through a lot of upheaval in the last few weeks. It's been a very stressful time. The accident, Doug being home, having to take care of him every day, Jason's funeral."

"That's all true," Christina said. "But the problem's deeper than that."

"What do you think is going on?"

"Doug can barely look at me. We haven't had a single conversation longer than two sentences since he came home. I've seen the way he is around you and Jim. How he is when other family members come over. He seems pretty normal then. It's only around me. It's like he'd rather be anywhere else."

"Is it really that bad?"

She nodded. "Feels like it to me."

"Do you want me to talk to him? See if I can find out anything?"

"It's pretty obvious what it is. Doug's trying to send me a strong signal that he doesn't want me to get any ideas about our relationship being anything more than friends, now that he and Courtney split up." She felt a rush of emotions rising, but she was determined to get ahold of them.

"Do you really think that's it?"

"I've thought about it a lot," Christina said. "It's the only thing that makes any sense." Marilyn reached over and patted her hand. Christina knew how Marilyn felt. She had told her many times that she had wished, and had even prayed, that God might someday bring Christina and Doug together. And she thought of Christina as her daughter, which made the next thing Christina had to say even harder. "There's something else I need to tell you." She looked away, swallowed. "I think it might be time for me to go."

"What? Go? Why?"

Christina sighed. "A lot of reasons. The biggest one is, with the way I feel about Doug, and all that's happened, I can't be around him this much, knowing he's never going to feel the same way about me. This is his home, and God's done a miracle changing his heart and bringing him back. That's what we've all been praying for. And he needs to feel like he can be himself when he's here. With me hanging around, he can't. Pretty soon, he'll be healed up enough to be able to go up and down stairs on those crutches. When that happens, he should be allowed to come back in this apartment where he belongs."

Marilyn was visibly upset. "I can't believe you're saying this. Where will you go?"

"Maybe I could still sign up for that St. John's College you and I visited near St. Augustine. I'm pretty sure I qualify for student aid, if I'm on my own."

Neither of them said anything for a moment.

Finally, Marilyn said, "There's got to be a better fix to this problem. I don't know what it is yet, but I'm not giving up until I think of one."

59

When Marilyn got back to the house, she was still upset. She walked past Jim and Doug in the living room. The credits were rolling on whatever TV show they had been watching. "Jim, before you start watching something else, could we talk?"

"Sure." He stood.

"You want me to pause this until you get back?" Doug asked.

"No, I'm sure I can catch up." He followed Marilyn into their bedroom.

She walked toward the corner and sat in the upholstered chair she used every morning during her quiet time. "Could you close the door?"

He did, then came over and sat on the edge of the bed. "What's the matter?"

Marilyn explained everything Christina had said. Jim listened carefully. When she finished, he said, "I'd really hate to see her go. She's like family now. But you and I both know how long she's felt this way about Doug. Do you see any signs of him ever returning her affection?"

She sighed. "No. If anything, I'd have to agree with her. Since he's been home, he seems to treat her with even less interest than before. I'm not sure he's doing it deliberately, like she thinks, as if he's trying to send her a signal. But either way, the result is the same."

"Then I think we have no choice but to help her, if she's truly set on leaving. I think it would be too painful for her to stay. Can you imagine how she'll feel if Doug starts showing interest in someone else?"

"No. That would be awful."

"How soon do you think she wants to go?" Jim said.

"We didn't talk about that. But I think soon."

"Well, maybe you can talk to her about it some more tomorrow. Tell her we talked, and that we'll do anything we can to help her."

Doug must've had a hard time last night. It was almost 10:00 a.m., and he was still asleep on the sofa bed. But as Marilyn walked past the office, she heard sounds that made her think he was starting to awaken. She began to get the couch ready in the living room.

As she finished, she heard the now familiar banging noises he made with the crutches when trying to navigate the space between the desk and the French doors. "Are you okay in there?"

"I'm getting it."

He made his way to the bathroom. A few minutes later, she helped him to the couch. Apparently, she wasn't hiding her mood as well as she thought. Just before she left him in the living room, he said, "Is everything okay?"

"Yes. Why do you ask?"

"I don't know. You seem a little tense. Something bothering you?"

Should she tell him?

"C'mon, Mom. I can tell something's bugging you. Have I done something?"

She didn't want to make him feel bad. If he didn't have feelings for Christina, then he didn't have them. There wasn't anything he could do about it. "You haven't done a thing, Doug. Really, I'll be fine."

"Okay, then. But you always tell me that if something's bothering me, it helps to talk about it."

He had a point. She walked around the couch and sat in the chair across from him.

"I'm just a little upset about a conversation I had with Christina last night."

"Christina? Is she okay? What's going on?"

Marilyn wondered how to say this. Maybe she should start with the thing that upset her the most. "She told me she's been thinking it might be time for her to move out. I don't just mean from the apartment, but to leave River Oaks."

"What? Leave?" He sat up. "She can't leave!" He was almost yelling. "Why would she leave?"

"It's kind of hard to say."

Doug was stunned. This was horrible news. "Is it some kind of secret? Would she be upset if you told me why?"

"It's not exactly a secret. I think she might be more embarrassed than upset if I told you. So I shouldn't —"

"If it's not a secret, then you've got to tell me. I need to know."

"Doug, I don't understand. Why is this upsetting you so much? You guys can still be friends if she leaves. It's not like you're all that close anymore."

Doug looked down, began rubbing his forehead. "But that's not how I want it."

"Want what?"

He looked back at his mom. "How I want

things to be between Christina and me."

"It's not? It seems like that to me. If anything, even more so since you've been home from the hospital. I've been watching. You guys seem even less like friends than you used to be."

"But that's just because . . . it's because . . . well, I've been such a jerk to her. Whenever she comes around, I keep thinking back to the look on her face that day."

"What day?"

"You know. When you guys came to St. Augustine and found me with Courtney."

"That was a bad day. But Doug, you've already said how sorry you are for that. You know we've completely forgiven you. I'm sure Christina isn't holding any grudges, either."

"How could she not be?"

His mom got up and walked over to the couch, sat by his feet. "Haven't you ever talked to her about it? Told her you're sorry?"

He shook his head no. "I've tried to so many times. But I can never find the right moment."

She rubbed his leg. "Doug, I don't think you need to wait for a right moment for something like that. You just need to tell her how you feel. Just be honest. She knows you've changed since that night in the hospital."

"You think she does?"

"I know she does. We've talked about it."

"I don't know if I *can* tell her how I feel."

"Why not?"

Could he say it? She knew Christina better than anyone. She'd know if Doug had even a sliver of a chance with her. "Because I love her, Mom." Tears welled up in his eyes. He blinked them back.

"You what?"

"I love her. But I've ruined it. She could never look at me like someone she could ever —"

"Doug?"

He looked up and saw tears in his mother's eyes. But she was smiling. Why was she about to cry, and why was she smiling? "What?"

"You *really* need to talk to her. You need to tell her how you feel. Tell her what you told me. I'd do it as soon as you can, the next time she comes over." She wiped the tears from her eyes. "You're the reason she wants to leave, Doug. She doesn't think you care about her at all."

Doug reached for his crutches and swung his legs off the couch.

"Where are you going?"

"I'm going over there to talk to her now."

60

Christina set her book down on the end table and got up to bring her coffee mug out to the kitchen. On the way, she walked past the window to the backyard, in time to see Doug hobbling across the walkway on his crutches. What in the world? She watched as he almost fell trying to get the door open.

Was he coming here?

He made a terrible racket climbing the apartment stairs. She came out to the landing to help him up the last few steps. "Doug, what are you doing here? You're going to kill yourself."

They made it through the doorway. "Christina, please don't go. You can't leave."

She helped him to the sofa. "Your mother told you?" *How could Marilyn do that?*

"Don't blame her. I could tell she was upset. I made her tell me why."

"What did she say? Did she tell you why I

need to leave?"

"Just that it has something to do with me, and you thinking I don't care about you."

"Well, that's not exactly it."

"Well, whatever it is, there's something I need to say to you. I've tried to say it a dozen times in the last few weeks. But I have to say it now." His eyes got all teary. "I am so sorry for the way I treated you. Even before, when we were friends, I was a lousy friend. A total jerk. And I hate the fact that you saw me there with Courtney that day. I can't get the look in your eyes out of my head. I should never have been with her. I don't even know why I was. It was a total mistake, everything about it. And I know you have every reason to want nothing to do with me ever again. But you can't leave. This is your family now. Everyone here loves you. My parents do. Tom and Jean, Allan and Michele, the kids. Even Uncle Henry and Aunt Myra."

He stopped to catch his breath.

She looked straight into his eyes. "I believe they do love me. Your family has been wonderful to me ever since I got here. I'd hate it if they weren't a part of my life anymore." Now she started crying. "But I still don't think I can stay."

"Why? Why not?"

She took a deep breath. She might as well just say it. "I can tell you don't want me around anymore. You barely even look at me. We've hardly said a word to each other since you've come home."

He leaned one of his crutches against the couch and reached for her hand. It startled her, but she took it.

"I don't want you to leave, because . . . I love you, Christina. And not like a sister . . . or like a friend. I've never felt this way about anyone. Do you think . . . we could ever be more than friends, after the way I've messed things up?"

Tears fell from her eyes. "You . . . love me?"

He nodded. "I think I've loved you for a long time. I was just too stupid and immature to see it. Can you forgive me?"

"I already have. A long time ago. I was leaving because I thought you didn't want me around anymore."

"Want you around? Are you crazy? I want you around all the time. All I ever think about is you." He dropped the other crutch, took her other hand, looked into her eyes, and said, "Christina, would you please stay? And not as my friend anymore but as the woman I love?"

She threw her arms around him and

kissed him. Gently at first, then with serious passion. She pulled back a few inches from his face.

"So that's a yes?" he said.

"Yes." And she kissed him again.

61

The following day was Sunday. At one point in church during worship, Jim had been so overcome with emotion he had to stop singing. Five seats down on his right, in the aisle seat, Doug stood on his crutches next to Christina, eyes closed, singing. Without any prodding, he'd asked to come with them to church that morning.

Jim looked around him. His other children and their spouses were nearby. His grandkids were in the children's ministry classrooms down the hallway. He flashed back to the first time he'd visited this church two years ago. He and Marilyn were separated. Michele was there, but she didn't even like him. None of his kids did.

And now look.

God had been very good to him. He hadn't done it according to Jim's plan, certainly not on Jim's timetable, and sometimes he did the exact opposite of what

Jim had expected. But here they were, all together.

After church, they drove back to the house on Elderberry Lane for an Anderson family dinner, the first time they had been able to gather this way since Doug had come home from the hospital. Even Uncle Henry and Aunt Myra had driven over from the coast to join them.

But besides the joy in Jim's heart was a growing sense of confusion. As much as he loved seeing the changes in Doug, he couldn't help but notice that every time he saw Doug, Christina was right there next to him. And the smiles on both their faces were constant and pronounced. Just last night, Marilyn had told him that Christina was ready to leave River Oaks, mainly because Doug seemed to care less about her now than he ever did.

But that wasn't what Jim was seeing this morning.

He asked Marilyn about it on the car drive home. She just smiled and said something *had* changed, but that she didn't want to ruin the surprise. When he asked her to please explain, she simply smiled and said, "Wait until dinner."

The table was set and everyone was in their

seats. Well, almost everyone. Doug was sitting in the corner spot where Allan normally sat, so he could elevate his leg. Once again, Christina was right next to him. Even now, Jim noticed the way she looked at him. Like a young woman in love. He watched Doug glance back at her, the same look in his eyes.

What in the world?

Jim was almost too distracted to say the blessing. But he did.

For the first ten minutes or so of the meal, Jim listened as Uncle Henry and Aunt Myra took turns sharing about a recent trip they had taken to Walt Disney World. They hadn't been to the theme park in almost fifteen years and couldn't believe how much it had changed.

Toward the end of their story, Doug jumped in and said matter-of-factly, "That's the first place I want to take Christina when I'm off these crutches. Can you believe she's never been to any of the Disney parks?"

It took every bit of Jim's self-control not to insist Doug tell everyone at the table what was going on. But he needn't have worried. He didn't have to wait long.

After all the platters of food had been served and everyone began to eat, the conversation momentarily quieted down. Doug slid his chair back, grabbed his crutches, and rose to his feet.

Needless to say, it got everyone's attention.

"Hey, everyone, feel free to keep eating. I just have a few things to say. Seems like the easiest thing would be just to say it with all of us here together. Because it really involves all of you. I've already said some of these things to Mom and Dad, and to Christina. But I need to say them to you guys too. The first thing is, I want to thank you all for the way you've been treating me since the accident. It's way nicer than I've treated any of you lately. Really, for the last couple of years. You all know this, but I kind of lost my way there. Hardly ever coming home. And I'm sure you guys could tell, even when I was here, I wasn't really. I'm very sorry about that."

He repositioned the crutches under his arms. "But this accident has opened my eyes, and really, so have a bunch of other things that happened before the accident. So I'm making some changes. Thought I might as well just tell you, so you wouldn't have to guess. The first one is, I'm not just home until I get better. I've decided to stay. I'm actually checking out which of the colleges nearby would be the best one to finish my degree."

Marilyn looked at Jim, gave a silent, celebratory clap. Jim certainly loved what he was hearing.

"The second one you've already seen," Doug continued. "Me going back to church. I really liked it this morning, and I really wanted to be there. Maybe for the first time ever. It's amazing how different church is when your heart's in a new place."

Uncle Henry looked right at Jim then nodded once and smiled. His eyes got a bit watery.

"The third change is . . . well, you might have noticed that one too." He reached a hand toward Christina, and she took it. "I know to all of you, Christina's already like family. She's been about the nicest and truest friend I've had, ever since I've known her. But I realized something else recently . . . that's not exactly what I feel for her inside. She's way more than that to me. I know I'm kind of new at this, but I've been praying about it too. And I think God may want us to be more than friends. I talked to her about it last night, and she thinks so too. So, I guess what I'm saying is . . . we're officially a couple."

Instantly, Marilyn and Michele started clapping. Jean joined in right after them, which, of course, got the kids clapping. Jim

446

was pretty sure they had no idea why. None of the men clapped, but Jim certainly wanted to.

"Well, I'm glad that makes you all happy," Doug said. "I know it makes me happy." He started to sit down. "My armpits are killing me, so that's about all I've gotta say. I love you guys."

He didn't get choked up the whole time until uttering those last four words.

About two hours later, Jim and Marilyn were enjoying coffee out on the veranda with Uncle Henry and Aunt Myra. They were mostly reflecting on all the wonderful things that had happened, not just today but all the way back to Michele's wedding. Just before that, it seemed like Jim and Marilyn's relationship was broken beyond repair and their entire family was on the verge of falling apart.

"It's been a rocky few years for sure," Uncle Henry said. "But I never gave up hope that God could turn things around. Myra and I saw what he did for us and our family, and we knew when you two started walking in humility and started pursuing God's ideas for your marriage and family, he'd be just as faithful to you."

He looked at Jim, smiled, and said, "With

the kind of things I heard Doug say this morning, I think it's fair to say the legacy of the Anderson family is heading in a totally different direction now than it was before you and Marilyn learned how to dance."

DAN'S INTERVIEW WITH GARY
ABOUT *THE LEGACY*

Dan: In the first three books of our Restoration series, the spiritual themes were drawn from one of your nonfiction books. With *The Legacy* that's not so much the case. Although both of us can relate to the themes depicted in the book, which are drawn from our personal experiences. We've both gone through the challenges of raising our kids in the faith, then seeing some of them temporarily drift away from "the straight and narrow."

What were some of the personal issues you faced when you became aware of your children's struggles and failures?

Gary: My favorite stories are about my son Michael. While in college, he began to date different girls, and I could tell he was not living as he had while growing up in our house. My wife Norma used to tell each of our three children that if they ever wanted to experience anything in life, just tell her and she would go with them. That sort of killed their enthusiasm for worldly things in high school. But new dating experiences in college seemed to be drawing Michael away from his biblically based life.

Things got pretty serious for a time, and when they did, I really struggled as a father. But eventually God turned things around. I think one of the things that helped was that Michael knew he always had my love, no matter what.

I told him often that I would always love him no matter what life path he chose. He had watched me as he grew up and told me that one day he wanted to choose the life of following Christ as I had. But he knew he was free to choose whatever life he wanted and it would not separate us one bit. I think parents need to express that kind of love, even when their children stray, so the children always know there's a way back.

Dan: Why do you think so many parents struggle with guilt over how their kids turn out or over the choices their adult children make?

Gary: Some of the guilt parents feel is misplaced. Especially when you know you've done the best you can, and your children still drift away. When they reach a certain age, your influence with them can fade. When that happens, they are responsible for their own choices. God doesn't hold us accountable for things we have no control over. But some of the guilt we feel might be due to ways we have treated our children as they grew up. Things we now regret. If that's the case, we should confess this to God and maybe even to them, spelling out the things we did wrong and asking their forgiveness.

If you can remain in harmony and love with your children as they grow up, they will tend to take on the same values that you have. But, if you offend them by your actions as they mature, they can hold on to their anger toward you. If this happens, they will tend to reject your values and lifestyle.

The relationship you build with them when they are young and the effort to maintain that loving and caring attitude toward them as they age is the basis for them desiring to remain your "friend" when they reach adulthood.

Dan: When we look at how well your children turned out as adults, even after some of them strayed for a time, it's obvious you learned some things about parenting that our readers who are still "in the thick of things" would love to hear. What are some of the major lessons you've learned?

Gary: Recently, I started a new book about how my wife and I raised our three children. Each of them are very different, but one is more like Norma and two are like me in personality. We actually wound up doing seven specific things that seemed, for the most part, to keep all of us in harmony and in love. Here's a brief summary:

1. We taught them and reminded them almost every day to highly honor God and other people. I would say things like, "What are the greatest things in life?" They might say, "Dad, we know." And I would wait until they would repeat what they already knew (because we had gone over it so many times). My oldest adult child is forty-seven now, and she still remembers repeating those.

important words back to me. What I've learned about this method of teaching kids what's important is that as they repeat these sayings back to you, they tend to remember them better, because they thought about the sayings regularly.

2. We also reminded them of the need to keep their anger level as low as possible each day. We told them that people who remain angry tend to lose their love for God and others. We reminded them that "holding anger in their hearts" would cause them many negative consequences. We would ask them, "How long can you keep anger toward someone or something?" They would say, "Until the sun sets each day!"

3. We taught them by example how to forgive each day. Forgiveness is basically realizing how much we each mess up each day and giving others the same grace that God gives us. We all have goofed up, and God is constantly patient with us, so let's cut others the same slack. We need to seek forgiveness if we offend others and forgive them seventy times seven times, if

needed.

4. We showed them by example how to turn every negative experience into something valuable for the future. God doesn't waste anything that happens to us and especially the negative things. He shows us how to find pearls in every pile of junk that hits us. This message is the main theme in a book I wrote called *Joy That Lasts.*

5. We explained how to choose a vocation from the strengths God has given and regularly asked them questions like: (a) Who is your Master? (b) What mission has God chosen for you to help you love people more? (c) What methods can you use to do the best job of serving people as you live out God's mission for your life? Greg and Michael, my sons, chose to serve marriages and families much like I did. Kari chose to love on the helpless, like widows and the fatherless. She wants to see all the orphans on earth adopted by families.

6. We taught them how to follow Jesus by "keeping his commands." And Jesus told us that his most

important command is to love others like he did (John 15:12, but read the entire fifteenth chapter of John). I eventually found that four of Jesus's teachings summarize almost everything else he said (Matthew 5:3; Mark 12:30; Mark 12:31; and Matthew 5:10–12).

7. We went camping every year as a family and discovered that camping bonded us like nothing else we did. Camping is basically "scheduled disasters." During these struggles, we all had to pull together. We still go on vacations together, and we love to hang out with each other just like we did back in the "good ole days."

Dan: It seems some older children and young adults need to experience the consequences of their poor choices before they can accept their parents' warnings and advice. What are some things parents can do during such times to keep from isolating themselves or pushing their children away completely?

Gary: As my children were going into their teen years, it was always my goal to stay in a close relationship with each of them as much as possible. We tried to attend church together. We played with them whenever we could. We attended their sporting events when possible. If I was out of town, one of my staff members would video their event and we would sit and watch it when I returned. We were so closely knit that it became obvious when any one of them seemed to distance themselves from us.

Either Norma or I would try to discuss the situation with them and get them to talk about it. We'd ask something like, "We can sense something might be wrong in our relationship with you. Are we missing something that we did to offend you?" Or we'd just talk and find out how they were doing and if everything was all right between us. If we found out that we had offended one of them, we'd listen carefully to understand how they were feeling, and as soon as we understood how we had offended them, we'd seek their forgiveness. They'd usually hug us or show us in other ways that we were back on track again.

We made sure to always work through any offenses with each other, because we reminded each other from time to time how important "high honor and low anger" is to any family. Especially to those who follow Jesus.

Dan: How important are things like prayer, faith, and hope when parents are faced with these kinds of challenges? What are some of the mistakes parents can make, or ways we can make matters worse?

Gary: I almost always tried to win my children over by example and minimized my lectures. I would even include them in developing my hopes and dreams. My children knew, for example, that I had some major ministry dreams that were totally impossible for me to do without a miracle from God. I would share my dreams with my entire family and see if they were okay with each one, and we discussed all the consequences each dream presented. Like, how much travel would be involved, how much time these dreams could involve, or any aspect of these dreams being given to us by God.

We even included them in things like vacation decisions, by taking the time to find out what had to be included on our vacation so that everyone could get excited about it. Norma almost always wanted to include shopping. Kari needed several books to read in a small motor home. Greg needed his music and either fishing or snorkeling. Michael needed something that included his brother. We all tried to live out the "honor concept" as much as possible.

If anyone was offended by a family member while we were together, we always took the time to keep our anger levels low by seeking forgiveness. We were constantly playing "bombardment." Taking one minute to say as many things as possible about why a person is special or outstanding. Everyone would join in to say something and it was like we were in competition to outdo each other. We might say, "Who wants to be bombarded today?" And we'd all join in when we picked one family member.

The closer the bond within a family, the easier the discussion if one of the family members starts heading in a harmful direction. My kids knew the importance of obeying their parents because of how clearly the Bible commands children to obey. But we never forced them to obey us if they questioned our request. Instead, we'd think of creative ways to get them to explore the truth or wisdom behind the command. When we let our kids discover truths on their own, it has a huge impact on their lives.

Dan: I know because we're writing fiction, we have to be careful not to get too preachy in the scenes where the characters are discussing spiritual truths. Are there any things in any of the chapters you'd like to elaborate on here? Any parting advice you'd like to share with parents who might be facing a prodigal son or daughter situation right now?

Gary: I think the most important thing is love. I've always told my children that they would have my love and commitment to them for as long as I lived. There was nothing that they could say or do that would keep me from loving them and valuing them forever. We used to say, what could you do or say that would cause my love to leave you?

They'd name a few things and I'd say nope, sorry. Or I would take their statements of actions that would cause my love to fail and expand their statements. Like, prison. I'd come and visit you regularly and bring you legal gifts or play basketball with you on the prison courts. We'd laugh and carry on about anything that they would say that could cause our love to fail. They always knew how important they were to us and, by the way, we are still saying how much we love them and want the best for them.

They also know how proud of them we are.

Kari is forty-seven years old, and her dream is to rescue all of the orphans in the world. Greg is forty-five and is the vice president at Focus on the Family, in charge of both marriage and parenting. Michael is forty-one and has his own ministry called "ER4Love: Save Your Marriage in 2 Days." He is developing Smalley Centers in major cities all over the world.

I'm super impressed with each of my children and their spouses and our grandchildren. Kari's husband is in charge of managing marriages, parenting, men's and women's ministries, and several other areas at the Assemblies of God headquarters in Springfield, Missouri. Erin, Greg's wife, also works for Focus on the Family, and is an author and speaker with Greg all over the world. She's a trained counselor and also a labor and delivery nurse. Michael's wife, Amy, is a trained marriage and family counselor, speaker, and author of marriage books. She is the leader in training professional, licensed counselors to perform 2-Day Marriage Intensives for almost divorced couples.

ABOUT THE AUTHORS

Dan Walsh is the award-winning author of *The Unfinished Gift, The Homecoming, The Deepest Waters, Remembering Christmas, The Discovery, The Reunion,* and *The Dance.* A member of American Christian Fiction Writers, Dan served as a pastor for twenty-five years. He lives with his family in the Daytona Beach area, where he's busy researching and writing his next novel.

Gary Smalley is one of the country's best known authors and speakers on family relationships. He is the author or coauthor of sixteen bestselling, award-winning books, along with several popular films and videos. He has spent over thirty years learning, teaching, and counseling, speaking to over two million people in live conferences. Gary has appeared on national television programs such as *Oprah, Larry King Live, Extra,* the *Today* show, and *Sally Jessy Ra-*

phael, as well as numerous national radio programs. Gary and his wife, Norma, have been married for forty years and live in Branson, Missouri. They have three children and six grandchildren.